THE
WINTERS
IN
BLOOM

THE WINTERS IN BLOOM

LISA TUCKER

ATRIA BOOKS

New York   London   Toronto   Sydney   New Delhi

ATRIA BOOKS

A Division of Simon & Schuster, Inc.
1230 Avenue of the Americas
New York, NY 10020

First Atria Books hardcover edition September 2011

ATRIA B O O K S and colophon are trademarks of Simon & Schuster, Inc.

For information about special discounts for bulk purchases, please contact Simon & Schuster Special Sales at 1-866-506-1949 or business@simonandschuster.com.

The Simon & Schuster Speakers Bureau can bring authors to your live event. For more information or to book an event contact the Simon & Schuster Speakers Bureau at 1-866-248-3049 or visit our website at www.simonspeakers.com.

Designed by Kyoko Watanabe

Manufactured in the United States of America

10 9 8 7 6 5 4 3 2 1

Library of Congress Cataloging-in-Publication Data

Tucker, Lisa.
    The winters in bloom : a novel / Lisa Tucker.—1st Atria Books hardcover ed.
       p. cm.
    I. Title.
    PS3620.U3W56 2011
    813'.6—dc22

                                                                    2010048089

ISBN 978-1-4165-7540-5
ISBN 978-1-4165-7575-7 (ebook)

*This book is for Judith and Greer, who convinced me I could write it,
and for Laurie and Miles, who taught me that the story never ends.*

We shall not cease from exploration
And the end of all our exploring
Will be to arrive where we started
And know the place for the first time.

—T. S. Eliot, "Little Gidding," *Four Quartets*

THE
WINTERS
IN
BLOOM

Part One

ONE

He was the only child in a house full of doubt. In bed each night, though it wasn't dark—the floor lights his father had installed—and it wasn't entirely private—the nursery monitor both parents refused to give up—he rehearsed the things he was certain of, using his fingers to number them. He was just a little boy, but he wouldn't allow himself to sleep until he'd gone through both hands twice. Twenty was a good number, he thought, though of course it paled in comparison with the number of doubts, partly because his parents had had so many years to discover them, but mainly because the doubt list was always growing, towering above him like the giant boy at his old school, the one his father had called a bully. The giant boy, whose name was Paul, had never done anything to Michael, but his parents *doubted* that Michael could learn in such an environment and took him out of that school. The three schools that followed had led to three other doubts, and now Michael was finishing first grade in home school, even though homeschooling had its doubts, too. *I doubt he'll get the socialization he needs*, his mother said. *I doubt we can teach him laboratory science*, his father said, *but we'll have to deal with that when the time comes*. And then the words his parents didn't have to say—*if the time comes*—because the future was always the biggest doubt of all.

"I will get bigger." Michael whispered it every night, holding up his thumb. Then he said, touching his index finger, "I will not die before I get to drive a car." He would force himself not to think of all the ways he could die, the hundreds of things his parents had told him all his life. He would also force himself not to daydream about what his first car would be like, because then he would fall asleep before he finished his counting and dream about rows and rows of shiny cars, all with headlights that looked like eyes and grills that looked like mouths.

In the morning, he was often very tired. When he slumped down for breakfast, his mother would put her hand on his forehead and ask if he was feeling okay. He hardly ever got sick, except when he was two years old and then he was so sick he had to spend weeks in the hospital, though all he remembered about that now was the pattern of elephants and monkeys on the nurses' clothes. His mother always made him touch his chin to his chest, even if he told her his neck didn't hurt. Sometimes she would take his temperature and inspect his throat and ears with a flashlight and push on his belly to make sure his appendix wasn't about to burst. Only after she was satisfied that he wasn't coming down with something would she ask, "Did you have any nightmares?"

He used to tell her, but he'd stopped when he realized that she and his father discussed his dreams the same way they discussed all the books they were reading about Raising Your Gifted Child. So he didn't tell her about the dream he kept having where the ocean came up to his bedroom window and he jumped in a boat and floated off. He only thought of it as a nightmare because he knew it should have been scary—if he was alone in the boat, this meant his parents must have drowned. In real life, he would have cried and cried for his parents: their love for him was one of the things he was most certain of; it was always somewhere in the first five things he counted every night. But in the dream, it never occurred to him to wonder where they were. He was sitting on a flat wooden seat in the middle of the boat, listening to the sound of the water lapping against the sides, blinking at the sun hanging so low in the sky it looked like he could row right to it. He felt like the biggest, scariest parts of the world were all gone, washed away by something that was winking at him in the soft fat cloud that floated overhead.

The lady who appeared that day was like the cloud, though she wasn't fat and she wasn't at all soft. Her arms were so skinny that when she bent her elbows, Michael thought of the paper clips he liked to twist apart when he was supposed to be learning geography. He didn't really like geography, though he loved the maps hung up in the room where he studied—the *schoolroom*, his parents called it, though it was nothing like school, because there was only one desk. The map of the city was right in front of him, and he'd stared at it so many times that he knew the lady wasn't lying when she said she was taking him to the ocean. He'd always wanted to go there, but his father said a jellyfish might bite him, or he might swallow a mouthful of dirty, germy sand, or, worst of all, a tide current might pull him out to the sea and he would never, ever come back.

The lady had asked him where he wanted to go more than anywhere in the world. She was so nice to him that he felt like it might be true when she said she loved him, even though he'd never seen her in his life until that morning. He was outside the house, in the backyard. It was the second day of the *outside alone half hour*, which his mother had decided he needed after she read a book about letting kids be *free range*, like the good-for-you kind of chicken. Michael didn't know what to do outside—his mother had told him to go ahead and do whatever he wanted, but he was afraid to touch anything, because dirt on your hands could make worms grow in your stomach, and he knew he should never climb a tree, he could fall and break his neck—so he walked around in circles and waved back each time his mother waved at him. She could see him perfectly while she did the dishes. So she must have seen the lady, and it must have been okay for him to go with her, like the lady said. *It's a surprise! Like on your birthday, except better!*

He knew he wasn't supposed to even talk to strangers, but the lady said she wasn't a stranger. *You're my little buddy,* the lady said, and she was crying, which made Michael feel bad for her. She was so skinny and sad, but in her car, she had lots of toys, just like she promised. She had toys he'd always wanted to play with, like robots with little parts that could break off and choke him, and bright red and blue and yellow cars that were probably made with lead paint. He was afraid to touch the toys at first, but then he decided that he wouldn't choke or swallow lead paint unless the toy went in his mouth. And why would the toy go in his mouth, when it was so much more fun to move the robot arms and pretend the cars were zooming up and down his legs, like the lady's car was zooming up the highway?

He might have had trouble believing that his parents had agreed to let the lady take him somewhere if he hadn't overheard them just last night, talking about how they had to change. *It can't be good for him to be trapped in the house all summer. Other children are out of school, going to camp, playing with their friends. The two of us are doing our best, but it's not enough. He needs more people in his life.*

His mother was the one who'd talked the most, but his father had made noises that sounded like agreement. So this trip with the lady that his parents had planned must be like the time they replaced the entire heating system in the house, rather than trying to get the old one fixed. *Sometimes you have to take extreme measures,* his father had said, and then he'd explained that an *extreme measure* was necessary when the problem was so big, the only way to deal with it was to give up on what you'd done before and start over from square one.

Being with this lady, sitting in a regular seat in the back of her car belted in with a regular seat belt, next to another seat covered with dangerous toys he'd taken out of a dangerous plastic bag, on the way to the ocean, was definitely an extreme measure. On some level Michael felt this, but most of him was just excited. The lady was happy now, too; her laughs sounded like Christmas bells. She had a really friendly smile and nice straight teeth, but when she pushed her hair back, he noticed a big scar on her wrist, and he wondered if it hurt sometimes, the way Mommy's scar on her knee did whenever it rained.

If they talked about anything important on the way to the Jersey Shore, Michael didn't remember it. What he remembered— and would for the rest of his life—was that afternoon on the boat. It wasn't a rowboat like in his dream; it was a big fishing boat with an upper deck and a lower deck and lots and lots of people. Michael was on the upper deck looking out at the wavy sea when a giant fish jumped straight out of the ocean and landed with a huge splash. It was a humpback whale, the fisherman announced, and everybody on the boat was pointing and talking when the whale jumped up again! It did it seven times, which Michael heard people say was amazing, because a lot of times these whale-watching boats went out for hours and didn't see anything.

It's because we're lucky, the lady said. She pointed at the whale's tail, which seemed to be waving before it disappeared back into the water. *It likes you.*

Michael closed his eyes tight, but when he opened them it was all still there: the bright blue sky and the soft pillow clouds and the endless ocean lapping at the sides of the boat. His hand was still tucked in the lady's bony hand, and the boat hadn't tipped over and the seagulls hadn't pecked his eyes out and the big scary fish wasn't really scary at all.

"It likes me," Michael whispered; then he grinned as big as he could, in case the whale was looking up at him through the water. In case the whale was like the lady, who'd promised when she appeared in his backyard that all she wanted was to be Michael's friend, more than anything in the world.

TWO

At some point that afternoon, it did occur to Michael that his parents had to be very worried, without even a phone call to tell them that he was okay. Of course he was right, though his assumption that his parents knew this lady would also turn out to be true. (Actually, only one of his parents knew her, and *knew* was hardly a strong enough word for the relationship they'd had, but as this was a long time ago, it was all the same to Michael who, like most five-year-olds, thought of his mommy and daddy as fixed in time, with barely any life before he was born, much less complicated lives before they got married.) Even his feeling that the lady loved him was true, though her love was a desperate, entirely unexpected response that he couldn't possibly have made sense of. But that his parents must be worried about him, that he understood all too well, even if he didn't understand why. It had never occurred to Michael to wonder if something had happened to his parents to make them so chronically afraid. Until that afternoon on the boat, he had no basis of comparison other than the parents of his classmates at school, during the short periods he went to school, but since those parents weren't in the classroom nearly every day, sitting in a corner, watching, as his mother or sometimes his father was, there was no way to tell what they were like.

Naturally, Michael had no idea that those other parents were often whispering about his mother and father, calling the Winters "ridiculously overprotective" and even "insane." It made the other fathers and mothers feel better about themselves; for if they were a bit overprotective at times—or more truthfully, *when* they were overprotective—at least they were nowhere near as bad as David and Kyra Winter.

The other parents never wondered why Michael's parents were this way, and no one else did, either: not the teachers at the four schools Michael briefly attended, not even the woman who'd been cleaning the Winters' house since Michael was three and a half. The teachers did try to reassure Kyra and David: they insisted the bigger boys weren't bullies, just high-spirited; that it was normal to catch colds the first few weeks of the school year; that Michael would have friends, if only they'd give it time—however, the teachers saw no mystery in the Winters' behavior. To be fair, they hardly had a chance to think about it, and not because they were busy with their students, but because they had so many worried parents who required constant reassurance. Yes, the Winters were more extreme, but they still seemed like a type the teachers knew all too well: helicopter parents.

The cleaning woman who came every Friday thought the Winters were nice enough. They gave good tips; they kept the place tidy; they didn't have any of the disgusting habits some of her other employers did. *Hey, they're a hell of a lot better than the guy who trims his beard in the kitchen sink.* She did notice that the little boy was always there, that he seemed pale and lonely and kind of weird. Once she tried to give him a toy that her own kids had out-grown. It was a stuffed bear, "to sleep with," she told him, because she thought it was sad that his little bed was as empty as a monk's. He thanked her three times—always polite, that little boy, unlike her own kids—but he explained that he had allergies and so he couldn't sleep with anything that might "harbor mold." She might have known this if she'd washed Michael's organic sheets the way she washed his parents', but his mother always insisted on doing them herself. Must be because of the kid's allergies, the woman thought, though she'd never seen the little boy sneeze or cough and part of her suspected these allergies were just something for the Winters to worry about. The cleaning woman had a theory that everybody needs worries. If rich people don't have any, she figured, they have to make some up.

Michael's parents weren't rich, but they were rich enough to have their house cleaned once a week. They were rich enough to allow Kyra to work at home. Indeed, both of them were home when Michael disappeared, as they told the police during their frantic call to report that he was gone. They'd called the police immediately, even though each of them felt sure they knew who'd taken him. Even though on some level, they'd always expected this.

Of course their child had been taken away from them; how could it be any other way? He was the best thing in their lives. He was a miracle not only because he was smart and beautiful and a thousand other absolutely perfect things but also because his very existence meant that his parents had let themselves forget about the fear. He was born because, incredibly, after so many years of unrelenting doubt, David and Kyra had allowed themselves a brief period of hope.

And now he was gone, and somewhere deep inside, they weren't even surprised. Because no matter how many locks they'd installed, the idea that they would lose what they loved best was always lurking around the corner, threatening in whispered memories, as close as the next breath.

If every marriage has three stories: the wife's, the husband's, and the story that is created when these two stories try to live side by side, in Michael's parents' case, their individual stories, as different as they were, had one common, overarching, tragic theme. They each came into the marriage with so many cracks inside themselves that it would have been nothing short of astonishing if having a child together had somehow sealed these cracks forever. Instead, sadly, all too predictably, their life together was shaped by their perpetual fear that *something* would happen; it had to, because they didn't deserve this perfect child. They didn't even deserve to be part of a family, because of what they'd done in the past. They never talked about this with anyone, not even with each other, but they thought about what they'd done in a startlingly similar way. Neither of them ever allowed themselves to use the beautiful word *mistake*.

squad. I wished my sister would get an F—or even a B—in Algebra. I wished my sister would have acne, and I wiped my face on her towel once or twice, trying to make her catch it from me.

None of Kyra's wishes came true, which most of her was glad about, because she did care about Amy. Their mother was gone; their stepmother disliked teenagers in general and Amy and Kyra in particular; and their father was a computer programmer with no real interest in raising children because he considered them mystifyingly irrational. Kyra and Amy had each other, period. If their relationship wasn't perfect, or even close to perfect, it was all they had. Sometimes after their stepmother had gotten mad at them for one thing or other, Amy and Kyra would retreat to their room and turn up the one song they knew their stepmother hated: "We are family. I got all my sisters with me."

The grown-up Kyra sometimes wondered if she and Amy had really given their stepmother a chance. Yes, the woman seemed selfish and irritable and really, really uncool—her most damning flaw, from the teenage point of view—but she'd been placed in a very difficult position. She was a thirty-seven-year-old, shy, never-married billing clerk when she met their father and found herself taking care of two girls who'd been without a mother so long they saw no use for her. Indeed, by the time they were fourteen and thirteen, respectively, Amy and Kyra thought they were far more skilled at child care than their stepmother ever could be.

They knew to use baking soda to get baby spit-up stains out of their clothes. They'd taught themselves how to diaper infant boys without getting peed on by using the old diaper as a shield. They could do a good job distracting screaming toddlers, winning the trust of suspicious seven-year-olds, and entertaining any child from babies to preteens little younger than themselves. They were the only two members of the Callahan Child Care Company. Amy had insisted on the name; she thought it would make their babysitting business sound professional. They even advertised on handwritten flyers stuffed in mailboxes. If people smiled at the girls' pretensions, they still used their services because everybody knew that those Callahan girls (Amy and what's-her-name) were good with kids.

Not that the girls liked children especially, but they liked money and they needed money for their college fund. Amy had planned it out perfectly, and the amount they required was pretty staggering, even for the state school where they planned to go: University of Missouri, Kansas City, where their mother had spent three years studying botany before she got pregnant. Amy remembered their mother talking about UMKC, and how happy she was then. Kyra didn't care where they went, as long as it was away from here.

Of all the dreaming teenagers in their little town, few would make it out and even fewer would stay out. Years later, Kyra would admit that she probably would have been one of those failed dreamers herself, if it hadn't been for her sister. Already a prodigious planner at fourteen, by seventeen, Amy had all the skills of a personal accountant. Everything they purchased went in the green ledger she'd bought from the office supply store: every T-shirt, every soda, even the twenty-five-cent gumballs Kyra liked to buy on her way home from the new McDonald's, where she worked after school. The babysitting company had been abandoned as soon as the girls could make real money at real jobs. Amy worked, too, doing data entry at the aluminum plant that was the biggest employer in town. She was the only teenager they'd ever hired, since those jobs were normally saved for the adults who needed them. But no surprise, Amy had somehow managed to convince them, so there she was, sitting at a reception desk rather than standing on her feet, wearing her normal clothes rather than an ugly uniform, coming home without the smell of hamburgers in her hair. And she made three times more than Kyra did, but she put all her money in their joint account and wrote the amounts in the deposit column and shrugged off their stepmother's question about why Amy insisted on sharing everything with her sister. Back in their room, Amy played the "We are family" song, though neither girl liked it anymore. "Just to bother her," Amy said. "Because it's none of her business."

Kyra's response to this was to make a joke under her breath, a dumb joke most likely, as her comic abilities had taken a nosedive once she hit high school. By sixteen, when she still hadn't been kissed by any of the boys Amy had tried to foist her off on, nothing seemed very funny to her. She wished she could ask someone what she was doing wrong, but the only person who wouldn't laugh at the question was Amy, and Kyra already knew what her sister would say. "It's just the guys in this town who can't appreciate you. You'll see when we get to college. It will all work out."

Obviously, Amy was as nice as ever, and Kyra, just as confused. Why *was* her sister sharing all her money? She'd never asked Amy to do that. In a way, it was insulting, as if Amy thought Kyra was too incompetent to make it on her own.

Kyra still went to confession; only the sophistication of her laments had changed. There was one Catholic church in town, and all three priests there had heard some version of Kyra's problems with her sister. But one of them, Father Tom, thought the girl needed something beyond more time on her knees reciting Hail Marys and Our Fathers. Father Tom was young, twenty-eight or twenty-nine; he'd majored in psychology and he recognized all the signs of sibling rivalry in Kyra, but he was also deeply spiritual. In fact, some of his beliefs were decidedly radical. His fellow priests might have been a bit shocked if they'd heard him interrupt Kyra in the middle of one of her tortured rants to ask if she'd considered the possibility that her sister was an angel.

"Are you joking?" Kyra sputtered. "Angels aren't real."

"Not in the ordinary sense, no," Father Tom said quietly. "But there are people in our lives that act as angels for us. They guide us and serve to demonstrate what God's love might look like."

"No way. I've seen her barf hot dogs out of her nose. She's nothing like God. Her sneakers smell."

Father Tom sounded like he was holding back a laugh. "I'm not saying she's physically an angel." Though Kyra knew he was probably thinking Amy looked like an angel. People always said that about her. She had white-blond hair, blue-gray eyes, and a lithe, dancer's body. But her expression was the main thing. *What a beautiful smile she has. She always looks so perfectly happy!*

"She's not an angel," Kyra insisted. "She talks about wanting to have sex way too much to be an angel."

Kyra threw this in hoping to shock the priest, but it didn't work. He asked her to just think about what he'd said. "You don't have a mother," he said, sounding more confident. "You may never have experienced truly unconditional love before. If your sister is offering this to you, you don't want to refuse God's gift."

As Kyra walked over to her evening shift at McDonald's, her thoughts were as dark as the winter night. If Amy was God's gift to her, what, then, was she? God's burden on Amy? It just wasn't fair.

After a few days, she decided that she wasn't sure about UMKC anymore. Maybe MU would be more fun. Columbia was a college town, after all. Maybe she wouldn't even go to college but would instead join the navy or the air force.

When she told Amy what she was thinking, her perfect sister finally got mad. It was the only big fight Kyra remembered them having—until the summer after her junior year in college, when everything went to hell.

"After all this?" Amy said, or more precisely, shouted. She grabbed the green ledger from the top of her dresser and threw it on Kyra's twin bed, missing Kyra's elbow by only an inch or two.

"It was your plan," Kyra said. "Not mine." She drew up her

knees, wrapping her arms around them. She wasn't an angel, but she was thin and flexible, too. In her case, the thin was called skinny. No boobs, no butt, nothing to set off her stick figure but her size 10½ feet and her too-pronounced chin. She had brown hair that she wore long and close to her face, hoping to hide that chin. Her smile, on the rare occasions that she smiled, was nothing like beatific. She couldn't ever remember feeling perfectly happy.

"So you were just pretending to go along?" Amy said, flopping down so fiercely on her own bed that the metal box springs rattled. "You were *humoring* me?"

Amy looked shocked, and no wonder. Their father humored them. It was one of their first realizations, after their mother left when Amy was eight and Kyra was seven. They didn't use that word, but they knew he was just pretending to listen. Pretending to care when they cried for Mommy, Mommy, Mommy.

"I wasn't humoring you," Kyra said. "It's just, I've never had this certainty that you do. About the future. And about . . . whether we have to go to the same school."

She looked away from Amy, but everything in their room condemned her. The money jar on the windowsill. The stack of UMKC brochures on Amy's white dresser. The dresser itself, as they'd discussed whether they would take it with them when they went to college. Amy was planning to work full-time for a year and wait for Kyra to finish high school, so they could be freshmen together and live in their own apartment. It would be right up Rockhill Road, in the area where their mother's college apartment had been. They'd seen the area only once, on a trip to Kansas City when they were so small Kyra was still in a booster seat. She didn't remember the trip, but Amy had the address. She had all the papers their mother had left behind in a box under her bed.

Amy was leaning back against the wall. She had her pillow grasped in her hands and she was twisting it hard—as if, her sister thought, it was a useful substitute for Kyra's neck. Kyra was waiting for her to say something, anything, but the only sound was the ticking of the old-fashioned clock that they'd found at the thrift store. They'd intended to give it to their stepmother for Christmas, but then she'd yelled at Kyra for leaving a spoon in the sink, so they gave her the usual boring black socks instead.

"Why do you care?" Kyra finally said. "You'll have like a zillion friends and a boyfriend and teachers who'll think you're God's gift." Not to mention priests, Kyra thought. She paused for a moment and looked at her hands. They were getting raw, both from the very cold winter and from all the hand washing at stupid McDonald's. She took a breath. "You don't need me."

"I can't go without you," Amy said. "I just can't." All of the anger had left her voice. Was she choking up?

"Yes, you can," Kyra said. "You'll do great. You don't need—"

Amy held her hand up. The tears were coming now, soft, Amy-style tears. No sign of the red, scrunched-up face that made Kyra herself so ugly when she cried. (She'd watched herself cry in the mirror, and actually cried more when she realized how hideous she looked.) But even so, Kyra felt sorry for her sister. Amy almost never cried.

"Don't you love me?" Amy's voice was breaking. Her long lashes were glistening with tears. "How can you not love me, sis? I love you more than anybody in the world."

Kyra felt so horrible that she went to Amy and put her arms around her and said she didn't mean any of it. She said she must have PMS, and hoped Amy wouldn't remember that her period had just ended last week. "Of course I love you," she insisted. "You are the biggest part of everything to me. I can't even imagine the future without you in it." Amy looked up, and Kyra nodded. "God, Amy, everyone loves you. You are the kindest, smartest, person in—"

"I'm not that great," Amy said. "I'm just trying really, really hard. And all those people don't love me. They don't even know me." Her tears were wetting Kyra's shoulder; her snot was dripping onto Kyra's purple shirt. She cried silently for a while. Kyra could feel her sister's chest shaking when she added, "Only you really know me."

Kyra wondered what Amy meant, what Kyra knew about her sister that other people didn't. It surely wasn't the mundane details of the body: the barfed hot dog, the occasional stinky feet, the mole on Amy's forearm that she had to keep shaving or face a long, curly hair growing out from its center that they both agreed was unfair and a little disgusting. It couldn't be their stepmother's random criticisms and punishments. She was hardly Cruella De Vil, and though Amy and Kyra complained about her constantly, part of Kyra knew she wasn't that bad.

Their father's indifference was more important, but Amy had told a few boyfriends about that. It wasn't exactly a secret anyway. Every teacher had remarked on their father's absence at the girls' school functions and parent conferences. Even the priests could tell their father was not a true parent to the daughters in the pew next to him every Sunday at Mass.

What did Kyra know about Amy that no one else did? She snored. Big deal. She had to work very hard sometimes to get her perfect grades. Harder than Kyra herself, actually, but this was a recent development. Kyra had chalked it up to Amy working so much at the aluminum factory. She hadn't let herself consider that she might be better than Amy at something.

Amy was crying harder when she stammered out the word *Mommy*. It wasn't strange; even seventeen-year-old Amy still called for their mother on the rare occasions when she cried. But it reminded Kyra of what she should have known immediately, why Amy thought Kyra knew her better than any of her friends. And why, in fact, she did.

When their mother left, it was a Thursday in July and so hot and humid the gnats stuck to their eyelashes. She said she was going to Overland Park, a suburb of Kansas City where their grandmother lived. Grandma was dying, and she had to go to take care of her.

Their father was at work. She was standing on the curb, holding a liquor store box, pressing its weight against her chest. She'd packed up nearly everything she owned: her clothes and her books and dozens of framed pictures of the girls. The rest of the boxes filled the back of her old Plymouth. In the passenger seat, she'd wrapped a blanket around two limp plants.

Amy had run after her, grabbed her arm, felt it slip in her sweaty hand. "Wait," she panted. "Take me with you."

"Granny is sick, kiddo. I don't think you want—"

"I can help!" Amy said. "I won't do anything wrong!"

Though Kyra barely remembered this, the child Amy was nothing like Amy now. The child Amy was always getting into trouble. Knocking over her milk glass. Melting crayons in the radiator. Breaking their mother's favorite blue bowl. Almost setting the house on fire trying to light a candle for a Barbie tea party.

It was all innocent enough, and it certainly had nothing to do with why their mother didn't come back. Though it was true that their grandmother was dying, it was also true that their mother and father had already filed for divorce. Irreconcilable differences. Full custody awarded to the father but only because the mother did not request custody or even visitation. She did request that she not be required to pay child support, but since she had no steady source of income, the father saw no point in fighting her on that.

Their mother said nothing about the divorce. Instead, she told Amy that if she was a good girl, Mommy would come back for her. It was either an incredibly cruel thing to say or at least very immature. Possibly both.

"Until I come back, though, I want you to stay with your sister." She pointed at the walkway, where Kyra was standing. Kyra was afraid of death. She didn't like to think of Grandma dying.

She couldn't imagine wanting to go with Mommy like Amy did. "You two take care of each other," their mother said, as she put the last box in the car. The closing of the trunk smacked the air and Kyra jumped.

Amy had to be pried off their mother and deposited next to Kyra. Their mother instructed Kyra to "hold your sister's hand." Kyra tried, but Amy managed to shake loose and she followed the Plymouth down the block, running as fast as her short legs would carry her. When their mother gunned the engine at the corner, Amy lost sight of the car and wailed her way back.

Their mother really did go to Grandma's, but when Grandma died, she traveled to all kinds of places, none of them even close to their small town. She sent postcards to Amy and Kyra; she wrote things like, "You should see the Pacific. It's FANTASTIC." "The Liberty Bell isn't all it's cracked up to be. Ha, ha." She never once asked how her daughters were. Kyra didn't care that much, since they obviously couldn't have answered her anyway. None of the postcards had a return address.

They never talked about their mother, not really. Up until Kyra was eleven or so, Amy would occasionally say, "We should save this for Mommy" when they found some treasure in the woods: a shiny rock, a perfect daisy, a snail or a butterfly. It ended one afternoon after Kyra yelled, "She's never coming back!" and smashed something to the ground, she no longer remembered what. But inside Amy's heart, it had not ended. This was what Kyra knew that no one else did.

As Kyra held her crying sister in her arms, she felt sad, but stronger, too. Her sister obviously needed her. When Amy had calmed down, Kyra thought how surprising it was that her sister seemed so perfect on the outside, yet on the inside she was as troubled as anyone, maybe even more troubled than most.

That thinking of Amy this way seemed oddly cheering to Kyra is probably forgivable. She was only a teenager. To the grown-up

Kyra, that day would always be memorable not because she'd discovered that Amy had problems, but because she'd been there for
her sister. She'd held her sister while she wept. And she'd told her
sister the truth, though she didn't know how true it was then—she
couldn't imagine the future without Amy in it.

FOUR

Sandra had put one of the senior nursing assistants in charge and left work only minutes after her son called with the news about Michael. Now she was in the car, stuck in traffic on 95, on the way to her former daughter-in-law's house. She had time to think, but rather than think about what had happened, she found herself thinking about David, what he was like as a boy. What he was like before Courtney.

He'd always treated women well; in fact, he was the kind of boy who respected women more than men—at least more than the old-style, hide-your-feelings-type men he associated with his father. From the time he'd started dating at sixteen years old, he'd demonstrated an enormous amount of compassion: for the girls who cut themselves because their daddies didn't love them, for the girls who refused to eat because they were desperate to be prettier, even for the girls whose mood swings included screaming at him for not doing something they were too unstable to know they wanted, much less ask for. Sandra watched as he took in these crazy girls the same way he took in stray kittens when he was little. Naturally, Sandra did not call David's girlfriends crazy in her son's presence. If anything, she talked herself out of her worries by finding the good in each of her son's choices: Isabelle, the cutter, had such a lovely voice; Miranda, the anorexic, was very smart; Jill, the queen of mood swings, was trying so hard to be normal, you just had to admire her for that.

As David went through high school and college, Sandra wished he would meet a woman who would be easier for him, someone who could take care of him for a change. She also wished he would break up with the ones who weren't easy. Instead, they left him when they tired of his steady reasonableness, his cheerful good nature, his inability to put an end to their fear of being rejected by giving them the criticisms they were always waiting for. He let them break his heart because he found the alternative unbearable.

"You are Prince Charming," Sandra said, to cheer him up, but also because, in truth, he really was back then. He was sensitive, kind, tall, good-looking, and intelligent—so much better in every way, Sandra thought, than herself or her ex-husband. Admittedly, Sandra had a few issues of her own in the self-esteem department. Though she rarely let herself think about it, deep down, she knew that David's unusual ability to take care of screwed-up women was, shall we say, at least partially homegrown.

Courtney was the one who stayed long enough for him to marry. It was her idea, to get married right out of college, but David was excited, too. He loved Courtney, and he really loved the idea of having a proper family. He dreamed of having two or three children who would be sheltered by a picket fence and happy parents. No apartment for his kids. No divorced father who could barely be bothered to visit and refused to attend his own son's wedding because "weddings are meaningless."

Sandra remembered the first time she was afraid for her son. It was after the wedding, at the reception, when she went outside to sneak a smoke. Courtney was out there, too, talking to one of the guys from the caterers. The guy was decent-looking, but what was Courtney doing laughing and chatting out here? Was it possible that she was flirting with another guy on her wedding day? Sandra stomped out her cigarette and threw the butt in the trash. When she went back in, she saw David dancing with Courtney's ancient grandmother. He was smiling and guiding her safely around the floor in the gentlest, most unobtrusive way possible. When he glanced at Sandra, she smiled and gave him a thumbs-up.

They didn't have a honeymoon because David had to settle into New Haven. Graduate school was starting in less than a week. He'd gotten a fellowship to study history; he was planning to get a PhD and become a professor. He was extremely dedicated to his work, while Courtney was . . . not. She was planning to use the next few months discovering what she wanted to do with her life. As if the expensive college paid for by her parents hadn't already given her four years to do this "discovering." David, on the other hand, was a scholarship student. He'd gone to college entirely on his own merits because his father wouldn't pay and Sandra had never made enough to save for college. She'd been lucky to support herself and David on her salary as a geriatric nurse.

Courtney's discovery process ended only six weeks later, when she turned up pregnant. David admitted that she'd told him she was using the pill. "So she lied to you, honey?" Sandra whispered into the phone, though she instantly regretted saying this. Courtney was not about to get an abortion. David was not about to divorce her. What was done was done. Why add trouble to what was already going to be big trouble for her boy?

"I think she just made a mistake," David said. "You know she's not that great at remembering details."

THE WINTERS IN BLOOM

Courtney fancied herself a creative person, and really, she did have some ability as a writer. At least Sandra liked her poems well enough. One of them was read at the wedding, and it had a lot of comparisons: marriage is like two vines growing together, marriage is like the passenger seat joining with the driver's seat of a car, marriage is like the financial merger of the moon with the sun. Some of it didn't make sense to Sandra, but she figured it was her own fault. She'd finished her BS in nursing, but she'd never taken poetry. She couldn't remember the last time she'd read a poem that wasn't a haiku written on the side of a bus.

"Child care is full of details," Sandra said to her son, tapping a pencil against her old kitchen table. "You have to remember to change their diapers, feed them, take them in for their vaccinations."

"I'm sure she'll be fine," David said, in that tone that made it obvious he didn't want to hear any more. He would never let Sandra criticize any of his girlfriends, and certainly not his wife. Though it sometimes frustrated her, Sandra admired this about him. She also liked that it went both ways. No one was allowed to criticize his mother, either.

But Courtney wasn't fine, unfortunately. She got very sick in her first trimester, a relatively uncommon condition known as hyperemesis gravidarum. Sandra had seen women with hyperemesis: basically, they couldn't stop throwing up, and it often meant going to the hospital for IV fluids. Now when David called his mother, he often sounded exhausted from taking Courtney to the hospital late at night and waking up at seven for his classes the next morning. He was taking three difficult seminars and he'd signed on to be a teaching assistant, to supplement his fellowship. He was also tutoring undergraduates. Whatever he could do to bring in the money they'd need when the baby came.

David was always extremely responsible. It was another difference between them. Courtney thought the world owed her an easy time of things. She railed against everything during her sickness: against their apartment, against their new town, even against David for getting her pregnant (no, the irony didn't stop her).

Sandra went to visit them as often as she could. She wanted to help, even though it meant driving five hours to New Haven and sleeping on their uncomfortable IKEA couch. They had only one bedroom, but she told Courtney that if she moved her writing desk out of the bedroom and into the living room, there would be space for a little nursery. "You can put a crib right here," Sandra said, standing between the two windows. "And a changing table under one window, and a little chest for the baby's things under the other."

"And just how am I supposed to write in there?" Courtney said. She'd already thrown up a dozen or more times that day. Sandra was trying to remember to feel sorry for her.

The truth was that she most likely wouldn't be writing, at least not for the rest of her pregnancy and the first few months of child care. But Sandra said, "As long as the TV isn't on, what's the difference? Neither one of you ever turns it on, do you?"

When Courtney frowned, Sandra thought she looked a little like that other Courtney, the one who was on the new TV show *Friends*. Like the TV girl, her daughter-in-law had an oval face, bright blue eyes, great skin, and near perfect features, but she also had thick red hair, which Sandra thought made her even prettier than the other Courtney. Sandra might have mentioned the resemblance if she wasn't sure her daughter-in-law had never watched that show. She knew they never turned on the TV, because she kept wishing they would. It might be something she and Courtney could do together. David was in his carrel at the library, working on a paper that was due on Monday.

"Writing requires inspiration," Courtney said. "You can't just do it anywhere like other jobs."

Sandra gave up, but four or five visits later (she lost count, she was up there so often), she found the desk had been moved into the living room. That weekend, she took Courtney to Toys "R" Us to help her pick out a crib. They also got a changing table with pullout wire shelves, because it was on sale. David was working again, tutoring a rich boy whose father paid him a hundred dollars an hour to help his kid write papers for history and English. Courtney complained about being alone so much, but really, David had no choice in the matter.

Sandra hoped all her visits would help Courtney feel less lonely. She and her daughter-in-law were definitely getting closer; at least Courtney seemed to be opening up more. It was a few visits later; they were sitting at a vegetarian restaurant, when out of the blue, Courtney said, "Did you ever feel like you didn't want your baby?"

Sandra was tired; she wished she could have a good steak. David was off running a review session for the class he was a TA for: "American History after World War II." He was excited because they were covering the sixties, one of his favorite decades, historically speaking. Sandra was a teenager in the sixties, but she didn't find that time exciting. If anything, she thought of it as one death after another: from JFK to Martin and Bobby. She'd kept a scrapbook of newspaper clippings about the assassinations and the riots and the war and the kids who were killed at Kent State. Her mother used to call her morbid, but her son thought she'd been a budding historian herself. Maybe so, but she'd never considered being anything but a nurse. She chose geriatric nursing because she loved taking care of old people. Even when she was very young, just getting started, she saw no real difference between the oldest patients—the ones stuck in wheelchairs, the ones who couldn't leave their beds—and herself. They were all just human beings with dreams and desires and pains and embarrassments. Plus, she didn't mind the bedpans and "old smells" that turned off many nursing students. Sure, it wasn't always pleasant, but it was a good day's work. It made her feel needed, which Sandra thought she couldn't live without. For her, it was the same feeling she had taking care of her baby.

But had she ever felt like she didn't want her son? Courtney's question unnerved her. The girl was six and a half months pregnant; it was far too late to get an abortion. Why was she asking this, when Sandra had just spent the day cheering her up? She'd taken Courtney for a manicure and a haircut, and helped her pick out three new maternity dresses. She was still too thin, still vomiting too often to really gain much, but the baby bulge had grown to the point that her jeans wouldn't fit even if she left them unzipped. Now, wearing her green-flowered dress, with that red hair neatly falling at her shoulders, she looked even prettier than usual. But she was frowning and her eyes looked so sad.

"I don't know," Sandra tried. "I wanted to get pregnant, so it was different for me. I'd also been married for a few years." What she didn't say was that she'd wanted a baby because her husband was a salesman and never home. It was a stupid solution, when you got right down to it, but she was still young enough to think that all her marriage needed was a baby for her to play with. Then she wouldn't be so desperate to see her husband that she was turning him off with her pleas and tears.

Courtney stood up and rushed in the direction of the bathroom. She'd only had a few sips of water and one bite of her quiche. Sandra thought about following her, holding her hair, but she was worried the waiter would think they'd left. And Courtney didn't really want that from Sandra. She didn't like to be mothered; she'd made it clear that she associated mothering with being controlled. Courtney's own mother had bossed her around at the wedding. That was all Sandra knew about the woman, but it probably explained Courtney's attitude.

Sandra spent five minutes or more looking around the restaurant. It was one of those places with stuff on every wall. Next to her was a dented oil can from the forties, and a large glass box with a dusty hat and chipped cane that looked like they were from another century. The place was packed with people. Her daughter-in-law had told her it was considered hip—or did she say cool? Whatever they called it now.

"Sometimes I hate this baby," Courtney said, slumping back into her side of the booth. Her face was pale. Her hands were trembling.

"I think that's normal with your condition," Sandra said. She'd looked it up, and it was, actually. "Once the baby is born, you'll feel—"

"Like I'm trapped with a screaming baby, in a town where I know no one, with a husband who doesn't care."

"David cares about you," she said, maybe a bit too firmly. She wanted Courtney to feel she could talk to her, but there were limits. And David had been killing himself to provide for her and the baby. He also told her she was beautiful all the time; he brought her flowers he'd picked by the side of the road; he cooked dinner whenever he was home. What more could she want?

When Courtney grew silent, Sandra said, "I know you're in a tough spot right now. What can I do to help?"

Courtney was twirling her straw in her water. She looked up and laughed, but it was a little bitter. "Let me go back in time to seven months ago?"

"I wish I could," Sandra said. Truer words had never been spoken. She would have given pretty much anything to get these kids out of this situation. Maybe David was ready to be a father—Sandra wasn't sure about that—but Courtney was so obviously not ready to be a mother. She worried about her son, but she'd also started to worry about the baby, her *grandchild*. It kept surprising Sandra: she was only forty-six and about to be a grandmother.

A song came on that Courtney liked and she cheered up, or at least, she changed the subject to something cheerier: David was taking her out to some fancy restaurant next week, for the anniversary of their first date. One of her new maternity dresses had been chosen specifically for the occasion. She also talked about something she was writing, a story about a woman who gives her uterus to a gay man, so that he can have a child. Sandra thought she meant the woman agreed to give birth to a child for the gay man, but no. "She hands the uterus to him," Courtney said. "Just like handing over a loaf of bread."

"But what does he do with it?"

"He puts it inside of himself, so he can get pregnant." Courtney's voice sounded a little annoyed, as if she were thinking: what else would he do with it?

Sandra was stuck on the basic facts of anatomy. There was no place inside a man where a uterus could go. And what would it be attached to? But all she said was "That's different," and Courtney took it as a compliment. She always wanted to be original. In fact, she gave up on this story a few months later, when, as she told Sandra, she discovered that someone had beaten her to it and written an entire novel about a woman who loses a uterus. "That one is lost, and mine is given away, but it's close enough," Courtney said, sighing. "It's like somebody else always gets my ideas first."

When they left the restaurant, Courtney was still in a good mood. Sandra drove carefully, hoping to avoid any bumps that might make her daughter-in-law nauseous. They got back to the apartment and David was there and happy to go on and on about how beautiful Courtney looked, from hair to eyes, from face to dress. He even mentioned her shoes, which, as Courtney pointed out, were the same brown Mary Janes she'd been wearing for months. David laughed and kissed Courtney's hand. "Well," he said, "apparently I've always loved those shoes."

The couple ended up on the couch together: Courtney resting her head on Sandra's bed pillow, David slouching on the other end, rubbing her feet. Sandra was sitting on a hard kitchen chair that she'd pulled into the living room. But she was feeling pretty good, seeing her son and his wife relaxing together and, best of all, watching TV. It was Courtney's idea to turn it on, and even though they didn't have cable, they got *Murphy Brown*, which was one of Sandra's weekly shows.

Over time, the visits to David and Courtney would become one big clump—Sandra couldn't remember if something happened in the winter or the spring, the sixth visit or the ninth, the flat-tire drive or the ice-storm drive, a weekend she called a "short vacation" or a midweek trip using her personal days—but she was positive that there were a lot of moments like this when everything seemed good. And when she added up all these positive times, she rested easier, convinced that her son's new family would be all right.

Later, she couldn't believe that she'd let herself forget what she'd learned in her marriage: it's not the happy parts that will tell you what will happen next. No matter how much you want them to, the happy parts—as long as they're only *parts*, and easy to recognize precisely because they're not the normal state of things—can only give you heartache. Even the good memories they provide aren't really good, because every one just reminds you of what you were too dumb to see at the time.

Sandra refused to believe that it was David's fault, what Courtney did. But she had no problem blaming herself for not figuring out what was going to happen and stepping in to stop it. Courtney was a twenty-three-year-old kid. Her parents were always too busy to visit. So the only adult around was Sandra, and her failure to save her son's first family would always be like a weight she carried on her back. And it literally aged her. She got arthritis by fifty, her hair turned gray, and her energy level dipped, never to come back.

Fifteen years later, she still hadn't cut back her schedule as a geriatric nurse, though she felt older than some of her patients, and much older that her sixty-one years. Luckily, her eyes were fine and she had no problem negotiating the traffic as she made her way to the quaint little suburb where Courtney lived. She knew David was wrong to suspect Courtney of taking his son—because she knew Courtney. It was the only secret she'd kept from David, who had changed so much over the years, sometimes she barely recognized the boy he'd been in the man he'd become.

Sandra didn't plan to deceive him, but someone had to take care of Courtney when she got out of the hospital. Her parents had essentially disowned her: what she'd done was a stain on their ordered life with their fancy friends. So Sandra found her an apartment in Philadelphia, nursed her back to something like sanity, and even helped her find a job as a technical writer. She saw her less often in the last few years, but they still kept in touch. Courtney never stopped being grateful for what Sandra had done, and for her forgiveness.

The row house where she lived had a heavy iron door knocker. Sandra picked it up and dropped it twice before she accepted that Courtney wasn't home. It was a nice day, cooler after yesterday's rain, so she decided to wait on the porch swing. It was only two o'clock. Courtney usually got off early on Tuesday, but maybe she'd had to run some errands. She'd never remarried; she had no roommates. She lived alone, in a life not that different from Sandra's.

A breeze blew up and the wind chimes on the porch were singing. Courtney had planted a little garden in the front yard: pink dahlias surrounding a white hibiscus, with yellow roses on the vine that climbed on the porch rail. It was a peaceful place to wait, but Sandra's hands were throbbing from her arthritis, which was always worse when she was nervous. Her stomach hurt, too; she wished she hadn't eaten lunch, though of course at lunchtime, she hadn't known what had happened yet.

She closed her eyes and thought of her grandson, Michael. He barely knew her, because David wouldn't let Sandra take the boy anywhere unless he was also with them. Sometimes she got confused, trying to remember what Michael was like when he was little. She'd stare at a picture of him, but in her mind, she'd see the other baby, the one she knew so well that she could quiet him with just a coo and a touch.

She had so many regrets. What if she'd told Courtney the truth that day in the restaurant? Sometimes you won't understand your child. Maybe you'll wish—just for a moment—that you'd never had them. But that doesn't mean you wouldn't die for them in a second. They become everything to you; of course that hurts sometimes. And even when they leave, they're always there, inside your mind, imprinted on your body: the arms that held them, the voice that sang to them, the eyes that cried for all their heartbreaks, from skinned knees to lost loves. So sure, I guess it's a hard truth, when you get right down to it. There is no you anymore without them.

FIVE

As hard as it was for Kyra to believe now, she couldn't deny that back in college, Zachary Barnes had been the kind of boy that attracted girls. He had long black hair and a stubble beard that made him seem cool, especially as he was from Seattle, which seemed strange and exotic even before the city became the cool center of the world thanks to grunge bands. He also seemed more grown up than other college boys because, in fact, he was. He'd spent six years in the army before he'd started at UMKC. He'd been out of the country, the first person she'd ever met who had.

Zach was often quiet, making him seem mysterious, like he knew things that other people didn't. Kyra thought he was wiser than every other boy at school—but he wasn't wise enough not to fall in love with Amy. It was almost the first thing he did at college, right after he signed up for his premed courses: he started dating the pretty girl in line behind him at the registrar's office.

He wasn't deterred when he found out that pretty girl wasn't in line to sign up for classes but to withdraw from school. He didn't tell her it was a mistake, because Amy could still make anything sound like a good idea, even quitting college after only one year to follow her dream (when did this become her dream?) of becoming a singer.

If only someone had thought to get Amy to a psychologist when she started having problems during freshman year. It was obvious even at the time that Amy seemed hell-bent on reenacting their mother's life, but Kyra didn't know why and she didn't know any psychologists. When Amy told Kyra that their mother had wanted to be a singer, too, and this was why she'd left them, it was news to Kyra, and she was mystified how her sister could know this when she didn't. Amy wouldn't say, but she glowed as she talked about their mother's voice. "It was so beautiful. I only hope I can sound half as good as she did."

Kyra didn't remember her mother singing, not once. Though she must have sung hymns at church and carols at Christmas and "Happy Birthday" at least a few times a year, her voice hadn't stood out at all. Sometimes Kyra thought Amy was making all this up, creating a better, glamorous, version of their mother. But the strange part was that Amy didn't need their mother to be talented, because Amy's own voice had *always* stood out. Even when the two girls sang along with "We Are Family," Amy sounded as good as the famous sisters who'd recorded the song. She'd been picked for every solo in grade school, and her high school chorus teacher had begged her, each year, to try out for the musical, but she was working and saving money for college and she didn't have time.

Zachary Barnes wanted to help Amy, and Kyra had given up trying to argue her sister out of her "dream." He knew a guitar player, a guy who called himself Peanut. Peanut's band was doing gigs in town, nowhere fancy, but they were making a living doing cover tunes. When Zach brought Amy to one of their rehearsals, Peanut decided they could use a "chick talent." And just like that, Amy wasn't a student anymore; she was a singer in a band.

Zach and Amy had been dating for nearly a year when Amy broke his heart. The first time. It was at a bar on the Country Club Plaza, the most upscale place Amy and the band had ever played. Kyra had just finished the last finals of her sophomore year, and she was only at the bar reluctantly, because Amy had begged her to come to the gig. She was sitting at a table by herself, as far away from the music as possible. The waitress was already annoyed that she was only sipping a Coke. If she'd been closer to the stage, the waitress might have carded her and thrown her out.

As always, she was impressed by how good her sister sounded, belting out pop songs like "We Didn't Start the Fire," and "Right Here Waiting." But the song that moved Kyra the most was Amy's cover of George Michael's "Faith." The song wasn't actually about religion, but the happy, up-tempo chorus line about having faith made her feel lonelier and strangely lost, like she wasn't sure where she belonged. It was partly because she and Amy hadn't been to Mass since they moved to Kansas City, but it was also because she felt like she didn't even know her sister anymore. Who was this girl standing in front of these four men Kyra had barely spoken to? Amy called the guys in the band her "mates." Kyra was almost positive she'd slept with Peanut, and she suspected she'd slept with Tim, the drummer, too. Amy rehearsed with them at a run-down house in the suburbs, and often, she was gone all night. She said they were "jamming," but she came home smelling of weed and sex. When she woke Kyra to tell her how well it had gone, she seemed drunk or high or both. Kyra tried locking her bedroom door, but it didn't work. Amy would knock and beg, "Hey. Let me in, okay? I have to tell you about the coolest thing! I want to give you a morning hug, too, you goofball!"

No wonder Zach loved Amy. Although she was no longer

the good girl she'd been, she was still so sweet and affectionate. Whenever Kyra was unhappy—at least on the rare occasions when she couldn't hide it—her sister worked so hard to cheer her up. She went to the bakery and got a half dozen of the giant cinnamon rolls Kyra loved; she spent hours straightening up her room and the rest of the apartment, knowing that Kyra got depressed when things weren't put away; she gently brushed Kyra's hair and worked it into braids. Kyra suspected that even her sleeping around was mostly driven by her desire to make the guys happy, to give them what they wanted, especially since, as she said, shocking Kyra, sex was "such an easy thing to do for someone." Everyone loved Kyra's sister, even the girls who otherwise would have called her a slut. Kyra did, too, though Kyra's love had become stern and unforgiving. She truly believed Amy was in danger of ruining her life. And then Amy announced that she was going to do another stupid thing, something almost as bad as quitting school: she was going to break up with the one boy who really cared about her.

Zach didn't know—or wouldn't let himself know—that Amy was sleeping with other people. When she told him she was busy, he accepted it. Maybe because she still asked him to come over at least two nights a week. Often, she would ask for his help with something like a leaky faucet in the apartment or the battery of her car, and then she would make him dinner and let him spend the night. Kyra could hear them laughing and moaning. Her face would turn bright red; she usually fell asleep with her pillow smashed over her ears. When she woke up in the morning, she got dressed and left the apartment as quickly as possible, so she wouldn't run into him in the hall. She didn't want to see his skin warm and pink from sleeping in her sister's bed, his hair tousled from her sister's touch. But she wasn't aware that she liked him *that* way. She hadn't let herself consider the possibility, because she was so convinced that Zach was the only thing standing between Amy and utter chaos.

"I know you're going to be mad at me," Amy said. She sat down at Kyra's table and took a big gulp of Kyra's soda. The band was on a break. She seemed too hyper, as she always did at her gigs, but she claimed it was simply the excitement of performance. "You think he's good for me, and I know you're right. But I'm not ready for this. I'm going to have to tell him I just think of him as a friend."

Kyra was stunned into speechlessness, but Amy quickly changed the topic to Kyra's finals, which Amy claimed she was sure Kyra had aced. "You're the star of the math department, Miss 4.0. You can say what you want about me"—she smiled a half smile—"though I wish you wouldn't . . . but you are an unqualified success." She grabbed Kyra's hand. Her fingers were so warm, even though she was wearing a low-cut tank top and a skirt that barely covered her thighs. Her blond hair was longer now, with a blunt cut that made the ends look very sharp. Sharp enough, Kyra thought, to give someone a paper cut, except of course it would have to be called a "hair cut," which made no sense.

Kyra never considered herself the star of the math department, yet it was true that she'd already taken an upper-level proof class and done well. She and Amy had started math together, in the same section of the same course, their first semester at UMKC. Kyra had gotten a perfect grade, while Amy had ended up with a C in that class and Bs or Cs in all her others, though she'd worked much harder than Kyra. That was the beginning of the end, as Amy stopped trying only a month or two later. She started saying things like "I'm not very smart" and "I'm not the type to be in college." After all her plans, she let UMKC go with as little thought as she gave to selling back her books at the end of the semester. Unfortunately, she was following their mother here, too, though their mother had hung on for three years, while Amy decided to leave after only one.

"I'm not going to say anything bad about you," Kyra said

slowly, "but I think you're making a huge mistake. He's really smart and sensitive and—oh, cripes." It was dark in the bar, but Kyra recognized Zach coming toward them with the big smile he reserved only for Amy. When he smiled like that, Kyra thought the whole world seemed better.

"Hey, babe," he said, and sat down next to Amy. He leaned over to give her a kiss, but she turned her face so he was forced to kiss her cheek. It was the first time she'd done this, so he had to be confused. Amy must have sensed that and thought the best thing would be to tell him right then. Or maybe she just wanted to get it over with. Whatever her reason, Kyra felt terrible that he had to hear this in a crowded bar, with Amy about to go on stage.

He didn't say a word; he just stood up and headed toward the exit. Amy was crying, but Peanut came over to tell her it was time to play again, and he hugged her and told her it was for the best. "We're musicians. We can't get entangled with day giggers, even cool ones like Zach."

Maybe he was joking about the stupid day giggers remark, but it infuriated Kyra. She left to find Zach. He was walking down Nichols Road toward the parking garage. She caught up with him right as he was putting the key in the door of his old yellow Jeep.

"She doesn't deserve you," she whispered, and then she impulsively reached out and folded him in her arms. When she felt his shoulders moving, she realized he was crying.

"I love her," he stammered. "I can't stand to see her do this."

Kyra thought by "this" he meant Amy breaking up with him. But no. He said something about Amy being in trouble, and Kyra figured out that he was worried about her sister. That was why he was crying. Kyra admired him so much at that moment. He was such a good person. She offered to go to his apartment with him because she knew he really needed someone to talk to.

He lived in a basement apartment not far from Kyra and Amy's place. Kyra had never been there, but Amy had told her it felt like a cave and she was right. It was almost as dark as the bar, with only tiny windows near the ceiling and wood paneling on every wall. Zach said it had been furnished with stuff the owners of the house above him didn't want. A beige Formica dinette set with two metal chairs. A brown-and-gray striped couch that was sagging in the middle. A yellowing white ottoman. A three-legged desk with a stack of schoolbooks serving as the fourth leg. A mattress on the floor in the corner, with the sheets twisted up and the blanket kicked to the bottom.

"I'm planning to move somewhere better at the end of the summer," he said. "I just need to work and save up a deposit."

"It's fine," Kyra said. She sat down on the far end of the couch to avoid the quicksand of the middle sag. "Our apartment isn't perfect, either. Don't worry."

Kyra and Amy's apartment was furnished with used stuff, too, from a thrift store, but the difference was their place looked pretty. They'd bought wicker baskets and wicker laundry hampers to store their books and clothes and shoes, and they'd painted their junk furniture white, to make the place look airy. They'd made their own curtains from cloud-blue sheets. They'd covered all the walls with the musician posters Amy loved, and the clocks Kyra was always picking up at garage sales. She had seventeen clocks at this point: the biggest, an old white one rimmed in black, three feet across, that used to hang in the front hallway of some elementary school; the smallest, no bigger than a quarter with cardboard hands, painted green and curved like fingernail cuttings. Her favorite present for her nineteenth birthday was a clock that Zach had found for her: a plastic raccoon with the time in his belly. On the hour, the raccoon's eyes moved and his tail swayed back and forth: twelve sways for twelve o'clock, etc. He said it was corny but Kyra thought it was perfect and she'd hung it over by her cuckoos and her clock with the lion's mane.

Zach mumbled something about how much more comfortable

he'd always felt in Kyra and Amy's apartment, which Kyra thought was an obvious reference to how comfortable he'd felt being with Amy. When he got out an unopened bottle of whiskey from the metal cabinet over his sink, she didn't disapprove. Of course he needed a little something to drown his sorrows. His heart was broken.

After he sat down on the other end of the couch, he poured the whiskey into two Welch's jelly glasses. "Last night, I told her she has to stop," he said. "I told her if she didn't agree to quit, I was going to have to do it. She begged me not to, but I said, 'It's for your own good.' I really thought she understood that I was only trying to help."

"Do what?" Kyra said. "I don't know what you mean."

He took a gulp of his drink. "It's the one thing she made me promise I wouldn't do." He looked up. "I have to do it though. I can't think of anything else to try."

Kyra heard loud footsteps coming from the ceiling and what sounded like marbles being dropped. She wondered how Zach could study here. He was a very good student. His professors had told him that if he kept up his grades, with his experience as a medic in the army, he was a shoo-in for medical school.

"Amy is using," Zach finally said. "Not just weed, which I don't care about. Coke, speed, whatever she can get her hands on to be up for the gig."

Kyra was stunned, but she knew she shouldn't have been. No wonder Amy was so intense at the clubs. She swallowed hard and peered at Zach. "But what did you tell Amy you were going to do about it?"

"This," he said, lowering his face. "Talking to you."

"She didn't want you to tell me?" Kyra took a big drink from her own whiskey. "*That's* what she begged you not to do?"

He nodded. "She respects you more than anybody in the world. If anyone could talk her into getting clean, it's you."

"She does?" Kyra was repeating this new fact over and over in her mind: *Amy respects me more than anybody in the world.* How could this be true? Because she got good grades? Big deal. UMKC wasn't exactly what you'd call a hard college. (Kyra had thought it was hard, until she started doing well. Then she figured it couldn't be.)

"Oh yeah," he said, leaning back, letting the old couch absorb him. "She thinks you're a genius. She said when you two were kids, you were the smartest girl in the whole town."

"That's just false," Kyra said. "Amy was the smartest girl. I was merely average."

"Only because you didn't care," Zach said, glancing at Kyra. "Amy told me about your mom leaving. She said it really hit you hard." He paused. "Must have been rough for both of you."

"Not really," Kyra said, because she believed this. But Zach pointed out this was another reason Amy respected her: she never complained; she was tough.

There was no point in arguing this with him. Instead Kyra listened as he talked about how wonderful Amy was and how he couldn't stand to see her hurt herself. He said he'd always hoped they'd end up married. He wanted to have kids with Amy. He wanted to spend his life with her.

They were both drinking pretty heavily—Zach was on his third tumbler, Kyra on her second—when Kyra realized she still didn't know what to do about Amy's drug problem. Of course she would confront her sister, but when that didn't work, then what?

Zach had been silent for a few minutes when he said, apropos of nothing other than the fact that he was getting drunk, "You're cute, you know that?"

"No." Kyra could feel her face growing warm, but she forced a laugh. "I'm okay-looking, but I don't think I'm even slightly *cute*."

"You are," he said. "And you're even cuter because you don't know it."

He was leaning toward her and she could hear her heart pounding in her ears. He came so close; he put his arm around her. When he whispered, "I wish I'd met you before I met Amy," his breath tickled her neck. But when she stupidly tried to kiss him, he said, "I can't." Then he leaned back and collapsed in on himself.

He looked so sad that Kyra tried to put her embarrassment aside. She told him he would get Amy back, though she didn't believe it. She said he would get someone better, which he refused to believe. She listened to his random memories about her sister for what felt like hours while he drank and drank his whiskey, though she herself had stopped drinking after she'd tried to kiss him. She didn't want to lose what little inhibition she had left or she might cry and ask him why no one ever seemed to like her.

When it became clear that Zach was far too drunk to drive her home, she helped him over to the mattress. He fell into a stupor immediately, and he didn't wake up when she pulled off his shoes and socks. He had great feet; she'd noticed them every time he'd been barefoot at their apartment. His toes were long and elegant and the tops of his nails were as smooth and rounded as ten little guitar picks. The calluses on the bottoms just made his feet more endearing to her. He'd been in the army. He wasn't some kid; he was a man who'd been willing to sacrifice himself to keep the country safe. (Well, that and to earn money for college.)

After she covered him with his fraying gray blanket, she knelt on the bed, looking at his face. She gently brushed a stray hair from his mouth. She traced his light brown eyebrows with her fingertips; she held his cheeks in her hands. She even touched her lips to his, but so lightly she wasn't sure if she'd made contact.

In her entire life, she'd never wanted anything as badly as she wanted him to wake up and pull her to him. But when it didn't happen, she stood up and started the long walk home. It was a beautiful night. The moon was hanging low in the sky and Kyra was looking at it as the tears started. She was giving herself a stern talking-to though, telling herself to *cut it out* and *be reasonable*. It only made sense that she and Zach should not do anything together until he was over Amy. And the truth was, even if he'd wanted to sleep with her as much as she wanted to sleep with him (or even half as much), it really wouldn't have been a good idea. She was still a virgin, and he had years of experience. What if she'd disappointed him?

It wasn't planned, at least not consciously, but it turned out to be only a few weeks later when Kyra finally lost her virginity with fellow math major and quasi-friend Ford Trundale. Ford was also a virgin, and nothing about their sexual experience was memorable other than that he burned her shoulders and chest with candle wax when he went to move the four "romantic" candles over to her side of the bed so he could see her body in the dark. She didn't cry out because Zach was in her apartment that night, too, down the hall in bed with Amy, who had decided that sex was allowed as part of their new, just-friends status. Amy had been up front that she wasn't going to be exclusive, and Kyra thought Zach was setting himself up for a massive heartache. At least Amy had agreed to quit whatever drugs she was using. When Kyra had confronted her about it, she'd promised that in the future she would stick to coffee and Vivarin to get her up for gigs. Kyra could tell she meant it; the only question was whether she could actually do it.

Ford Trundale. Kyra had more or less forgotten everything about him except his name, when, a decade later, she and David had been dating long enough that they were ready to talk about past lovers. Naturally, she started with the boy named after the car. She tried to make it funny by connecting the boy with Ford's biggest automotive failure, the Pinto, a car her father had briefly owned. Her joke had something to do with blowing up at the wrong time, but of course there is no right time for a car to blow up, and David just looked confused and a little sad.

They were sitting on a blanket at Fairmount Park. They'd packed a picnic lunch, but they hadn't opened anything but the wine. David felt around for a flat spot in the ground and set his glass down carefully. He picked up Kyra's hand and kissed her palm. "Why are you joking about this guy?"

He was so sincere. It was one of the things Kyra loved about him. She immediately realized she'd handled it all wrong. "I didn't joke about him then," she explained. "I would never have hurt him like that." It was true. She'd picked Ford because he was moving to California the next week. He'd been accepted as a transfer student at UC Berkeley. He didn't want a girlfriend; he just wanted what she wanted: to stop being a virgin as soon as possible, and definitely before turning into an adult, meaning age twenty.

"I don't care about him," David said. The sun made his hair look auburn. His big brown eyes seemed so innocent. "Did he hurt you?"

David had a bedrock belief that men hurt women far more often than women hurt men. Kyra assumed this had started in his childhood, but she wasn't sure what had happened, other than that his parents had gotten divorced. What she was sure of was that David treated all the women in his life with the utmost respect: from his mother to the people he worked with to an overburdened waitress or grumpy dry-cleaning clerk. No surprise, he also spoke very highly of Kyra herself. He talked about her as though she was beautiful, brilliant and, just as important, extremely responsible. He knew she'd been a scholarship student as he was. He loved that she'd worked hard for her success. And he concluded—though he didn't share this part with Kyra or even fully admit it to himself— that his wonderful girlfriend was incapable of doing something as rash and irresponsible as what his first wife did.

Kyra didn't know what had happened in David's first marriage, but she sensed that he viewed her as a much better person than his former wife and, frankly, as a much better person than she actually was. Of course she told him that Ford Trundale had burned her with the candles, and accepted his sympathy for that, because anything else would have led to what she'd felt for Zach and what she'd done to Amy and all the things she didn't want him to know.

She already knew that David was going to be the love of her life, and she knew all too well how lucky she was to have found him. Most of the time she was deliriously happy, but occasionally she would find herself stricken with fear that he would realize the secret truth that she'd been running from since the last time she saw Amy, and maybe even before, maybe since that hot summer day when her mother left—that there was something wrong with her, something inside herself that she couldn't see or change, which eventually, always, would make her impossible to love.

SIX

David had not hesitated to tell the police that he believed his ex-wife had taken his son. They promised to investigate; for now, though, they needed answers to some questions. Many of the questions were exactly what anyone would expect—the what, where, when, and how of what had happened to their son—but some of them seemed bizarre. That's what David thought anyway. And he certainly didn't expect to end up in a conversation with a detective about the philosophical theory that even very young children had some rights to self-determination.

It started when the first two officers wondered why they'd chosen homeschooling. The police were from the city: David assumed they'd dealt with murders and domestic violence and robberies and drug busts, and yet they talked like homeschooling was some kind of *crime*.

"And you're not religious?" one of the officers asked. Sitting at their dining room table, he seemed like a giant. His hands were so big that when he picked up the coffee mug Kyra had given him, the mug became invisible.

It was the second time for this question. David repeated the answer. No. He and his wife were sitting on the other side of the table, holding hands. He thought his hand was sweating—or was it Kyra's hand? He could feel her trembling, but at least she'd stopped crying and saying it was all her fault. She'd done absolutely nothing wrong. She was in the kitchen; David was in his office. She'd gone down the hall to ask David if he wanted her to pick up vegetables for supper tonight, and when she came back, Michael was gone.

This time, David also told the police, thinking it might help somehow, "We do believe in God, though."

"Does your god allow Michael to attend school?"

"Of course," David said, and, once again, explained that their decision to homeschool was based on Michael's educational needs, pure and simple.

"Does your son have any friends?" the second officer asked. He wasn't small, but he seemed small next to the other one. He was older, with wisps of gray hair coming out of his ears.

"How is that relevant?" David said.

The officer just stared. Kyra whispered, "Because he could be over at one of his friends' houses now."

"All right then, no. But he's only five years old. He'll make friends," David said firmly. "But he can't get back these years if he spends them in a school where he's afraid to be himself because the teacher can't control the classroom bullies."

"Was your son bullied?" the giant officer said. He put down his coffee cup and picked up his pen and pad. "I'll need the names."

"You think another five-year-old kidnapped him?" David snapped.

"He wasn't really bullied," Kyra said. "But he was only four years old—" She broke off because she was crying again. David squeezed her hand. "He'd started a year early," David explained, "because he was gifted. Some of the other boys seemed a little threatening. We were just worried it wouldn't be a good environment for him."

"What do you mean by *threatening*?" the second officer asked. And David tried to explain. And the large one asked another question. And on and on, until the officers were satisfied that homeschooling had nothing to do with what had happened to Michael. But then the older officer went in another ridiculous direction.

"Do your beliefs keep you from taking Michael to the doctor for medical treatment?"

"Of course not," David said. Kyra stood up and said she wanted to talk to the lead detective, who was upstairs, examining Michael's room. In the meantime, David told the officers that yes, their son's vaccinations were up to date, and moreover, he was at the doctor's office more than most children because he had allergies. "If you want to call his doctor, her name is Sheila Upland. She's an excellent pediatrician. I can give you her number if you like."

The giant officer said yes, they wanted the number. He said the police would have to call Dr. Upland to see if there had been any "incidents." "Has he ever been in the hospital?"

"Yes," David said. "He had—"

"Then we'll need those records, too."

"But it has nothing to do with this. He had—"

"No need to discuss it, Mr. Winter, until we get the records."

"But it was meningitis when he was two!"

"He was sick—got it." The older officer looked at David. "It's okay, I'm writing it down. We're only trying to help you here."

When Kyra returned, a man was walking behind her whose mere presence silenced the other officers. His name was Detective Ingle. He looked about forty, very thin, with a red nose that made him look like a drinker. His voice was gravelly but so quiet David had to concentrate to hear him.

The detective sent the officers outside to do another sweep of the backyard. Detective Ingle leaned against the dining room hutch and explained how the investigation would proceed. It all made sense, and it had a calming effect on David, who hoped that this man knew what he was doing. David hoped Kyra felt calmer, too, but he wasn't sure. She'd said she had something to do and disappeared in the direction of her study.

He was still wondering what his wife could possibly have to do right then when the detective cleared his throat. "Hope you don't mind, but I'm curious. You told my colleagues you have no recent pictures of your son. Why's that?"

At least this was actually relevant to finding Michael. David was angry with himself for not having a picture the police could use. It had been fourteen months since the last photo, and, as the detective pointed out, children grow very quickly. It was true: Michael at five and a half looked very different from the picture on the mantel of the fireplace. He was taller, of course, and his blond hair had darkened considerably. His hair was cut shorter, too. His baby face had turned into the face of a little boy.

David tried to explain to the detective that they were only trying to hear and respect their son as much as possible. At four, Michael had started acting like having his picture taken was having something stolen from him. He hated it, and so they were waiting until he didn't, simple as that. "Convincing him to try tomatoes took almost two years," David added, hoping he didn't sound defensive. "But now he loves them."

The detective was stuck on the phrase *hear and respect*. "Hope you don't mind, but I'm curious," he said. Apparently his favorite sentence. And if I do mind? David thought. Does that mean you're not curious anymore? "Let's say your son wanted to run out in traffic. Would you let him?"

"Of course not," he sputtered. "That's absurd."

"So you decide what you're going to hear and respect?"

"The issue of the rights of children is complicated," David said. "And it's irrelevant to finding my son."

"Unless your son decided that he wanted to leave this morning." Detective Ingle rubbed his hands together, as if they were cold or in pain. "Would he have a *right* to take a little trip if he wanted?"

David couldn't resist explaining that the children's rights movement was never about giving children more rights than adults. And adults have to let their families know where they are. "It's part of basic respect for the people you live with." He shook his head. "But the point is that Michael would not decide to take a trip by himself. He's not that kind of child."

Detective Ingle paused for a moment. "Would you say he's an adventurous boy or more fearful?" He shook his head. "I think I can answer that myself."

The man looked like he was trying not to laugh. David found it difficult to swallow back his anger. "Protecting your child is not wrong, Detective. Frankly, I think you would know this if you had a child. I assume you don't."

"You're right." Ingle shrugged. "Don't have kids, never wanted kids. You got me there."

David might have felt as if it was a victory, getting the man to admit it, except that *none* of this had anything to do with finding Michael.

Detective Ingle walked from the hutch to the table and back again. He was looking at the light pouring in from the kitchen "Tell me something. Do you remember how old Michael was when he decided he wanted to be homeschooled?"

"He didn't decide that. We did. Because we're his parents and—"

"You know better?"

"No, we know, *period*. A four-year-old has no idea what homeschooling is."

"You could say the same thing about a photograph, couldn't you? And the value of eating tomatoes?"

The consequence of the choices in those cases was completely different. It was a simple matter of logic, but David saw no point in continuing this conversation. He was tired of this guy pacing around, looking down on him, instead of doing his damn job. He was considering contacting someone to complain about the detective—the university community liaison? a lawyer?—when one of the police officers came in to tell Detective Ingle that they needed him to come and look at something in the backyard.

David hoped it was a clue, but at this point, it seemed possible that they needed to discuss why Michael didn't have a swing set. The detective could rub his hands together and act like he'd proved that David and his wife were inconsistent, because if Michael had wanted a swing set and they'd refused to give him one, then they weren't hearing and respecting him. But if he hadn't even wanted one, they'd screwed him up so badly that he didn't hear or respect himself. Either way, they were failing as parents, which seemed to be what the detective really wanted to prove, though David had no idea why.

At least they weren't suspects in Michael's disappearance. David was walking down the hall to find his wife when he overheard one of the officers talking on the phone. "No way. Their kid is everything to them. Trust me, these two are the kind who got on a nursery school waiting list the day after they got married."

In other circumstances, David would have laughed. They hadn't even bothered to use a cliché that fit with homeschooling.

SEVEN

Of course the officer was wrong: David and Kyra had not signed on to a nursery school waiting list the day they got married. In fact, one of the founding principles of their relationship was that they would *never* have children. Even the place where they met seemed to support this decision, at least from David's point of view.

The Mütter Museum in Philadelphia is one of the world's only medical museums. Among the exhibits are numerous skeletons, jars full of brains, and a woman whose body was buried in a chemical that turned her fat into soap. On that particular day, David had come to the museum to prepare for a history class he'd gotten stuck teaching for a group of med students who were contemptuous of any class that wasn't science; he hoped to spice up his lectures with bizarre facts. Kyra was there because it was a Saturday, and she had to go somewhere. It was one of the goals that she'd stuck on her refrigerator: Explore the City. Each week, she forced herself to find some well-reviewed spot in Philadelphia and stay for at least two hours. Only then would she let herself escape back to her apartment, the only place she felt comfortable in her new town.

In the seven months since she'd moved here, she'd made very few friends. She'd come to Philadelphia to take a job writing math test questions for a textbook company. The people she worked with were all married, with the exception of the administrative assistant, an older woman, who might as well have been married given how much time and energy she spent talking and thinking about her ex. They invited Kyra to their homes for Friday night dinners or Sunday barbecues, but she was always the only person who came unaccompanied, and though it didn't make her that uncomfortable, she could tell her coworkers felt sorry for her and so she'd starting making up excuses not to go. She'd met a few people in her apartment building; she knew them just well enough for a hi-how-are-you exchange in the elevator or the laundry room in the basement. She'd also had a few dates, guys she met through personal ads primarily. They were rarely anything like their descriptions. In fact, she'd sworn off personal ads when the last guy turned out to be not only boring but also fifty-one years old. In his ad, he'd called himself "young enough," which was not exactly a lie, since he was surely young enough for something.

At the museum she ran into David—literally—when she was leaning in to read one of the information cards on the "wall of skulls." He was moving right, she was moving left, and they walked into each other. It would have been a mere excuse-me moment, except for the fact that she tripped over her own big feet. She felt like a clumsy idiot, not to mention that the contents of her purse spilled all over the floor.

He knelt down to help her collect her things. He didn't hesitate to pick up her Tampax; she noticed that and wondered if he was married, though he wasn't wearing a wedding ring. She guessed he was a little younger than she was, which turned out to be true, though his hair was already graying. It was cut long, curling over the collar of his blue button-up shirt. He had a large forehead that made him look intelligent and dark brown eyes. His pale skin looked perfect, like he'd never had acne or even been sunburned. But it was his smile that made her decide that there was no reason to be embarrassed. It was such a friendly smile, without a hint of mockery, as if he was incapable of laughing at someone who'd fallen down.

Kyra had never understood why so many people considered falls—and spills and punches and kicks and hits—funny. She didn't like slapstick, and she especially detested *The Three Stooges*. Every guy she'd ever met just loved those idiots. The last guy she'd dated considered himself an expert on the show, and had spent a whole dinner expounding on the merits of Curly versus Shemp.

When the stranger reached for her hand to help her up, she felt her face get warm. She stood up as straight as she could, with her purse clutched tightly to her body. She was trying to think of what to say now that they'd gotten past his apology and her insisting it was her fault. A family was headed over to the wall of skulls, which meant they would have to move on.

What happened next was a matter of debate. As Kyra remembered it, David repeated his apology and started to turn away, but before he could leave, she screwed up her courage and said, "I think you owe me a coffee." David, however, thought that the coffee had been his suggestion. He told her this a few months later, after they'd been together long enough to reminisce about the day they met. He also remembered his motive: "You seemed a little off balance."

They were in her apartment, a studio on the top floor of a high rise in Rittenhouse Square. Kyra had chosen it because of the large window that provided an expansive view of her new city. They were cuddling together on her small bed, their talk punctuated by the soothing sound of the ticking of Kyra's clocks. It was snowing outside. The big, fat flakes were floating so slowly, like they were never planning to hit the ground.

"Are you saying you were doing me a favor?" She leaned up on her elbow. "What if I'd been an old lady? Would you still have offered?"

"I hope I would have," he said, and he obviously meant it. Kyra smiled. "But admittedly, it was easier with you."

"Why's that?" She leaned against him. "Because you knew I had a purse full of your favorite flavor of gum?"

"You did, didn't you?" He smiled. "But no, I think how pretty you were trumped the gum. And that you seemed so kind."

"In what way? Like good-to-meet-you, let-me-fall-on-the-floor-in-front-of-you kind?"

"Remember when you were looking at the exhibit of surgical instruments?"

She nodded. It was when she first got to the museum, long before she ran into David. She remembered thinking it was so creepy. "I thought of it as the 'instruments of torture' display."

"Do you remember the boy that was making jokes about chopping up his little sister?"

"Yes." She was surprised that David knew about this. He'd never mentioned it before. "I wondered where their parents were."

"So did I. And I really admired you for getting the boy to stop. I think it was the way you said it. So matter of fact, without making the boy feel like he was in trouble. You said, 'Look at her face. See how sad she is. Do you want her to be sad like that? You're her brother. She needs you to be brave, and show her nothing can hurt her in this scary place.'"

Kyra surprised herself with how pleased she was that David had witnessed this. "Well, I used to be a professional babysitter," she reminded him, and forced a shrug. She'd already told David about the Callahan Child Care Company—and a little about her sister. "As professional as you can be at fourteen years old anyway."

"You're very good with kids," he said, looking into her eyes. "Are you sure you don't want any of your own?"

They'd discussed this already, on their first real date, actually, when they went to dinner in Old City. David had asked her if she'd noticed all the abnormal fetuses at the Mütter Museum. She told him she had, and they were horrifying. "All the things that can go wrong," he said quietly. "That's why I don't plan to have children."

Now she sat up with the sheet pulled to her neck. She watched the snow for a moment before she said, "I'm sure." She leaned down and gave him a kiss. "We can always get a dog if we need something to take care of."

They discussed this topic at least three more times before David asked her to marry him, and Kyra always said the same thing: she was sure. She moved into David's apartment on Fitler Square, which was large enough for two people but not three. She loved David's neighborhood, and she no longer felt like a stranger in the city. David knew everything about Philadelphia because he'd grown up here. His mother still lived in the apartment where David had spent his teenage years after his parents' divorce.

David's mother was another reason Kyra felt like she'd won the lottery finding him. Sandra brought them fantastic lasagna and delicious cakes, made them a lovely quilt, cried with joy at the wedding, and insisted that Kyra call her anytime if she needed anything. Kyra felt close to David's mother in a way that she'd never felt close to her stepmother or her own mother. She wanted to see Sandra more often, but after they'd been married about eight months, when she finally asked David why he rarely suggested inviting his mother to their apartment, he said, "I love my mother, but we have issues. Like every family, I suppose."

They were standing in the kitchen. Kyra had just unwrapped

the last portion of Sandra's latest food gift, a glorious caramel flan. David was making himself a cheese sandwich. She took a quick bite and mumbled, "Issues?"

"Give me a minute."

Kyra walked over to their tiny kitchen table, piled up all the bills and junk mail, and sat down with her flan. She ate it slowly, but still, she was finished before David joined her. He ate his food slowly, too. She watched and waited until the only thing left on his plate was a piece of lettuce that had fallen out of the sandwich. Finally she tried, "Is this about your parents' divorce?"

"Why would you think that?"

"Because your mom told me she should have left earlier. I know she blames herself for letting your dad treat you the way he did."

Kyra was proud that she knew this, that Sandra had felt comfortable enough to talk to her like a friend. They'd had several girls' nights out on Wednesdays, when David was teaching his late class. They'd even gone to a spa together one Saturday, because Sandra had a coupon. Her mother-in-law said she wasn't normally the spa type but joked that if they exfoliated enough dead skin cells, they might uncover her missing waist. Sandra was a little heavy, but Kyra thought it looked good on her. She seemed so soft and maternal. Even her gray hair seemed the perfect frame for her delicately lined, heart-shaped face.

"Mom is wrong about that. It's not her fault that Dad could be an ass. And he was a lot worse to her than he was to me. If anything, I should have protected her more. I was thirteen. I could have told Dad to leave her alone."

Kyra said, "Thirteen is still a child," but she respected him for believing this. She remembered herself at that age. She had no sense of responsibility for others. All she wanted then was to be better than Amy at *something*.

The phone rang—a grad student David was advising. When

her husband returned, he was holding his sneakers. He was bent over, tying them, when she said, "You're not going to tell me?"

She was counting on the fact that her husband was not the kind of person who would say, "Tell me what?" And she was right. He said he was going to talk about it, but he wanted to take a walk together. She nodded. She already had her shoes on. Only David insisted on living in socks wherever he could get away with it.

They walked over to South Street and across the bridge to West Philadelphia. The same path David took every day to the university; he obviously wasn't walking to see the sights. They'd just gone past the bookstore on 34th and Walnut when David said, "It's very simple, actually. I would have told you before but it never came up." He squinted at the sun rather than look at Kyra. "My mom is very close to my ex-wife."

His pace didn't slow at all. He was a fast walker, and Kyra was a little out of breath. "Courtney?" she said stupidly, as though David had more than one ex-wife. "What do you mean?"

"She thinks I don't know, which makes it even worse. She wants to keep their relationship a secret from me."

A group of students were walking toward them, crowding the sidewalk. David and Kyra separated as they moved to the edges and waited until the kids passed. It was a beautiful April day, almost 70 degrees. It finally felt like spring.

He rubbed his forehead. "I found out about this while I was still in New Haven. It was the third anniversary of Joshua's death. I don't know why I decided to go by the grave that morning. I usually waited until after I taught my classes. "

He didn't speak for another block. Kyra could feel her heart pounding from nerves and from trying to keep up with him.

"I was walking out of the cemetery when I turned around and saw them. My mother and *her*, holding flowers. Kneeling at his grave."

He still hadn't slowed down, but Kyra could hear the emotion he was swallowing back. She reached for his hand and finally he stopped walking. She pulled him into her arms at the corner of 40th and Spruce, and he let her hold him, but he didn't cry. It was another bond the two shared: neither of them had ever cried in front of the other.

Whenever David talked about his baby, Kyra's heart ached for him: from the first time he'd told her about Joshua, after they'd been together for about five months, to this moment on the street and every time in between. Kyra had shed so many tears for her husband's loss, but only at night when he was sleeping, or in the car when she was alone. She still thought her face looked hideous when she cried, but the main thing was that she wanted David to continue to believe she was calm and steady and responsible—and nothing like his first wife. He'd mentioned once that Courtney cried constantly, and that was all it took.

"Why didn't you ask your mother about it?" Kyra said. They'd been walking in silence for a while when this question occurred to her. They were back on the bridge, going toward Center City.

"Because I know what she'd say." He crossed his arms. "My mom forgives people, that's what she does. She did it over and over with Dad. She doesn't seem to understand that some people don't deserve to be forgiven."

"But at least you could have told her how betrayed you felt. It might have brought you closer."

Now that Kyra was thinking about this, it struck her that her mother-in-law was concerned about her relationship with her son. Sandra had never directly asked Kyra why David didn't call or come over more often, but didn't that just prove the point? Her mother-in-law was so careful with her questions, like she'd been relegated to permanent outsider status in her son's life.

"I don't think it would have," David said. "I think it would have pushed us apart, because she wouldn't have understood my position. She would say something like 'the past is the past,' forgetting that I'm a historian." He forced a smile. "The past is never over for us."

Kyra doubted that her mother-in-law would forget David's profession. Sandra tried to read every article David published, no matter how obscure the academic journal. She'd even tried to read his dissertation, all 237 pages, though she'd never mentioned this to him because she was afraid she hadn't understood most of it. Kyra hadn't read his dissertation because, as David said, it wasn't all that interesting outside of his field, which was twentieth-century American history, specifically, the impact of the fifties and sixties on American notions of work and the work ethic. David had actually discouraged Kyra from reading it, and joked that it was too much work to read that many pages about work.

It was so odd for Kyra, who knew nothing about being mothered really, to understand that Sandra was trying hard to be a good mother. She understood it better than David himself seemed to.

She didn't know what to say to her husband. Of course he felt betrayed by Sandra's relationship with his ex-wife. Even Kyra felt strange thinking of her mother-in-law hanging out with Courtney, possibly going to the spa with her, too. It wasn't until David was in the shower that she realized she was actually a little jealous. She'd seen pictures of Courtney in an album on the bottom shelf of Sandra's media console—pictures of all three of them: David, Courtney, and little Joshua. Courtney had looked so confident of her right to be with David. Kyra, on the other hand, still marveled that a man like her husband would even look at someone like her, much less marry her and share her life.

Did her mother-in-law like Courtney better? Kyra wished this thought hadn't sprung fully formed into her mind, while she was snapping beans for dinner, but now that it had, she felt so much worse. And there was no way to fix it. Even if she had the nerve, she couldn't discuss any of this with her mother-in-law without breaking David's confidence.

Kyra knew all too well how easy it was to lose touch with someone you loved, but even as she gently pushed her husband to see his mother more, she found herself seeing Sandra less often. She continued to enjoy her mother-in-law's company, but she just couldn't trust her, knowing she could keep something like this a secret from them. In addition, though Kyra didn't fully understand this, now that Sandra was associated with Courtney in her mind, some of the feelings Kyra felt for her husband's ex-wife were spilling onto her mother-in-law. And unfortunately, Kyra had a *lot* of feelings about Courtney.

They'd been married for only a year or so when David admitted that what had happened with Joshua had changed him from a person who was usually optimistic to a person who feared the worst. Kyra had already discovered how true this was. If she was ten minutes late from work, her husband called her cell; if she dropped the soap and he heard the thump in the shower, her husband came in to check on her; if she got a cold or cut her hand or had a bruise she couldn't account for, he begged her to go to the doctor. He even worried that he was oppressing her with all his worries. "Ironic, I know," he said. "I wish I could relax about all of this."

It was all Courtney's fault, that much Kyra knew. Although David's ex-wife had not been found guilty of a crime, she was responsible for what had happened to the baby. And the older Kyra got, the more she blamed this woman she'd never met for David's anxieties and even for something that seemed to be missing from her own life, something she couldn't put her finger on. Indeed, by the time Kyra was thirty-two, she actively hated Courtney, especially when she thought about the pictures of Courtney and David and their child. Especially when she imagined what David must have been like, back when he trusted that he could have a family of his own.

EIGHT

Although Sandra didn't like cell phones—the buttons were too small for her arthritic fingers; she felt like she couldn't hear the person on the other end unless she sat very still, with the earpiece glued to her ear—she always had her cell with her, stashed in the pocket of her purse next to her medicines. It was convenient when someone at work needed her, but the real reason she carried it was to placate her son, who had given her several long lectures about the dangers of going without a phone. She knew he was just worried, so she didn't remind him that somehow the human race had survived before the invention of all these annoying devices.

It was a little after three o'clock; she was still on her former daughter-in-law's porch, dialing the number of the software company where Courtney worked. The receptionist told her Courtney wasn't there, which she expected, but she also added that Courtney had left the company after an extended sick leave. "She's sick?"

Sandra said—or shouted. She was never sure how loud she had to be. The phone was tiny, way too small for her head. If the earpiece was on her ear, the mouthpiece didn't come past her cheek.

"I believe so," the receptionist said. "All I know is that she resigned a few months ago."

A few months ago? Why hadn't she mentioned this to Sandra? And if she was unemployed—and possibly sick—why wasn't she home? Sandra had knocked a half dozen times and rung Courtney's home phone a half dozen more, even though it was such a discouraging sound, the bright ringing of the phone echoing in the deserted house.

Sandra had given her cell phone number to Courtney reflexively, in case her former daughter-in-law had an emergency; however, she'd never thought to ask Courtney for hers. Why would she need that? They talked only once or twice every few months, usually on a Sunday afternoon, when both of them were puttering around their houses. They talked about what they'd planted in their gardens or new recipes they'd tried, books they found interesting or TV shows they were following. Courtney used to ask about David, but after he married Kyra, her questions became much less frequent, and soon after he had Michael, she stopped asking all together. Sandra figured her former daughter-in-law had finally accepted what she'd been telling Courtney since she got out of the hospital: that David wasn't angry with her; he'd just moved on with his own life.

That this wasn't exactly true never stopped Sandra from saying it. The girl desperately needed to believe that David had forgiven her, and Sandra figured maybe he had forgiven her somewhere deep in his heart. Certainly, it didn't seem possible that her son would never forgive his ex-wife. Holding on to anger like that couldn't be good for David. And he didn't even know Courtney anymore, if he ever had; they'd been so young. Otherwise, how could he be so convinced that Courtney had taken Michael?

David had promised to call after he talked to the police. He kept his promise, but Sandra couldn't help noticing how curt he sounded, like calling his mother was nothing but a task on a long to-do list. At least he had some relatively good news. The detective in charge felt sure it was someone the family knew, and whoever this person was, their intention wasn't to harm Michael.

At first Sandra didn't understand how this detective could be sure of that, though she was immensely relieved, and even more so when David told her a note had been left.

"Why didn't you tell me this before?" Sandra said.

"They just found it in the back of the house, slipped under a rock by the porch steps." He paused. "It says that Michael is fine and he'll be back in a day or two."

She took a breath. "Well, that's encouraging, isn't it?"

"Come on, Mom. We're dealing with a lunatic who stole a child from his own backyard. Why should we trust what she says?"

"It's a woman?"

"One of the police officers said the handwriting looks female."

"But it doesn't look like Courtney's handwriting, does it?"

"I don't know." He sounded distracted. "The police are going to check that. They're also going to run fingerprints."

A lifetime ago, Courtney had been fingerprinted. Though the charges had been dropped, David was obviously assuming they still had the fingerprints on file somewhere. Sandra had no idea if that was true. She knew very little about how the police worked other than what she'd seen on television.

She watched someone get out of a truck across the street. It was Courtney's neighbor, Rita, a friendly woman and quite the talker. Sandra waved with her free hand and pointed at the cell phone, and thankfully, Rita headed in the direction of her own porch.

David was still talking about the letter. The woman who wrote it said to think of her as a babysitter. She also wrote that she loved

Michael. She claimed she was part of his family and just wanted to get to know him.

Sandra swallowed hard. The words sounded familiar. She remembered when Courtney had said something similar to this. But it was almost six years ago, right after Michael was born. She wanted to know if David would allow her to just *meet* the baby. "I won't even touch him," she said, which broke Sandra's heart. "I just want to see if he looks like . . ."

Sandra had said no, because she knew David would say no. But she'd given Courtney a photograph of little Michael, dressed in a sweet yellow-and-white romper, asleep in his bouncy seat. Courtney had thanked her; neither of them had mentioned the resemblance.

The wooden slats of the porch swing were digging into Sandra's back. After she said good-bye to David, she stood up and headed down the walk. There was no point in staying here; the police would be arriving soon enough. Obviously, they'd have to question Courtney. At this point, even Sandra couldn't be a hundred percent positive that she hadn't done it, though it was so hard to fathom that sad girl doing something like this, after she'd worked so hard to have an almost normal life.

When Sandra was back in the car, she let herself cry, but only a little. She had to be there for her son—there was no time for a big boo hoo.

She'd just merged onto the highway when she considered telling David's father what was going on. If only she could tell Ray and have him offer to help in any way he could. If only Ray would be a decent man and a decent father for once in his life. But even the thought of turning to Ray made her realize how desperate she was. Yes, she wished she had someone with her right now, but Ray was the last person to call in a crisis. He'd never had much sympathy for other people's problems, mainly, Sandra thought, because he'd had so few problems of his own. He rarely even got sick, which allowed him to continue with his cruel belief that sick people were *weak*. This, in particular, had always infuriated Sandra, who, after all, knew a heck of a lot more about sick people than Ray ever would.

In a way, her ex-husband had led a charmed life. Though the things he did echoed forever in the lives of the people around him, he himself seemed to remain forever untouched. It was unfair, yet Sandra had given up wishing the world would teach Ray a lesson. The truth was the only people who needed the world to teach them a lesson were people who hadn't been paying attention to the lessons their lives had already given them. People like Ray, whose inability to pay attention had cost him two wives—Peggy, the woman he'd married after Sandra, had left him, too—and most important, his son.

Of course she never regretted marrying him. She couldn't, because the marriage had given her David. But in every other respect, getting together with Ray was proof of how stupid she'd been. Her high school boyfriend and first love had escaped to Canada when he got drafted. By the time Ray came along, she was twenty-one and finished with her nursing degree. Most of her friends were either engaged or already married. And Ray was undeniably handsome; people said he looked like that actor Christopher Plummer. He seemed incredibly sophisticated because he'd been to South America, or was it because he knew how to make martinis?

She'd been married for three years when she had her baby, more than enough time to discover that marriage was no remedy for loneliness. Having a baby wasn't, either, though little David could be downright good company at times. In fact, all these years later, she still remembered what an excellent companion her baby had proved to be during the swimming competitions of the Summer Olympics. She'd watched the games on the old-fashioned rabbit-ears television while five-month-old David sat on the rug, surrounded by pillows, chewing on his rattles. She was on the floor with him, so she could retrieve the rattles when he dropped them. He was too young to crawl or even scoot yet. She held his hands together to clap every time Mark Spitz broke another record. Her baby grinned and laughed, and she pointed at the screen and told him, "Maybe that will be you someday!"

Sandra had once dreamed of being an Olympic swimmer herself. Every summer when she was a kid, she'd spent her days in the water, swimming back and forth, while her little brother, Beau, timed her with the old railroad pocket watch their uncle had given them. She got faster and faster, but she could never catch Debbie Rendell, the star of their local swim team. By the time she was a teenager, she'd stopped going to the pool to swim, though she still went to sun herself with her friends. They would get into the water only when they were very hot, and then only up to their chests, so they wouldn't have to put on swimming caps and flatten their hair.

When Ray came home, they were holding the ceremony after Mark Spitz won the 100-meter freestyle. She greeted him, and nodded at the television, so he would know what was going on. It was all so thrilling.

"You know I don't like sports," Ray muttered, and walked out of the room.

The fact that she considered following him shows how foolish she was. Mark Spitz had set world records in every race. He was the greatest athlete of all time, as the newscasters kept saying. She wasn't going to walk out on an American making history in hopes of getting a smile of approval from Ray.

When the program was over, she rocked David and put him to bed. Finally, she went to the kitchen, where her husband was sitting at the table, going through the receipts in his briefcase.

As often happened, she found herself suddenly feeling sorry for him. He looked tired, and he was undoubtedly feeling neglected.

She asked if he'd had dinner on the road. When he said no, she got out the ham and Swiss and started piling it on the rye bread, the way Ray liked it, with tomatoes on top. She could feel him watching her, and so she made small talk about the day, nothing about the Olympics, probably some cute thing that happened with David.

He didn't say anything until she set the sandwich in front of him; then he said, "I don't want *that*." He even crossed his arms and rolled his lips together, as if his hands might move against his will and force the sandwich into his mouth.

It was after nine. The baby had gotten up at five-thirty in the morning and napped for only forty-five minutes all day. "I thought you were hungry," she said, as evenly as she could manage.

"I am. However, the last time I checked, a sandwich is not dinner."

She was twenty-four years old, which was considered a full-grown adult back then. She had a child and a mortgage and a husband, same as most of her friends. And yes, she knew that the adult thing to do would be to cook something he liked and wrap up the sandwich so he could have it tomorrow for lunch. If he hadn't said "the last time I checked," she might have been able to do it, despite how tired she was. But he sounded so damned smug, and he looked positively imperial sitting there, looking down on the poor rejected sandwich.

So she picked up the plate and walked across the kitchen and dumped not only the sandwich but also the plate into the garbage. She heard the ceramic dish snap in half as it hit the side of the metal can.

Her husband mumbled something to the effect that she was nuts. She wasn't really listening. She already knew she was going to regret what she'd done. It was a nice plate.

NINE

If you have been happily married for a few years, and you are over thirty, the people around you will often hint—or even say—that you don't have much time left to make The Decision™. This was the situation in which Kyra found herself seven years ago when she created a Word file, *Pro and Con For You Know What*. She planned to keep a journal of her thoughts and record her daily mood (1 for Yes, −1 for No, and 0 for Unsure) for a full year. Of course she knew the final result would be a negative number, possibly three digits, maybe even −365. She was positive she didn't want a baby. This was purely a test—and Kyra liked tests; she wrote them for a living—to prove conclusively what she already knew.

The biggest argument against having children was always her husband's feelings, but right after that came her own guilt about what had happened with Amy. Most days, it was easy to record a −1 in the journal and go back to her life. Her first positive number came about two weeks into her test, when she was on the bus, coming home from work. She was pushing her way down the aisle, trying to find a seat, when she saw a baby settled on his mother's lap. Such an ordinary scene, but this time, she was stopped in her tracks; she couldn't even make her lips form the polite words "how cute." She just stared, like the baby was a messenger from another world, come to tell her—what? *Don't forget to have one of me. You know you want to.* Or even, *it's wrong to lie to yourself.*

She grudgingly wrote a 1 in the journal that day, though she knew the baby messenger was wrong. She most certainly did not know that she wanted one of his kind. And to her relief, the test continued to prove her right. After keeping score for two months, there were far more −1s than 1s. Her tally had been negative the first week and the first month and it had remained negative so far. Good.

Most of the arguments she wrote in the journal were also against the idea. Beyond the big issues, she had a lot of pragmatic reasons why having a baby would be bad:

1. They'd have to move, and she loved their apartment. They'd probably have to leave the city to afford a bigger place. She wasn't a suburbs-type person.
2. They'd have to buy all that baby stuff: a crib, a stroller, a changing table, a car seat, a rocker, clothes, toys, etc, etc. It would be so expensive, and so daunting to deal with now that she'd just been promoted.
3. She would gain a lot of weight. What if she couldn't lose it later? What if she ended up fat for life?
4. She might die. It was unlikely, but not impossible. It would be so much better if it were impossible.
5. She was probably infertile anyway. She had no evidence to support this, except for karma. If karma existed, she would never be able to have her own baby.

Unfortunately, number five was one thing she couldn't just write down and dismiss. She spent a disturbing amount of time worrying about being infertile—disturbing because why did she care? Several pages of her Word document had nothing but the question: "What if I *can't* have a baby?" She estimated that at least half of her 1s were based on nothing other than this fear. Finally she decided to make an appointment with her gynecologist. He ran some blood tests first. A week later, he gave her a thorough exam, and told her that though he couldn't be sure, everything looked to be in working order.

"No reason not to start trying," he said. "You might be pregnant before you know it."

"Thanks," she said. "But I'm not planning to get pregnant."

"What?" He was washing his hands, not really paying attention.

"People always want what they can't have." She was still in the paper dress, but she was sitting up and relatively comfortable. She lifted her finger to emphasize her point. "But if I can have it, then I don't have to want it, right?"

"True," he said, and laughed. "Seriously though, you should start trying soon. You're thirty-two. I'm sure you know that fertility declines sharply in a woman's thirties, and by the time she's forty, she—"

"I know, but I don't want children. I feel so much surer of that now. Thank you."

"You're welcome?" the doctor said. He looked thoroughly confused, but Kyra was too happy to care. Since it was possible to have a child, she wouldn't have to want one anymore. She marveled at how simple it was.

It was Friday night, her favorite night of the week to be with her husband, and, she noted, as she walked in the door around six, another reason not to have a baby. After teaching all week, David was usually in a fabulous mood, and this Friday was no exception.

He was already home, and he'd brought steaks and asparagus and bread and a bottle of Kyra's favorite Chablis.

"I just fired up the broiler," he said, kissing her. "How was your day?"

"Same old," she said, feeling a bit guilty. "What did you want to do tonight?"

"Whatever you want, my darling wife. After all the grading I've been doing for the last two days, I could hang upside down by my thumbs and not mind." He leaned back and grinned. "I'm saying I'm game for the games."

The games were Kyra's logic puzzles. She had several books of them, and she loved solving them with David. They didn't require any math knowledge, which she emphasized, though David was right when he said she had an advantage. Still, he won fairly often, at least a third of the time, and winning wasn't really the purpose. It was the two of them thinking together until they revealed the beautiful pattern of the puzzle. Beautiful to her, anyway. David said it was interesting and fun, but she could tell he didn't see the point to all this. In a way, there wasn't a point—which was the point. These intricate patterns had absolutely nothing to do with their lives. They could think about them forever without running into a real problem. Like what David should do about the grad student he was working with who seemed depressed. Or how Kyra should deal with the new boss who was alienating everyone in the department. Or David's mother, who seemed so fragile after a bout with pneumonia last winter. Or Kyra's complicated feelings about her father's death from a heart attack last January. Or Amy, who hadn't come back for the funeral—another shocking sign that her sister had really meant it when she'd said that Kyra would never see her again for the rest of their lives.

How could Amy have meant that?

When they worked the logic puzzles together, Kyra forgot

about all of it. She even forgot about the question of whether she wanted a baby. But the next morning, she wrote −1 without hesitating. If they'd had a baby, they wouldn't have had that lovely evening, eating David's perfectly cooked steaks and asparagus topped with sea salt while they discussed how to get the robots across the bridge in puzzle number 142.

The baby would constantly be there; that was a huge problem with the whole idea. The baby would be like a *very* needy stranger forcing him- or herself into David and Kyra's life, which was going quite well, thank you. They could talk and drink and laugh and have sex whenever they wanted. Why would they want to trade this quiet life for the chaotic reality of parenthood? Why would anyone, when you got right down to it?

She had day after day of peaceful −1s until a few weeks later, on Saturday, when they went to a barbecue at Quon and Li's house. Quon was a colleague of David's who lived way out in the suburbs, in a cute borough called Doylestown. He and Li had two kids in grade school and a fourteen-month-old toddler. Kyra liked Li, even if spending time with her was always a challenge. Everywhere the toddler went, Li followed, and Kyra could either follow, too, or just stand in the kitchen like an idiot. So she followed and tried to continue her conversation with Li as the baby pulled open a dresser drawer and dropped sweaters on the rug, or took books off the bookshelf, one by one, until all of Li's women's history books were flung about the room as if the bookshelf had been hit by a hurricane. In fact, Kyra thought of the toddler as "Hurricane Baby." "I know I'm spoiling him," Li had explained, smiling. "I can't help it. He's my last one."

The picnic made everything harder because the outside world was not amenable to being childproofed, meaning everywhere Hurricane Baby went was potentially dangerous. The other two kids were playing soccer with David and Quon. They looked like they were having fun, but Kyra couldn't be sure. She and Li had followed Hurricane Baby from the swing set to the tree to the front yard. Finally, at the back fence, they'd been able to stop long enough to look at each other while they talked, thanks to the toddler's fascination with the neighbor's barking German shepherd.

Li was discussing an article she'd read in the *New York Times*, something about airlines lowering their fares to certain cities—Kyra couldn't be sure of the details because Hurricane Baby's squeals kept revving up the dog. By the time Li said she had to run into the house to go to the bathroom, Kyra was desperate to follow her right up to the bathroom door, anything to get away from this noise. But she could hardly object when Li asked her to stay here and watch Ping. "I'll be right back," Li said. She kissed the baby. "Mommy loves you."

Ping was too in love with the dog to let out his usual where's-Mommy wail. Kyra couldn't tell whether the dog reciprocated Ping's feelings, but she did know enough about dogs to keep the toddler from sticking his little hands through the fence, where he might get bitten. Ping was actually pretty cooperative; at least he was after she said no and pointed at the house, to show him where they were headed if he didn't follow this rule. The poor baby was not doing anything wrong when the dog circled back in his yard and charged right for them, easily hopping the fence and landing on Ping, knocking him backward. Maybe the dog was just being playful, but Ping was screaming and Kyra was horrified. She pulled the dog off the baby so fast that, later, she couldn't even tell David how she did it. The next thing she knew Ping was in her arms. He was crying, but more from fear than from pain. He only had little scratches on his legs. Kyra, on the other hand, had two bites on her forearm that were gushing blood all over Ping's green polka-dot onesie.

A moment later, everyone was there: Li, who anxiously examined her baby and pronounced him basically unharmed; David, who said Kyra needed to go to the ER; Quon's boys, who said that dog had bitten a neighbor kid; and Quon, who asked his boys why they hadn't ever mentioned this. Then the neighbor and owner of the dog came over, an older man, but Kyra didn't hear what he said because David was leading her back up to the patio. Li came with them and gave David a few clean towels to wrap the wounds until they got to the Doylestown Hospital.

The news was as good as it could be under the circumstances. The shepherd had had all his vaccinations. Though the bites looked horrible, once the ER doc cleaned them up, they only required about a dozen stitches each. The color came back to David's cheeks and he seemed almost normal, if a little shaken. Kyra had no idea how she seemed, but her shirt and jeans were covered with bloodstains. She couldn't wait to get home and change.

They still had the long drive back to the city. They were about forty-five minutes away from home when David turned down the radio and said, "I keep thinking how cool this is."

"What?"

"That my wife can wrestle a German shepherd and win." He grinned. "It's like discovering I'm married to Superwoman."

The pain pill the ER nurse had given her made her woozy and tired and overly emotional. It must have. Otherwise, why would this remark have made her feel so bad?

When she didn't say anything, David reached for her hand. "They're not going to put the dog down, honey. I told you before, the owner agreed to keep him inside or on a leash. And Quon and Li like the old guy. It's going to be all right."

Kyra had been worried about this earlier. She didn't want the dog to die for simply doing what dogs were designed to do: fight back when someone they don't know seems to be attacking them. But David was right; the dog would be okay. She wasn't upset about that.

"Even if I really was Superwoman," she said. And stopped. Could she really be about to say this?

"What?" David said.

She glanced at him. "It wouldn't matter, would it?"

"Matter how?" He waited. And smiled. "Come on, you know I can't stand it when you don't finish your thought."

"It's nothing," she said. "I was just thinking that even if I really was Superwoman, you still wouldn't trust me enough to have a baby with me."

"Whoa . . . wait a minute." He let go of her hand. He sounded shocked and even a little frightened. "Where did that come from?"

"I'm just saying I'm not your ex, David." She looked out the window, and of course some happy-looking woman was pushing a double stroller down the block. "I just saved Hurricane Baby, and I don't even really like him. I mean, he's cute. But even if he looked like a toad, I would have saved him."

"I know you would have." David's voice was quiet. He didn't talk for a few minutes while he drove to the exit ramp, merged onto the highway, and settled in the middle lane. "What's this about?"

"I'd be a good mom." She thought back to that hot July day when her own mom left. "I mean, I might be. It's possible."

His hands tightened on the steering wheel. "I didn't know you wanted children, Kyra."

"I just wish you believed that I *could* have kids and not destroy them. That I'm a good person who would do anything to keep a child from being hurt."

Including losing Amy? Wasn't that why Kyra had done what she did? Or was it something else, something ugly and unforgivable? If she could go back in time, she wouldn't do it again. Didn't that have to mean, on some level, that it was wrong?

David was sputtering something to the effect that he didn't understand what was happening. Unfortunately, neither did Kyra.

"Look," she finally said, "I don't want kids. Not really." She sighed and took back his hand. "I'm sorry. It must be the pain pill."

He let out a long breath. "Are you sure?"

She nodded. "But I don't think I want a dog, either. Maybe a cat?"

"Good idea." He waited a moment and said cautiously, "Any cat would be lucky to have you taking care of it."

The words flew out of her mouth before she could stop herself: "Is that supposed to be the same as being a good mom? Because there is a difference between a cat and a baby, you know. A big difference." She sounded so angry. God, what was wrong with her? Could a pain pill really do this?

"No, of course not," he said quietly, and squeezed her hand. "I'm sorry."

Kyra could tell the argument was over. No matter what she said, now that her husband knew she was not herself, he would be unfailingly gentle, kind, and nonconfrontational. She appreciated this about him, but she was also inexplicably sorry that the strange discussion had ended, even though she was the one who changed the topic to the boring problem of their leaky dishwasher.

She had no idea that this conversation had made an impression on her husband until a few weeks later. She was in their bedroom, about to put the sheets on the bed, when he told her, "You know, you really would be a good mother, honey." Kyra was surprised how happy this made her. She billowed the ivory sheet in the air and asked him to tuck in the other side. After he helped her with the pillowcases, she reassured him that she didn't want kids. That was the end of that, until another week had passed and he said the same thing again. Maybe Kyra smiled this time? In any case, before long, it had become a kind of routine with them, like "you hang up first" when they were dating. David would say, "Another reason you'd be a good mother," after Kyra had cooked a good meal or taken care of their bills or done basically anything that was mildly nurturing, and she would reply, "If I wanted to be a mother, which I don't."

Her journal backed her up on that. Indeed, the total was −92 on the night when she and David were in bed, kissing, and, after she rolled over to stand up, he reached for her and asked her to stay.

"But I need to put in my diaphragm," she whispered.

"Leave it," he said, touching her breasts.

"What?"

"You don't need it."

She could feel him pushing against her. She wanted him badly, too, but she forced herself to move away.

"Do you realize what you're saying?"

"I think so." He laughed softly. "Birth control prevents pregnancy. Ergo, if we don't use it, we could get pregnant."

She swallowed, trying to digest this news. After a moment, she said, "Aren't you afraid something will go wrong?" She was thinking: this can't be true. David is always afraid.

"Something could go wrong if we don't have a baby, too. And believe it or not, I believe everything is going to be all right." He kissed her neck. "Now can we please go back to—"

"But why did you change your mind?"

"I think I'm ready to have a family. And I realized if I want to really know you, I need to know you as more than my wife and my best friend and a logic genius." He brushed his lips against her eyelids, her nose, her cheeks, and her chin before leaning up on his elbows and smiling gently. "I can't wait to meet you as a mother, honey."

At that, Kyra began to cry. It was the first time in the three and a half years they'd known each other that she let herself cry in front of David. Of course he was surprised, but he assured her that she did not look even slightly hideous and that he still viewed her as a calm, reasonable person who was just as strong. "Even Superwoman cried occasionally," he said, but Kyra knew he was making that part up. David was not the comic-book-reader type.

A few weeks later, Kyra opened her *Pro and Con* file for the last time. She wrote a short note on the last page: *When the baby grows up, I'll let him or her read this file and know how hard I struggled with this decision.* But when she was seven and a half months pregnant, she got up one night and deleted the file from both her computer and her backup disk. She did not want her child, a boy, according to the ultrasound, to find this and wonder if his mother had really wanted him. And God/the universe/whatever needed to know that all those negative numbers hadn't actually meant anything to Kyra. She didn't want to be punished for her doubts, and so the universe needed to understand that she was absolutely, unambiguously in favor of having this child.

David was constantly nervous that something would go wrong with the pregnancy (of course), but even as Kyra tried to reassure him, she had a terrible fear of her own that she never talked about. She remembered when Amy told her that a pregnant woman wants her baby more than she's ever wanted anything. Now she knew how true that was—meaning if karma existed, she was in big trouble. Maybe she deserved to be punished, but her son didn't. "Just let him be all right," she told God. She was still in her office; her hands were resting on her abdomen, where she could feel her baby kicking. She wasn't sure why he always kicked more at night. It was almost as if he wanted her to wake up and think about all this.

After a few minutes, she escaped into the comfort of her logic puzzles, like she always did. She figured it couldn't be good for her baby to feel her stress or hear her cry. Better to talk to the little kicker about the proper order of spaceships organized on their launchpads by color. "If the first spaceship lands on a red launchpad," she said to her stomach, "the second spaceship must land on the green launchpad or the purple one."

Another kick.

"I think you're right." She smiled. "Let's try purple."

TEN

The afternoon traffic was getting heavy, and Sandra pulled off the highway to get a coffee at a fast-food place and use the bathroom. Back in her car, she swallowed her arthritis medicine down with the bitter-tasting brew, and realized she wasn't sure where to go. If she went to David and Kyra's house, she might just add to the stress and chaos. Surely the police were still there, questioning the neighbors, tapping the phone—whatever it was they did in a case like this. And her son hadn't asked her to come, had he? When she'd asked what she could do to help, he'd said he'd let her know if he thought of anything and hung up quickly, like she was a nosy neighbor offering him an unappetizing casserole.

In college, David used to brag that Sandra was not only a good mom but also a good *friend*. Of course every child's relationship to his mother has to change over time. Sandra knew that, and she tried hard not to feel bad when David pushed her away. It was part of motherhood, or so she'd heard: resigning yourself to whatever role your grown-up child decides to give you in his life. Her grandmother had had a saying about the need to let go of your kids, something about a mother only being a river for her children to bloom in the future. Since her grandmother had grown up on the Susquehanna, a lot of her sayings involved water.

Still, sometimes Sandra couldn't help wondering if she was making a mistake just accepting the wall David had put up between them, especially as the wall had never been there until what had happened with Courtney. If her son was hurting on the other side of a wall, she couldn't do anything to help him. She wouldn't even know. And he'd changed so much after the baby died. Certainly it was a devastating loss, but there was something about his reaction, even at the time . . . well, it wasn't exactly normal, was it?

She was back on the highway, sitting in the slow lane behind an eighteen-wheeler that wasn't bothering to inch up; the traffic was that bad. So there was nothing to do, nothing to distract her mind from the memory she'd been fighting since David's first phone call today. It was by far the worst moment of her life, when her son had called that morning fifteen years ago to tell her that her grandson had died.

Though she'd been sound asleep, she'd managed to get dressed and on the road in twenty minutes. The thought of her son dealing with such a tragedy by himself, surrounded by strangers in the garish light of an unfamiliar hospital, had made her put one foot in front of the other. Somehow she made it to New Haven without running off the road or into a truck. By the time she arrived, the lawyer Courtney's parents hired had arranged to have her moved from the police station to a psychiatric hospital. Which left David alone in the apartment—except he wasn't at the apartment. In just a few hours, he'd already moved his books and clothes and essentials to a two-bedroom place rented by another grad student. A guy named Brennan. That was all Sandra knew about him, but she was glad David would have somebody with him for the next few days and weeks, and possibly longer.

David wanted to talk to his mother alone, but he didn't want to go back to the old apartment. They ended up meeting at the same "hip" restaurant where Sandra had taken Courtney when the girl was pregnant and depressed. It was close to Brennan's house. David was waiting at a table when Sandra arrived. He stood up, as always, to give her a hug, yet it wasn't their usual long, warm embrace. He felt oddly stiff in her arms, but she assumed he was holding himself back so he wouldn't cry in public.

He admitted he hadn't slept or eaten since it happened. Sandra suspected he hadn't showered or changed clothes, either. He was wearing navy pants and a rumpled white shirt with what appeared to be a pizza stain on the cuff. He clearly hadn't shaved or combed his hair.

For the first fifteen minutes or so, his comments seemed random. He mentioned that he felt cold, and wondered if the restaurant was actually cold. He said it might rain later. He said his advisor had called him, a sympathy call. "Apparently everyone in the department already knows." His voice was so far away and tentative, Sandra wondered if he was on something, and then she realized he probably was. The hospital would have given him a tranquilizer of some kind.

The only time he sounded more focused and sure of himself was when he said that he was going to divorce Courtney.

"Don't decide anything right now," she said. She was picking at her salad, trying not to scream at the perky waitress who kept interrupting them to ask if David had changed his mind about ordering some food. He was drinking lemonade, which had been his favorite drink since he was just a little boy. She felt her chest tighten.

"I don't need to wait," he said. "I know I will never be able to live with her again."

Sandra noticed his eyes were watering constantly, the way they always did when he was very tired. "How do you know that?" she said softly.

He leaned back. "I know myself."

It was true; David did know himself unusually well for someone his age. And among the things he knew about himself—Sandra was positive on this point—was that he was a sensitive person. "Too sensitive," his father used to say, along with a variety of other things that were much more offensive. Her son had always been the type of man who could cry: when one of his crazy girlfriends broke up with him, when a college buddy had a diving accident, even when he watched a particularly sad or sweet movie, though his tears over movies would often be blinked off and laughingly denied later, as when Courtney accused him of crying during *Groundhog Day*. "If I was crying, and I stress the *if*, I was crying for the poor groundhog." He was looking back and forth from Sandra to Courtney. He pushed out his chest and took on a French accent; Sandra had no idea why. 'You humans use me without even knowing who I am! But I am not a hog at all . . . I am a rodent!'"

Had David cried at all about his baby yet? On the phone this morning, he'd sounded quiet and numb. Then he'd spent the day moving to Brennan's apartment. He had to be still in shock.

When she gently suggested that maybe he needed to grieve before he could make any decisions about his future, he said he couldn't do that.

She looked at him. "Can't do what?"

"I don't think I can grieve." His eyes closed for a second. "It may change, but it might not. I never cried about Dad. I don't—"

"That was completely different."

"Because leaving Dad was necessary. But breaking up our family affected me more than anything that had happened in my life . . . until . . ." The waitress arrived with another lemonade. He thanked her and waited another moment. "I've never cried about it. Even when I realized Dad wasn't going to try to change though it was the only way to have a relationship with me."

"You were very angry, honey. That protected you."

He lifted his chin. "And I'm divorcing Courtney now."

Wasn't her son basically admitting that his anger at his wife was keeping him from feeling his sadness about the baby? Sandra felt sure he was, but she also felt sure it couldn't last. He would have to face it eventually, and so she insisted on staying in town, even though she was out of personal and vacation time, to be there for him when it happened. When David didn't suggest that she stay in his old apartment, she checked into a cheap hotel over by the highway and met up with her son whenever he was free. She held his hand and hugged him repeatedly, whether he was stiff in her arms or not. She told him it would get better, and he went to all of his classes and taught his sections and acted like some version of his normal self. But he never laughed, and he admitted he couldn't sleep without Valium. The doctor at the ER had given it to him, just as Sandra thought. Sandra told David it was fine as long as he didn't use it for more than a few months. She herself was doubling up the Ativan she took for her occasional anxiety, so she could sleep without dreaming of the baby.

Sandra had attended to the burial, but it was almost three weeks before David was ready to have a small service at the cemetery. It was a quiet, quick affair and her son seemed all right when it was over. He told Sandra that the only thing left to do was pack up the things. When she offered to do it for him, he seemed immensely grateful. Everything was to go in storage, until Courtney was better. Let her decide what she wanted and what to give away.

Sandra went over on a Wednesday afternoon, while David was in his seminar on the history of American manufacturing. She'd barely gotten the key in the door when a little girl was at her elbow. Her name was Lupe, and Sandra had seen her around the apartment complex several times. She was a scuffed-up-looking girl, maybe seven or eight, with scabs on her knees and hair that needed a trim. She had four brothers and three sisters, or so she said. It seemed impossible that such a large family would live in one of these small apartments, even if they had the larger, three-bedroom model.

"Hi, Joshua's granny," the girl said. Sandra had told the girl to call her that the first time they met, almost five months ago, when Josh was only days old.

Sandra flinched, but she looked at Lupe with an expression that she hoped seemed pleasant enough. "I'm really busy today. I'm sorry, I can't talk like we usually—"

"I know he died. Everybody knows because the ambulance came and the police came and it was really loud."

"Oh," Sandra said. She had the door opened and now she was headed back to her car, to begin hauling in the stuff she'd brought with her: garbage bags, two dozen or so empty boxes she'd gotten from the office supply place, paper towels, a variety of household cleaners to get the apartment ready to rent when all the things were hauled away. She'd arranged for a truck to come this afternoon. As long as the place was emptied out today, David would get his deposit back, and they could use the money he saved in rent to pay the storage shed charges.

Lupe insisted on helping, though Sandra had told her twice that she could carry it all herself. The girl had the strangest way of lugging an empty box. She held it pressed against her legs, like it was keeping them warm, which, Sandra realized, it probably was. It was the last day of November, but Lupe was dressed in the same black nylon shorts she'd been wearing nearly every time Sandra had seen her. The shorts were too big and boyish, most likely a hand-me-down from an older brother.

Sandra and the girl stacked the cleaning supplies on the kitchen bar and the boxes on the floor by the refrigerator.

"He sure had a lot of stuff," Lupe said, looking around the small living room. The rug was covered with Josh's toys, many of which Sandra had bought. Her most recent purchase—a stuffed elephant with ears that crinkled and a belly that honked like a horn—was sitting on the couch, next to Josh's rainbow blanket. One of Sandra's favorite things to do was to lay Josh down on the bed, after she'd changed his diaper, and dance that blanket in the air while he giggled and reached for it. If he got his dimpled hand around a blanket corner, he'd squeal for joy.

"Are you sad?" Lupe said.

"Of course," Sandra snapped. She took a breath and reminded herself that Lupe was just a child. "Don't you think you should go home now?"

"I can't. My momma told me to stay with you until she gets here. She's coming over to help. She went around to tell her friends after I saw your car in the parking lot. Her friends want to help, too."

Oh Lord, Sandra thought, but before she could tell the girl to please let everybody know she didn't need any help, a woman was at the door. Her name was Delilah and she was holding a baby who was so big, his knees were circled with rings of fat. "This is Cody," the woman said. She shoved the baby in Sandra's arms. And so there Sandra stood, holding some stranger's baby, half in and half out of the door, while a parade of three other women marched right past her and into her son's apartment.

"Are you friends of Courtney's?" she stammered. Her first thought was that they didn't look like people associated with the university, but what she really meant was they didn't look like people who would be associated with her daughter-in-law. Courtney had grown up in a very sheltered world. She once confessed that, until she met Sandra, she'd never known a grown-up who was paid by the hour rather than on salary, other than the immigrants her parents hired to do cleaning and lawn care.

The women shook their heads and one even looked confused, like she'd never heard Courtney's name before. Sandra noticed that someone had brought food: a plate of fruit sitting on the coffee table, and a Crock-Pot that smelled like chili placed in the kitchen next to a dish rack of bottles, each set upside down to dry.

Baby Cody was heavy but good-natured. He kept leaning back to smile at Sandra. She tried to smile back, but it wasn't in her, and eventually he broke down crying. His mother took him back, and Sandra was thinking about what to say to get these people to leave her alone when the woman who'd brought the food introduced herself as Lupe's mother, Yolanda.

"You're the grandma," Yolanda said. "My daughter likes you . . . You talk to her. Your daughter doesn't talk to no one. Don't want to speak bad of her though." She made the sign of the cross. "I'm sorry about what happened to the baby."

"Thank you," Sandra said. "She's not my daughter," she added numbly. Even if these women didn't know that Courtney had been arrested, Sandra did, and her anger at her daughter-in-law was so intense that, more than a few times, she'd woken herself up screaming at Courtney. She'd even dreamed that she had her hands around Courtney's throat.

She tried to tell Yolanda, and Cody's mother, Delilah, and the other two women, whose names she'd already forgotten, that she didn't need any help. That she was fully capable of doing this herself. And finally, that she *wanted* to do this herself, to have this time with her memories.

Had she lost her voice? Why was no one listening? Two women had already gone into the bedroom with empty boxes. Delilah was on the floor of the living room, keeping one eye on her baby while she loaded up toys into a garbage bag. Yolanda was in the kitchen, doing up a few dishes that had been left in the sink. Only Lupe was paying attention to Sandra, and the girl's only response was to shrug.

"I don't want this!" Sandra shouted. Now that she'd yelled, other shouts were bubbling up, against her will. "Oh my God! I can't take this! I just want . . . I want . . ."

Then Yolanda was at her side, and one of the other women, too. They led her to the couch where she'd slept so many times with Joshua in his bassinet next to her. She didn't realize she was crying until Delilah put Cody on her lap, and she saw her tears dropping onto his fuzzy, brown baby hair.

David wasn't the only one who hadn't really grieved yet. Sandra's excuse was that she'd been trying to be strong for her son, and this was true, but she was also afraid that if she let herself start crying, she'd never be able to stop. If she'd just loved her grandson, the pain would have been bad enough, but she'd been in love with him, which made it unbearable. It was a secret that only mothers (and grandmothers) knew: that the feelings for a baby could be more intense than the most all-consuming schoolgirl crush. Every wall of Sandra's house had pictures of Joshua. Each time when she came home from visiting New Haven, she always left one of her shirts unwashed, so she could put the fabric against her face and be back there, holding him in her arms.

Cody lifted his hand to her cheek, the way babies do, but it seemed like sympathy. She cried harder, and Lupe sat down next to her and patted her knee.

Did she sit there crying the whole time? It was possible. She really didn't remember what she did during the hour or two while these strangers packed up her son's apartment. They didn't sing or hum or even talk much, but what they did say was respectful. One of the women remarked, "What a beautiful boy," as she carefully wrapped up one of the framed pictures of Joshua on the bookshelf. The two in the bedroom punctuated their packing of Joshua's clothes by mumbling "so sweet" or "little one." At some point, one of the women brought her a mug of chili and Lupe fed it to her like she was an invalid. Or did Lupe feed it to her because

Cody had fallen asleep and Sandra didn't want to move her hands, for fear of waking him?

She knew she had every right to be furious with these women, for barging into her life and acting like putting another baby into her arms would make it any easier—except that it had turned out to be true. She would always remember the way that fat baby had nestled into her shoulder, as though it was still a safe place to be. As though she hadn't failed to protect her son and his family. As though she hadn't lost her ability to soothe someone, even if she could do nothing to make this any easier for her own baby, David.

When Yolanda and her gang of gals got ready to leave, Sandra didn't think to ask for their addresses, to send them a thank-you card. She insisted Delilah take the toy Cody had fixated on: a clear ball with green and red gears that spun and rattled when you rolled it. She also gave Lupe one of Courtney's demitasse spoons because the girl clearly loved it; she said if she had a spoon like that, her ice cream would last longer.

And then they were all gone, and everything was packed, and the bathroom and the kitchen were clean, and there was nothing left to do but wait for the truck. As she sat on the couch, looking at the shadows on the walls where Courtney and David's art prints had been, her mind drifted to her father. She missed him so much then, even though he'd been dead for thirty-three years. It was another hard fact, and something Sandra would never have believed when she was young: you never get over the ones you lose.

Sandra was in grade school when her father started showing signs of the leukemia that would rupture his spleen and kill him when she was thirteen. Though she wouldn't fully understand what had happened to her dad until she was in nursing school, even at the time, she could tell what a struggle it was for him to take her and her little brother, Beau, to the pool or the park or just out in the backyard to rake leaves. He was much skinnier than the other fathers, and much, much more exhausted, but he did everything they did and more. He insisted on coming to every one of Beau's piano recitals and every one of Sandra's swimming meets. He read to the kids every night: another adventure of the Happy Hollisters or a chapter of *The Boxcar Children*, Sandra's favorite book. She remembered him gently lifting her up and carrying her to bed when she fell asleep. She remembered the afternoon he hung a tire swing in their backyard, to cheer her up, because she'd had the chicken pox and missed the town theater's production of *Cinderella*. In fact, her father was part of nearly every fond memory of her childhood.

He was a veteran of the Second World War, so he knew firsthand what it was like to have someone close to you die. He wouldn't tell his kids about the deaths he'd seen, but he did tell them stories about all the hardships the men experienced: the lack of food and sleep, the tattered clothes and boots, the cold rain that made their bones ache. But somehow, all of his stories ended up being funny, and while Sandra and Beau were laughing, her dad would shrug his thin shoulders and conclude, "Life has a way of going on."

When Sandra was a child, she thought it was a happy saying, like "Hang in there, baby," on the popular poster with the orange monkey hanging from a tree. Now she could feel the truth of what her father must have felt during the war, the irony behind his funny stories.

By the time the truck came, it was getting dark. David had been saying for days that it was time for Sandra to go home, and she knew he was right, though she'd been dreading this moment. Once she was back in Philadelphia, the crisis stage would be over and this would become a permanent fact of her life, something that was just true. If she were no longer able to react to it, there would be no choice. She'd have to live with it—and somehow, so would her boy.

ELEVEN

Michael Gabriel Winter was born on June 23 at 2:14 AM. He weighed 8 pounds and 11 ounces, and received a perfect Apgar score. He was absolutely healthy when Kyra and David took him home to their house in West Mt. Airy, which was like a suburb, with its yards and parks and kids and strollers, but still inside the Philly city limits. They'd bought a three-bedroom stone house with a sunroom built on the back. Kyra had placed a rocker in the sunroom, so she could nurse her baby and watch the sunrise.

The house had been painstakingly childproofed before Michael took his first breath. David had done it in the last months of her pregnancy. He'd gotten down on his hands and knees and crawled all over the house, pretending he had the eyes and reach of a toddler. Which of course Michael would not be for months, but since David couldn't know exactly when their son would become mobile, better safe than sorry. That was pretty much a theme with him. If something bad *could* happen, they might as well expend the energy making sure it did *not* happen. Within reason, as David liked to add, though most people wouldn't think it was reasonable to put locks on the attic windows, since even Kyra couldn't operate the door to the attic, meaning it was unlikely that a tiny baby—or even a twelve-year-old kid—would get up there and squeeze himself into a window that was too small for anyone but a two-year-old to fit through.

When David's sabbatical was over and he went back to the university, Kyra spent all her time with her baby, using his naps to finish work for her textbook company. The manager wanted her to come back full-time in the next few months, and she planned to. But then she and David started looking into the alternatives for daycare. They visited several places, and he took notes like a good academic. For example:

1. Home Daycare with Cindy
+ Cindy lived in Erdenheim, which wasn't that far.
+ Cindy only took care of four children, only one of which could be under a year old like Michael.
+ Cindy's house was thoroughly childproof. (Imagine David on his knees at the house of a woman he just met, deep into "toddler vision," while Kyra walked back and forth with the baby against her chest, hoping to soothe his colic.)
+ Cindy had a degree in early childhood education.
+ Cindy was opposed to using "time outs." She felt, as David and Kyra did, that it was too cruel to isolate a misbehaving child.
+ Cindy didn't even own a television.
− Cindy let a toddler cry for too long. It was exactly forty-nine intolerable seconds—Kyra counted—before Cindy picked up a little girl, though the toddler was grabbing at her leg and sounded hysterical. (That this

crying had also led to Michael starting to wail didn't
help.)

Conclusion: Michael would not be staying at Cindy's
Home Daycare.

And so it went, twelve daycare places in all, each with a fatal flaw
from David and Kyra's point of view. Some of the flaws were argu-
ably serious—the vague smell of cigarette smoke in the kitchen,
the children rewarded with junk food for staying quiet—but most
were like hearing the crying toddler at Cindy's, or watching a
daycare worker at the local college center hold one of the pre-
school children with no visible affection, like the poor child was a
sack of potatoes, David said. They just couldn't bring themselves
to let their baby be taken care of by any of these strangers. They
would have to arrange something else.

Kyra told her boss she wanted to work at home for the fore-
seeable future. This was five years ago, when the economy was
still going strong, and the manager agreed. She had to take a pay
cut and change her status to "contractor," but she didn't object.
It was doable, if not financially ideal. They were lucky they had
this option.

They were lucky in a lot of ways, and Kyra never forgot it
for a second. Sometimes after she put Michael in his crib for a
nap, she would walk around her house, making a mental inven-
tory of all the wonderful things in her life. Her husband's office
obviously reminded her of her fabulous husband. The guest bedroom made her think of her mother-in-law, who had come to
stay with them when Kyra had the flu and had taken such great
care of both Kyra and the baby. (Oh, how she wished David
would let Sandra be a bigger part of their lives!) Her own office
made her think of writing the tests, which she still enjoyed. The
playroom made her think of her baby, of course, and his wide,

toothless grin whenever he saw all those colorful toys. And her bedroom, which made her think of—having sex, which surely she and David would get back to having at some point. Parents have sex, after all; they must. How else could any family have more than one child?

By the time Michael was a year old, David and Kyra *were* having regular sex again, once a week anyway, yet they never seriously considered having another child. David would smile at Michael and say, "He deserves all our attention." David was an only child, so he probably didn't know how important a sibling could be. Kyra did, and it hurt her to think of the brother or sister Michael would never have—and especially the daughter she would never have—but she was not about to tempt fate by wishing for more when everything was going so well.

It really was going well, despite how tiring it was to deal with all of David's worries and her own. The first time they'd taken Michael to Sandra's apartment, when the baby could barely crawl, he'd managed to get his hand stuck in Sandra's old VCR. The hand was extracted with only the barest of scratches across Michael's little knuckles, but David and Kyra were mystified. How could this have happened with three adults in the room, all three paying attention? David said that his mother's house was obviously too dangerous. Sandra winced, but she only said, "I guess this is a sign that it's time for me to throw away the VCR and move to using a DVD player like the rest of the world." Later, David called his mom to apologize, but they begged off going to Sandra's again for a long, long time. Her house wasn't childproof. It was unfortunate but undeniable.

They felt safer at their own house, until Michael was fifteen months old, and he ate the little white silica packet that Kyra had casually left in the shoebox of her new black loafers. Both she and David were horrified when their baby stumbled out of the closet with white powder on his lips. Even after they called poison control and discovered that the Do Not Eat on the packet did not mean eating it would cause any harm, they couldn't relax for days. What if it had been poison and Michael had died or gotten brain damage? They'd thought they were being vigilant, but obviously they weren't being vigilant enough. They would just have to work harder. They would have to *imagine* the dangers before they were confronted with them.

Since David had a better imagination, he came up with many more potential dangers than Kyra did. He decided that one of the lawn chairs on their patio, for instance, had to be tossed out. The chair had an adjustable back, and *if* Michael ever got his hand caught in the metal adjustment device, he could lose a finger. The drawers of their bedroom dresser, which Michael liked to pull open—just like Hurricane Baby—had to be latched, because if Michael pulled a drawer out all the way, it might fall on him and break his foot.

Kyra wondered why Quon and Li hadn't thought of this. She'd gone over to hang out with Li twice since Michael was a toddler, and both times she'd been surprised by how dangerous their house was. The gate on their stairs was wobbly and easy to knock over, and their oven didn't have a safety lock. Still, she might have gone over again if Ping hadn't knocked Michael down while the two of them were "playing." Kyra had babysat enough to know this was normal, but she didn't care. Four-year-old Ping looked like a giant compared to her sweet sixteen-month-old.

But it was fine really—exhausting but wonderful, too—until Michael was two and a half years old. David had been invited to give a paper at a conference in London in November. Kyra hadn't even thought of going with him, because she knew he would be busy most of the time. Though the conference was in England, the subject was American history, his field, and his paper was on a hot topic, the rise and fall of labor unions. He was thrilled that he was finally going overseas, and Kyra was thrilled for him, if a bit jealous. They'd gotten their passports together, before they had Michael, but neither of them had had a chance to use them yet.

David had a lot of work to do before the conference. They didn't really discuss it, and then, a week before he was set to leave, he came home and surprised her with three tickets. "I got us a little row on the plane all to ourselves," he said, putting the tickets on the kitchen counter. "Both to London and back." Kyra hugged him and Michael giggled and answered, "Yes!" when David asked him if he was ready to see Big Ben. "He probably thinks you mean Big Bird," whispered Kyra. As if to confirm her hunch, a moment later, the toddler had retrieved his Elmo doll from the bottom of his toy chest.

The flight to London wasn't as bad as Kyra had feared. It was eight and a half hours, and Michael didn't sleep more than three, but he seemed thrilled to be allowed to watch video after video on the computer and never be told it was time for bed. Poor David had to get up the next morning to be at the conference at nine, four Philly time, but luckily Kyra was able to sleep in, with Michael snoring softly next to her.

The conference lasted five days, and each day, despite the rain, Kyra bundled up her little boy and took him to see the sights: Buckingham Palace, Big Ben, the London aquarium on the River Thames, Trafalgar Square, and St. Martin-in-the-Fields. Most of the time they didn't stay nearly as long as Kyra would have liked, and even so, she had to buy a lot of toys as bribes. Michael's favorite was the red double-decker bus like the ones he'd seen on Piccadilly. Kyra liked this toy, too, because it was made of wood by an ecologically friendly company that promised no splinters and no lead paint.

At night, they would have dinner with David: sometimes in a restaurant, but more often in the hotel, so Michael could play on the floor while David and Kyra relaxed and ate and drank a little wine. Their son didn't like restaurants, primarily because he didn't really like eating, but the doctor said it was normal for his age. As long as they gave him healthy foods, they didn't need to worry. He would eat when he was hungry.

The entire time they were in London, Michael probably ate six bites of chicken, a third of a slice of bread, a half of a very small salad with everything but the lettuce removed, and two grapes. He also drank his orange juice, some of it anyway, but he refused to even sip his milk; he said it smelled "funny." He didn't look any thinner when they left, but Kyra thought he had to be. She also thought he seemed "off" in the cab to Heathrow airport, but she couldn't put her finger on what was different. He was talking and pointing at the buses and other cabs. When David showed him one of the red phone booths, he laughed like he'd been told a seriously hilarious joke.

They were in the security line at Heathrow when Kyra suddenly felt sure Michael was getting sick. He wasn't rubbing his ear or complaining about his tummy; he was just holding her hand, but that was strange enough as he never held her hand for more than a few minutes without being told to do so. And his eyes looked a little glassy. Or something. She kept looking at her son, wondering what was going on.

Her husband had a stack of articles to read before he got back to Philadelphia. They were through security and sitting near the terminal, and he was in the middle of a paper written by a woman from Harvard who disagreed with his thesis about the labor movement, when Kyra told him she was worried about Michael.

He looked up at Michael, who was sitting on her lap, holding his double-decker bus, spinning the wheels against his leg.

David said, "He seems all right to me."

"I don't know," Kyra said slowly. "Maybe we should delay our flight. That way, we could see if—"

"Honey, even if he is getting a cold, flying won't make it any worse, will it?"

"What if it's not a cold? I asked him if his throat hurt and he said no."

"That's good, then." He squeezed her hand in an absent-minded way. "Don't worry."

Before she could say anything else, he'd gone back to the article. He was scheduled to give a report on the conference to his department the next morning. He also had two classes to teach tomorrow. Of course he wanted to get back.

She turned Michael around in her lap so she could look at his eyes again. They weren't watering or red, but they looked, well, glassy. It was the only word that described her little boy's weird, faraway stare. It was almost as if he couldn't focus his eyes. She wondered if this was the first sign that he needed glasses. Maybe it was something simple like that.

When they boarded the plane, Michael insisted on walking himself to his seat. Kyra was relieved, though he still kept his hand clutched in hers. The first hour of the flight was notable only for how quiet her little boy was. He was watching a *Sesame Street* video, but he didn't try to sing along or point at Elmo the way he usually did. His whole face seemed to have that faraway look. By the time the video was over, he was shivering.

"Are you cold, sweetie?" Kyra said. He nodded and she got out his favorite blanket from the diaper bag. She put it on his legs, but her hand went to his forehead. Normally, she went straight to the thermometer without bothering with the forehead test because Michael's fevers were always relatively low: 99.5, 100.3. But he wasn't usually shivering like this, either.

He was burning up.

"David," she said. "He needs Tylenol."

He dropped his article and reached for the diaper bag. In the meantime, she unhooked Michael's seat belt and leaned over to pick up her sick baby. He felt like a dead weight in her arms. His breaths were coming twice as quickly as usual and he was whimpering.

They managed to get the Tylenol drops down the little boy's throat, and Kyra held him and waited for the drug to work to bring his fever down. After a half hour or so, it had helped; he no longer felt warm when she touched him. But he wouldn't smile; he didn't even look at the pages as David read his favorite book about trains and trucks. He kept his eyes shut and his face burrowed into her shoulder, as if the cabin lights were bothering him.

When he finally fell asleep, Kyra closed her eyes, too. She wanted to rest just for a minute, but almost an hour and a half went by before she woke up when Michael vomited down the front of both of their shirts.

David handed her a wet wipe, but she didn't have time to wipe herself off before Michael vomited again. He hadn't eaten much all morning, but now that he'd started vomiting, he couldn't seem to stop dry-heaving. The people in the row next to them gave concerned looks, but no one knew what to do for the little boy, including the flight attendant who came by to see if they needed anything. The first time they told her no, but the second time, about fifteen minutes later, David said, "I think he needs a doctor."

"Sir," she said, "I know it's rough being on a long flight with a sick little guy, but it's going to be all right." She smiled sympathetically.

Kyra tried to move Michael over a little, to take the pressure off her left arm, and he let out an awful scream. "I'm so sorry, baby," she whispered. Her eyes were burning with tears.

"He needs help," David said to the flight attendant. When she didn't move, he said, "Now!"

A moment later, they heard the announcement, "If there is a doctor on board please make yourself known to the cabin staff." The only doctor on the plane was a psychiatrist in his seventies, but he remembered enough of his medical school training to recognize that Michael was very sick. When the old man lifted up the little boy's green and white shirt, there was a rash that hadn't been there before, a rash that had developed in minutes. Kyra felt her body go numb when the doctor said the horrible word: *meningitis*.

What happened after that would always be a blur. Somehow they got through the next few hours as the aircraft moved over the ocean. When the plane landed, an ambulance was waiting on the tarmac. The next thing Kyra knew, they were at the hospital, and Michael was in the ICU, in a coma. The doctor in charge told them it was unlikely that he would live through the night.

She remembered sitting on a hard plastic chair, sobbing into her hands. But where was David? He was there, of course he was, but she had no memories of him trying to comfort her or letting her comfort him. She didn't remember them ever holding hands or putting their arms around each other. And he never cried at all; she was certain of this, because it surprised her even at the time.

Michael survived the night, but the next morning, the doctor told them their baby still might die; it was only less likely than before. And even if he didn't, he might have to have his legs amputated. He might have brain damage. He might have permanent hearing loss. He might be blind. The list of possibilities was terrible, but Kyra focused all her prayers on the only thing that mattered. As long as he was alive, she could keep going.

She had no idea if David prayed. She didn't remember seeing him in the hospital chapel. She didn't remember him being there when the priest knelt down with her in Michael's room to say prayers to the Virgin Mary. Her mother-in-law was kneeling on the other side of the priest. Sandra was always there, bringing her coffee and food and lotion for her hands, which were so dry they were bleeding. The hospital had lotion, but Sandra said hers was better. Kyra remembered sitting in a chair while her mother-in-law patted the lavender-smelling lotion onto her knuckles and palms. Neither of them spoke. Michael had had a seizure that afternoon. The doctors had done a scan and said he did not have brain damage. Yet.

Where was David? Why wasn't he part of this memory? Even the night when Michael turned a corner, it was Sandra who she remembered being with her, not her husband. Though it was almost three in the morning, after the doctor told them the good news, the two women began to giggle like girls. They didn't want to wake up Michael—now that he could be woken up like a normal little boy—so they went into the deserted relatives' lounge, where Kyra finally agreed to let Sandra comb out her long hair. It was a tangled mess after days of living at the hospital, but Sandra was so gentle. At some point, Kyra blurted out, "I wish you were my mom," but she forced a laugh.

"Your wish is granted." Sandra laughed, too, and touched Kyra's forehead with the comb, like it was a magic wand. Then she looked into Kyra's eyes, which had filled with tears. "Aw, sweetheart." She put her arms around Kyra. "I am your mom."

"She is," David said, smiling. "With all the rights and privileges attaching thereto."

And just like that, her husband came into focus, sitting on the overstuffed chair on the other side of the lounge. Had he been there all along? That was the part she would never be sure of.

In the months that followed, whenever they talked about the hospital—not often, and always in language so vague that no one who wasn't with them could have known what they were referring to, calling it "what happened with Michael," or just "that November"—Kyra listened carefully to what her husband remembered, looking for points of intersection, places where he *should* have been in her own memories. But she didn't admit that she couldn't see him. She was afraid of what it might mean about her marriage, especially as David seemed to have changed so drastically since that flight home from London.

If only he had talked to her about what he was going through. Instead, he focused all his attention on making sure nothing like this ever happened again. He bought and read books about childhood diseases that were dense and difficult, intended for pediatricians. He learned the signs of all kinds of illnesses, and he taught Kyra what to look for, too. It was David who figured out that Michael was allergic to mold spores, and David who decided Michael was also allergic to dust mites—after the mold remediation contractor had spent months tearing open the walls of their house and Michael was still sneezing. They hired someone to clean every week, and David or Kyra vacuumed Michael's room every day. As David always said, "We have to be on the safe side."

Part of Kyra knew that the *safe side* was a chimera, like the pot at the end of a rainbow, but she didn't argue with her husband. She was afraid, too, now that she understood just how fragile her family's happiness was. Michael had completely recovered, yet it felt like a great chasm still separated her from David. Gone were the days when they would broil steaks and do logic puzzles. They had more time now that Michael was older and a better sleeper, but they'd lost the inclination to do anything together other than work harder, ever harder, to protect their precious little son.

Part Two

TWELVE

I t was the middle of the afternoon, and Michael had a big mosquito bite on his elbow, but he was still happy to be on the boat. For the last few minutes, he and April had been on the lower deck, in line at the concession stand. April was the lady's name, or at least she'd told Michael to call her that, "like the month." They were about to order hot dogs, which Michael was excited about, though he hoped they were the healthy kind: turkey or chicken or at least all beef. He'd already told her he didn't want French fries. He loved how they tasted, but he'd heard his father say that fried food is *a heart attack waiting to happen.*

Now that he'd been with the lady for a few hours, he'd had time to daydream about what it would be like when he got home. He was proud that he could tell his parents that he'd held April's hand and sometimes the rail, too, that he hadn't had any drinks with caffeine or sugar, that he'd tried not to scratch his mosquito bite because he remembered it could get infected if he scratched, that he hadn't talked to strangers or forgotten to wash his hands in the bathroom or eaten (much) unhealthy food. He'd even let April take his picture after she'd told him that her camera wasn't the digital kind but old and really special: you could hold the photo in your hand and watch it come to life. He liked watching the pictures develop so much that by the time April gave her camera to a white-haired lady, to take a photo of the two of them, he smiled right on cue. April's cheeks looked pink in the picture, but his didn't. It was another thing he could tell his parents: that he'd insisted on wearing sunscreen, though April had had to buy it on the boat where it cost twice what it would have cost on land. But she said it was okay. "I don't want you to get burned," she said, and smiled. Then she said under her breath, "I should have thought of this earlier." But Michael told her everybody forgets something. "Even my daddy," he said. "And Mommy says he has the memory of an elephant."

While he was eating his hot dog (so yummy, but unfortunately not the healthy kind), April was asking him questions about his mom. She was sucking on a mint; she had thrown her hot dog away after one bite. Where does your mom work? What does she do there? Does she like music? What songs does she listen to? Michael answered them all as well as he could. He knew the name of his mom's company, but all he knew was she did something with math. "She really likes numbers," he said. "Four is her favorite, just like Big Bird's." He was about to tell April that Big Bird had a song about four, but then April started humming it. He thought the song was too young for him, but still, he couldn't resist chiming in when April got to the chorus: "I just adore four; the number—one-two-three—for me!" But afterward, he clarified, "I really like six better."

April smiled. "I think I know why. You have a birthday coming up soon, don't you?"

He thought nobody in the world knew about his birthday

except his family. His birthday was in the summer, which meant you never got to bring cupcakes to school and celebrate—and he didn't have a school anymore anyway.

"It's June twenty-third, isn't it?" She smiled and handed him a napkin. "And you'll be six."

His hot dog was long gone, but April was pointing at his upper lip. He wiped it with the napkin and handed it back to her. He could feel himself grinning.

"Let's think of today as an early celebration. We can do whatever you want now."

She stood up, and they started walking toward the ramp. The boat had just docked, and everyone was rushing off, but April said they were in no hurry.

Michael was thinking. There were so many other places he wanted to go: how could he pick just one? But then he remembered a kid at his second kindergarten saying that Six Flags in New Jersey had a giant Ferris wheel. One of Michael's books had a Ferris wheel on the cover. He loved the idea of a wheel that could take him so far up that he would feel like he was part of the sky. But when he'd asked his parents if he could go, his father said it wasn't a good idea: the Ferris wheel might break, or, more likely, Michael would pick up a germ from all those children standing in line, some of them sick, no doubt, with parents who were too irresponsible to realize that their sick child could infect hundreds of other kids.

He didn't want to get sick. Plus, shouldn't he be going home soon? The sun was still way up in the sky, but the light looked sort of yellow-orange, which his mom always said was a sign the sun was getting tired. He didn't want his parents to get so worried they would decide this day had been a mistake. But on the other hand, in case they did decide that, he should do everything he could now, while he still had the chance.

"If you want to go back home," April said slowly.

They were off the boat, in the parking lot. Michael felt like his legs had turned into stiff boards now that he was walking without the motion of the waves. He thought about it for less than a minute before he told her no, he didn't want to go home yet.

After he told her about Six Flags, she nodded and pulled out a cell phone. He wondered if she was going to call his parents—and sort of hoped she wasn't, so they couldn't say no—but instead she called the theme park, to see how late they were open. "Nine o'clock," she said, hitting the off button. "We'll make it."

"What is that?" Michael said, pointing to the phone's screen. It was very blue, light blue and dark blue and several shades in between, with white blobs that could be clouds or snow on top of mountains.

"It's called utopia," she said. "Do you know what that is?"

He shook his head.

"Well, I didn't know, either, when I picked that background for my phone, but today, I do."

He wasn't sure what she was saying, but he forgot about it when she leaned down and kissed him. Her breath smelled like lemons, from the mint she'd been sucking on since she threw away her hot dog. Which reminded him to ask why she did that. Wasn't she hungry?

"I don't really eat," April said, and opened the back door of her gray car. He hopped in, and she belted his seat belt and then got into the driver's seat. When he asked her why she didn't eat, she shrugged and looked at him in the rearview mirror. "I've been told it's something very wrong with me."

"You should only eat if you're hungry," Michael said. He was just repeating what his parents had told him a thousand times. "The clean plate club is not a health club."

She laughed. "Good one. Maybe I'll try that on the doctors." She started the car. "But in the meantime, we're off to Six Flags. More of our utopia."

Michael had been reading since he was three years old—he'd

learned accidentally from watching his parents read to him; that was why they had started calling him gifted—but if he'd had to spell the word April kept using, he would have been way off. It sounded so goofy: You-Toe-Pea-A. He wondered if it was something on the computer, like YouTube, which his parents used to watch political speeches.

They were driving away from the beach, toward the entrance to the highway. He was playing with his favorite toy, the red windup robot, watching the robot try to walk on the armrest vibrating from the engine of the car. April was trying to explain what *utopia* meant.

"It's like the perfect place, buddy. Like everything we've seen today: the whale breaching and the ocean waves and even the crisp white paper sleeves that held the hot dogs. It's you and me singing together. It's your mom loving numbers." She took a breath. "It's you loving your parents so much and them loving you. Does that make sense?"

It didn't, but he was distracted trying to find the robot's key, which had fallen onto the floor. He knew he couldn't reach it with his seat belt on, but he wanted to see it. Then he wouldn't worry that it was really lost.

A few minutes later, he heard April say something. He couldn't make out the words, but her voice was so scared that he looked up. In the rearview mirror, her eyes looked big and her face looked as pale as his, even though she hadn't used sunscreen. "I have to pull over," she said, and then she did, so quickly that she didn't use her turn signal and the car behind them honked.

She leaned her head against the steering wheel. He couldn't see her face, but he could hear her breathing fast, like she'd been running for miles. When he asked what was wrong, she said, "I'm feeling sick," and then she was totally quiet. Michael was quiet, too, because he knew people who are feeling sick don't like to talk.

After a while, he looked down and there was the robot key, peeking out from under the passenger seat. He didn't know whether he could take his seat belt off now, but he didn't really care that much about the key anymore. He was scratching his elbow, wondering what his mom and dad were doing. Normally, when his dad got home from the college where he worked, they would all take a break together and have something to eat. But seeing Michael was the best part of the break, according to his parents, though for Michael the best part was the goofy songs and funny stories.

As he stared out the window at the empty street—nothing but a brown field, a rusted truck, and a seafood restaurant that said Out of Business on a big white sign—he wondered if his parents could still have fun without him. But he wasn't really worried about how they were doing. Maybe this was because, if they weren't having fun, neither was he anymore. And if they were sort of scared, so was he.

THIRTEEN

Courtney knew she was in trouble when she put on a slouchy brown jacket, her floppiest hat, and sunglasses, and drove to the West Mt. Airy neighborhood where her ex-husband lived. She had too much time on her hands, but a normal person with free time does not spy on her ex-husband's family. The problem was she couldn't stop herself. She felt as if she was tumbling down a steep hill with no branches or brush or even rocks to break her fall.

It had all begun on a Tuesday night in October, when she went to her favorite deli after work and ordered a mushroom cheese steak. Such a normal thing to do. Yet a few hours later, she had vomited so much blood that her perfect white bathroom looked like a crime scene. Her legs were wobbly, but she managed to drive herself to the hospital, all the while telling herself that this was merely a precaution. "There is nothing wrong with me," she said to the foggy windows of her car. It was after midnight, and the streets of her little town were nearly deserted.

When the hospital released her two days later, she followed up with the gastroenterologist, a smart, friendly man with the unfortunate name of Dr. Downer. Dr. Downer ran a tube into her stomach and found "suspicious cells." It looked like cancer, but he couldn't be sure because her stomach was so inflamed. "Do you take ibuprofen?" he asked, and she nodded. Didn't everyone?

One wall of the doctor's office was covered with a poster of the digestive system. Courtney was staring at the part under the transverse colon called the jejunum. She wondered if the word derived from the same Latin root as *jejune*, which meant silly or childish. Meaning the jejunum was the silliest part of the digestive system?

He took out a pad and wrote prescriptions for two kinds of pills to reduce stomach acid. He told her to avoid citrus and a bunch of other foods, none of which she ate that much anyway. Then he said, "You have to reduce your stress. It's very important."

"I've always been a nervous kind of person," she told him, twirling a piece of her hair between her fingers. It wasn't true, but it might as well have been. She'd been like this for years and years now.

"Then it's time to change." He looked so serious, which scared her, as it was probably meant to.

As she left his office, she told herself that she would do it, somehow. She would become so calm that people would remark how serene she seemed. She would become a person who was so calm that she couldn't have cancer and die.

Though she meant this, still, a month or so later, she'd surprised herself at how well she'd succeeded at her goal. People at work *had* remarked that she seemed "relaxed" and "peaceful." At meetings now she sat still as a sphinx, not chomping on candies or biting her lips or twirling her hair. The only tic she had left was ChapStick. She used it every hour, sometimes many times in one hour, and she never went anywhere without a tube of it in her pocket.

The people in Courtney's department knew she'd been in the hospital, but they didn't know the rest of it. She hadn't told anyone about the suspicious cells—not because she was afraid they wouldn't understand, but because she didn't want her office to change from the safest place in her life to another place that reflected back her image of herself as a person who had problems, a person who wasn't normal enough to belong anywhere.

If only she'd told Betty Jean, her supervisor, about the cancer scare, she might still have her job. Or maybe not. Courtney no longer had any idea. Betty Jean wasn't a bad person, but she had a very short fuse. She'd directed her anger at Courtney a few times, always about some little thing in the documentation that Betty Jean had suddenly decided to care about and huff and puff until Courtney cared, too. Everyone in their department knew that Betty Jean was like this, but everyone, including Courtney, knew how to defuse the situation by nodding along and taking copious notes, some of which would later be thrown away. It wasn't that hard to handle. It was really nothing compared to the other things that Courtney had been through, which was why it was so odd, what happened on that particular night in December.

Courtney was working late, but her project was relatively unimportant. She was merely helping out because Betty Jean had asked her to. She was planning to go home soon, even thinking about ordering a sandwich from her favorite deli: the first time she'd dared to go back there since she'd gotten out of the hospital, though Dr. Downer had assured her that the deli was not responsible. It was either an ulcer or it was those dangerous cells, lurking inside her stomach, waiting until they could be biopsied for the third time at the end of February. Surely the inflammation would be gone by then, as Courtney was taking the medicine and eating the special diet and being calm. She'd even stopped tearing at her fingernails. Her hands looked so clean and young. She liked to click her new nails on her desktop.

When Betty Jean came roaring into her office at about six thirty, to tell her the letter she'd written was completely unacceptable, Courtney had already shut down her computer and taken out her keys from her purse. The problems Betty Jean had identified were trivial. If only Courtney had written down her suggestions and said nothing more. But she was so afraid of losing her inner peace that she begged Betty Jean to talk about this tomorrow. When that didn't work, she claimed she had a headache, which was true. Finally, she blurted out that all of this was unnecessary. She was working from a sample letter—and Betty Jean herself had written the sample. Most of the stylistic problems the woman was so obsessed with had been taken directly from the sample. So it wasn't possible that the errors were that serious, was it?

"You never listen!" Betty Jean was shouting, standing over her. Was she pounding her hand on the desk or on her own forehead? "Everyone has this problem with you. Don't believe it? Trust me, people talk around here, and you're getting a reputation. You're not going to make it in this company if you don't learn to shut up and listen!"

Courtney had been doing technical writing for a long time, but she'd only been at this particular company for ten months. She was the newbie; still, she felt sure it wasn't true that everyone had a problem with her. But when Betty Jean took the sample letter from her desk and ripped it up, barking that it was no justification for Courtney's mistakes, Courtney started to cry. And Betty Jean kept yelling for at least ten more minutes, because in truth, the woman didn't know how to handle the fact that she had made someone cry. The next morning, though, she must have realized something had gone wrong because she went to Human Resources to report an "incident" with Courtney Hughes.

Olivia, the HR rep who summoned Courtney upstairs, "just to talk," agreed that it sounded like she hadn't done anything wrong. Of course the Incident would have to be investigated, which Courtney expected now that it had become the Incident, capital I. But Olivia said Betty Jean was known to have some "anger management issues." "You're not the only person who has been on the receiving end of her temper," Olivia said, sighing and crossing her small hands. "I'm speaking off the record, of course."

There was a record? Courtney knew she shouldn't have been surprised: HR departments were notorious for viewing everything as a potential legal problem. One of the coworkers she had lunch with hinted that she could sue for something or other, but she didn't want to sue. She wanted her job to go back to the way it had been before: peaceful and calm and the best distraction she had from the question of whether cancer was destroying her stomach lining even now, while she was eating an innocent salad.

Though Betty Jean had started all this, she didn't try to hide the fact that she was very unhappy with Courtney. Day after awkward day, the older woman childishly exited the lunchroom when Courtney came in and pretended not to see her if they passed each other in the hall. On some level Courtney was aware that her very presence was now a challenge to one of Betty Jean's personal myths: that she was boisterous and funny and good-hearted, the kind of person the younger employees liked. It was mostly true, that was the strange part. Betty Jean was almost sixty years old, but she still wore black Converse shoes, jeans, and hoodie jackets. She was the only one in the department who had given Courtney a present for her birthday. It was a bottle of wine, and Courtney didn't drink, but still.

At the beginning of January, though the investigation was still in the early stages, Olivia decided that Betty Jean needed to at least do the professional thing and say she was sorry for losing her temper. Courtney was called to the HR conference room on

Monday morning. Olivia was already there, and Betty Jean came in a few minutes later, ostensibly to deliver the apology.

She did seem sad. She cried through most of the half hour— though she denied all of the things she'd yelled that night. She hadn't done anything but wad up the sample letter, but even that wasn't something she was sorry about. Yet Olivia kept nodding encouragingly, as if Betty Jean's nonresponse was exactly what she'd been hoping for.

The meeting was drawing to a close, and Courtney's feet were tapping an anxious rhythm on the carpet. She was eager to go back to her desk—and get back to being calm. She'd never seen the point of this apology anyway. What did it matter if Betty Jean denied everything? That was what she always did, and it wasn't that big a deal.

Courtney wasn't really listening at the end. She heard the word *afraid* coming from Betty Jean's mouth, but afraid of what? The older woman was wearing a nice blue sweater. Her hair was half gray, half brown, but clean and long. And she looked happy all of a sudden. It was the strangest thing. Courtney would never forget how Betty Jean had smiled, seemingly out of nowhere. "She was so upset," Betty Jean said, pointing at Courtney. "It was late and we were the only people in the office." She took a deep breath. "I became afraid of her. I thought, 'This woman is going to hit me.'"

Courtney felt the blood drain from her face. Had her mouth dropped open? She was trying to pull air into her lungs, but she couldn't seem to catch her breath. It felt like her heart was lodged in her windpipe.

She sputtered, "Have to—" and stood up and ran into the hall. About halfway to her office, she realized what was happening to her. She was having a full-fledged panic attack, the first one she'd had in over ten years. Her chest hurt, and she was gasping so loudly that she shut her office door so her coworkers wouldn't get worried and call an ambulance. She put her head between her knees and stared at the green rug until she could breathe again. Then she unlocked her desk, took out her purse, and went home.

She called in sick the next morning and for the rest of the week. She had no choice: her heart started to race every time she thought about going to work. At night when she woke up, covered in sweat, her heart was pounding so loudly she thought the sound was responsible for waking her. When she couldn't fall back asleep by reading a dull writing manual, she got up and baked bread or rolls or anything that required kneading. Sandra had taught her that kneading was better than yoga to calm the nerves. This was a long time ago, when she first got out of the psychiatric hospital and Sandra had had to drag her out of bed and stand her in the kitchen and place her hands on the warm, silky dough.

Though Olivia called and tried to explain away what Betty Jean had said by claiming Betty Jean had felt "judged" and "humiliated," "cornered" and "trapped," she also admitted that the question of whether Courtney was "physically threatening" to other employees could not be left out of the investigation now. But she acted like Courtney was silly for worrying about the outcome—and about what other outrageous things Betty Jean might make up if she continued to feel cornered. "She's worked here a long time," Olivia said. "Everyone on the management team knows her." When Courtney hung up, she wondered why Olivia had shared that last part. How was that supposed to help?

Silly or not, Courtney was so worried that she woke herself up on Sunday night, crying that she was innocent. She went to work on Monday, but she had another panic attack when she looked in her schedule and discovered that she was expected to work with Betty Jean that very afternoon. So she went home again and stayed there, calling in sick day after day, until HR told her if she didn't come back, she'd be fired. When she impulsively quit instead, they all seemed relieved: HR, because they could stop wondering if they'd violated some rule and given Courtney cause to sue, the department manager, because HR would stop investigating his department, and Betty Jean, because she could go back to strolling confidently down the hall, barking out orders, as usual.

No one seemed to feel particularly bad for Courtney (except for the receptionist, who'd taken all her sick calls and thought she really must be desperately ill). Most of the people in Courtney's department had no idea what had happened and some had heard rumors that she had money and didn't really need the job. She did have a small trust fund from her grandmother, but it wouldn't be enough to live on now that she had to pay COBRA to keep her insurance. She didn't have a husband or children; she didn't have many friends in the area. Working had always been the biggest part of her adult life. Indeed, she had never *not* worked since Sandra had helped her get her first job all those years ago.

As she handed over her ID badge, she broke down sobbing. They wouldn't let her spend even a few minutes saying good-bye. HR procedures required that when someone quit, they had to be escorted out of the building by security. She was devastated, but she felt she had no choice: she had to leave for her health. They would never fire Betty Jean, and she wasn't even sure she wanted them to. She just wanted to remain calm.

But unfortunately, without a job to organize her life, she couldn't find her way back to being calm. Her lovely house, so carefully furnished with her grandmother's antiques, had changed from her nightly after-work refuge to her twenty-four seven prison. She kept waiting for someone from work to email that they were sorry or call to invite her for lunch or *something*, but they never did. A few friends from her old job sent her sympathetic texts, but they were all busy with their families and their lives. If only she had a boyfriend to call, but she hadn't had a date in almost a year, since she'd ended it with Stefan, and the fact that she even thought about calling him now was a very bad sign.

She'd chosen Stefan because he was smart and funny and he'd

seemed safe because he was an artist. He was so dedicated to his painting that he lived in a dump for the high ceilings and good light. He had no money. Of course he would never want children. She was right about that, and she was right that he wouldn't be shocked if she told him what had happened with her baby. It was one of the best nights of her life, the night he painted her after she told him about Joshua: a beautiful portrait full of so much love and understanding that he said he could never use it in one of his gallery exhibitions. It wasn't edgy or dark; it didn't fit with the rest of his work. But then he did find a way to use it. In fact, it became the centerpiece of his next exhibition when he entitled it *Medea*, after the Greek goddess who killed her children in the Euripides play.

As day after lonely day went by, Courtney became more convinced that she really was seriously ill. Her skin was dry; she was always cold—except when she was suddenly burning up—and she had so little energy she stopped going to the gym. And the worst part was her poor heart, which was always pounding, pounding, pounding, though she couldn't say why.

She could sleep all she wanted to now, and yet her body wouldn't let her sleep for more than a few hours at a time. She was tired of throwing away moldy bread, so she'd given up baking. Instead, most nights she paced around her house like a nervous ghost, trying not to think about how unfair it was that *she* was the one who'd lost her job, trying not to be nostalgic for the office she used to have, the calming rows of pencils and pens, the coffee mug with the corny company logo, the modern art prints she'd chosen for her office walls that made her colleagues joke that she was too hip to work at a place like this.

When the idea of going to see Joshua's half-brother Michael first floated into her mind, it seemed like a life raft. Sandra had given her a photograph of him as a baby, and the resemblance was striking. She only wanted to have an idea what Joshua would have looked like as a little boy—what would be the harm? It would be so easy to arrange. She knew where David lived; she'd looked up his house on Google Earth. But she wasn't a stalker. And so she successfully resisted the urge until after the first week of March, when she found out that she did not, in fact, have cancer.

The nurse called to tell her the results, already a good sign, as all the other calls had come from Dr. Downer himself. But something had gone wrong; Courtney wanted to believe the good news, but she just couldn't. She was clearly sick, even if she didn't have stomach cancer. She wasn't sure what was causing her illness—and neither was her regular doctor; he was doing a battery of tests—but she suspected her heart was giving out. She could always feel it now, banging in her stomach and her ears and her hands. Her grandmother had died of a heart attack. Of course her grandmother was much older, but Courtney's life had been such a disaster, her heart had probably aged much faster than a normal person's.

And so one day, she found herself driving to Mt. Airy. She still resisted the word *stalking* for what she was up to—though she did sit in her car for several afternoons, watching their front door, waiting for them to come out and walk to the neighborhood co-op. She assumed they belonged to the co-op. It was a cute place, filled with healthy, happy people: exactly the kind of place David's family would belong, in Courtney's imagination anyway.

His new wife was not beautiful, but she was tall with long hair and long legs, and she moved in such a cautious, gentle way that it wasn't hard to see the appeal. The best word to describe her was probably *careful*: a word no one would ever use to describe Courtney, with her fidgety fingers and bitten-down nails and car full of empty candy wrappers and skittish, thumping heart.

But as she moved around the co-op that day, she tried to be careful. Even though she was wearing her disguise, she kept out of Kyra's line of vision. Surely David's wife had seen the photographs Sandra kept. She had to be at least somewhat curious about the woman—or more likely, the monster—he'd been married to.

Luckily, Kyra was busy filling up her cart. Too busy to notice that her son had turned around in the vegetable aisle to wave at a short woman in a green floppy cap. Courtney waved first, but still, her face lit up when the little boy lifted his hand and returned the greeting. The only problem was her heart, which was hammering like it was going to beat its way right out of her body. She was afraid she might die on the spot, but she couldn't leave, because Michael was smiling so shyly and sweetly. She had to stay in this aisle as long as this little boy smiled at her, even if her heart wouldn't cooperate, even if it decided to finally break.

FOURTEEN

March 28

Dear Mother,

    I'm writing to you though I know you probably won't ever see these words. How pathetic, right? Someone call the wah-ambulance. I'm only doing this because my psych doc has been pressuring me for months about this letter-writing idea. He thinks it might break through my "denial" about what happened to me and help me deal with my feelings about you, which is an even bigger deal to him. I told him it wouldn't change anything, but he wore me down until I finally agreed to give it a try.

    Over the years, I've made up dozens of stories about you. In one story, you were a missionary helping native peoples deep within the rain forest. In another, you were in an accident in Florida and were still being rehabilitated. Or you'd married a scary man who kept you locked in a cabin deep in the Canadian wilderness.

    My doc pointed out that all the stories had one thing in common: they didn't just explain why you hadn't contacted me, they provided a reason you couldn't. They made you make sense to me. The doc says I have a deep need for everyone to make sense and this is what led to what he calls my "habit of inventing reality." This habit or whatever it is goes way beyond making up stories about you. I've been doing it all my life. I didn't even know there was anything wrong with it.

It probably sounds like I'm some kind of freak who lives in pretend world, but I don't think I am. Until last fall, I was on the debate team, which is nothing like stories and all about being reasonable. I was pretty good at it, though sometimes when I was supposed to be working on a real debate, I would write down what I would say and what you would say, if I was going to try to convince you that you shouldn't have abandoned your daughter. And I guess that was a story, too, since you were talking, though at least I was trying to just stick *to the facts.*

The doc told me once that I treat facts like they're enemies. The truth is, I like facts fine, but they seem so narrow. The fact that you left, for example. What does that tell me that I can use?

In the fake debate, you always began with what I figured you must really believe: "That girl has nothing to do with me. Yes, I gave birth to her, but that doesn't mean I owe her anything now." I tried beginning with the classic: "Do you realize what would happen to society if everyone acted like you, Mother?" This is called "Kant's Test of the Universalized Maxim," according to my debate coach. Kant was a philosopher who thought that one way to judge if something is wrong to do is to think how you would feel if everybody did it. Unfortunately, it didn't do much for my side of the debate, since you could say, "Well, everyone wouldn't act like me," and that would be hard to counter, since most mothers don't want to desert their kids.

I also tried the nature argument, which goes something like "Even animals know they must take care of their young and humans should not defy the natural order." This is called an "argument by analogy." First I had to show that animals are good mothers and then make an analogy to human mothers. But it turned out that there are animals that desert their young. Some animals even eat their babies. So that argument went nowhere as well.

You: "Well, I didn't eat you. Aren't you grateful for that?"

Me: "Was eating me on the table? Pun intended." (I've always loved stupid puns. I hope that's not on some mental illness checklist.) "I mean, you're not a cannibal, are you, Mother?"

You: "All right, Miss Smarty-pants. I didn't have an abortion, then."

Me: "Thank you for calling me Miss Smarty-pants. Let's keep it formal, since we don't actually know each other."

You: "Seriously, young lady. Everyone told me to have an abortion. I was so young, but I didn't do it. That should mean something to you."

Me: "Yeah, it should. I wish I was more grateful about that."

Which I honestly do. I have no idea if you considered abortion, Mother, but you did give birth to me and that really is something. I wish I was glad about it, but I'm not really glad about anything anymore. I've let my friends go. I've dropped out of everything. I basically never leave the house now that I've finished all the credits I need to graduate.

Worst of all, I have no story that explains me to myself. It's a bigger problem than it sounds like.

The doc thinks I might have agoraphobia. He's wrong. I don't have a fear of places, I have a fear of people. I can go pretty much anywhere as long as I'm alone. I know every inch of this town: from the creek behind the strip mall to the hill at the edge of my neighborhood that I used to think was a mountain when I was a kid. As cheesy as this sounds, I called it "God's Mountain," because I thought I could talk to God there. I didn't like church because it was too warm and I have low blood pressure (inherited from you?) and so I was always close to fainting by the time the service was over. And at God's Mountain, I was alone. I thought God could hear me better if He wasn't being bombarded with the prayers of everybody in the building.

Hello, God, it's me. Will you bring my real mommy home?

You: "I didn't realize I was being invited to a pity party."

Me: "So you're still talking in my imagination, even though I'm no longer remembering our imaginary debate? That's probably a bad sign, but OK. You're right, I don't want this to be a pity party, though I think that's what my doc intends these letters for. I wasn't feeling sorry for myself *though. I was thinking about my eight-year-old self and feeling sorry for her. She was so much cuter and sweeter. Even my stepmother thought I was such a sweet, well-behaved girl that she trusted me to be fine if she just left me alone most of the time."*

You: "Are you hinting that your stepmother didn't take care of you? Don't you think that's a bit cliché?"

Me: "Cliché, Mother? Ouch. But OK, I'm not saying my stepmother is some kind of witch. She's just nothing like me. And I think she sort of dislikes me because I'm related to you and you were Dad's first love."

You: "I was, that's true."

Me: "Were you really?" (Yeah, I know, I'm making this up. I'm not that crazy. It's just that I like the direction my imagination is going.)

You: "Oh definitely. Your father thought I was the prettiest girl he'd ever seen. He told me I was beautiful all the time."

Me: "I knew you were really pretty. Believe it or not, I have zero pictures of you. Dad said all the ones he had were ruined in a basement flood when I was a kid. But I knew you were pretty because my stepmother mentioned it once."

You: "Well, your stepmother is probably just jealous. Ignore her."

Me: "Easy for you to say, since you don't live here."

You: "Look, I'm getting tired of talking about this. Blame me for your problems or don't blame me. Whatever floats your boat."

Me: " 'Floats your boat?' Now that's a cliché."

You: "No need to be snotty. Would you prefer, 'Whatever bakes your biscuit'? How about 'Whatever melts your butter'?"

Me: "Well, they're OK, but—"

You: "How about 'Whatever blows up your skirt'?"

Me: "That one is just crazy, Mother. At least the butter/biscuit suggestions had a down-home, southern feel. The blown-up skirt sounds like something a pervert would say."

You: "How would you know anything about perverts? Oh God, I hope this isn't one of those letters girls write to confess that their fathers have abused them."

Me: "Come on, you know Dad isn't a pervert. He's a totally normal person who works and mows the grass and fixes stuff around the house, all the normal things. It's not his fault that he has no idea what to do with a messed-up daughter. My stepmother thinks I'm not grateful for all the stuff my dad does give me: a roof over my head, clothes to wear, appointments with the shrink, my own car. She's wrong: I know how lucky I am to have all this. I just wish it could fix me."

You: "I met your stepmother once. Did you know that?"

Me: "Um, yes. I just wrote that imaginary sentence where you said you did. My dad never talks about your visit, but I remember it. You gave me a stuffed turtle and a puzzle with thick pieces shaped like fruit."

You: "Are you sure about this? I don't remember a puzzle or a turtle."

Me: "No, I'm not sure. I feel like it happened, but nobody else agrees. Both my dad and my stepmother say you've never come to see me. Not once. But I remember it so well. It's like my first memory. You were wearing a purple shirt and black pants. You had a really cool watch with big hands and a green face that glowed in the dark."

You: "That watch sounds—"

Me: Sorry to stop you in midsentence, but I'm being summoned for church. It's Sunday morning, did I mention that? They drag me to church every week, and there's nothing I can do to get out of it. It's pretty much to be expected here in Summerland, Missouri, home to twenty-nine churches and exactly one tiny library. I may need a shrink, but I need God, too—that's what I'm told, and they're probably right. After all, when you really need a reason for your life, who better to give you one than God?

FIFTEEN

At the beginning of April, when Courtney found herself still alive—if not well—she went to see a psychic. She used to think astrology and shamans and psychics were completely absurd. But this was back when she was so young that she found the idea that life had no meaning not only brilliant but also cool and even enjoyable. *Of course life lacks meaning. What kind of fool pretends that it doesn't?*

The office of the psychic, or "intuitive" as the woman preferred to be called, was on top of a pizza parlor. As Courtney climbed the steps, she felt slightly nauseated by the strong smell of grease. The intuitive introduced herself as Evelyn Rose. She was a large woman in a shapeless olive dress that was fraying at the neckline. She'd come highly recommended—by anonymous people on the Internet. But even anonymous recs were more than most psychics had, though Courtney realized it was possible that Evelyn had posted them all herself.

The room was dark with the exception of the candles burning on the large mahogany buffet against the back wall and one dim floor lamp in the corner by a door. She took Courtney over to an area where two love seats faced each other. In the middle was a small round table with nothing on it. No crystal ball. No tarot cards. Not even the divination stones that Courtney associated with her mother's annual trips to Santa Fe.

Her mother had been seeing psychics since Courtney was a little girl, but her mother had also had a psychiatrist who made house calls. Yet there was nothing wrong with her, or so she said. All of this was simply about "learning happiness." Courtney herself had not gone near a psychiatrist since she'd been released from the hospital years ago. This trip to Evelyn Rose was the closest she'd come to letting anyone know about the problems she was having. She had no idea if this woman could help. If she couldn't, Courtney would chalk it up as a wasted evening, but the evening would have been wasted anyway.

She sat down on one of the love seats and pulled down the back of her shirt over her jeans. Evelyn Rose sat down across from her and made small talk. But her eyes never left Courtney's face.

"How does this work?" Courtney finally said. She still wasn't sleeping, and she was much too tired to keep discussing the new farmers' market and the weather.

"You want to know about the future," the woman said. "But first, I need to ask a few questions about your past."

Courtney sucked in her breath and bit her bottom lip. And waited.

Evelyn Rose leaned forward. "You have done something that you are not proud of, yes?"

"Yes." Nearly everyone her age had done something in the past that they weren't proud of, hadn't they?

"You have lost someone very important to you."

Courtney nodded. Again, at her age, who hasn't?

"You blame yourself for this loss."

She nodded again, but she crossed her arms to protect herself.

"And other people also blame you?"

She looked at the wall behind Evelyn and waited a moment. "I suppose."

The woman took a deep breath. "Are they right?"

Courtney was blinking and biting her lip. "Don't you already know?" she said, more than a little irritably.

Evelyn didn't respond. After a moment, she stood up and smiled. "All right. Would you like a drink before we go on?"

A few minutes later, while Courtney was sipping weak raspberry tea, Evelyn waved her pale hand and said they could move on to the future now. "Fate is going to bring someone new into your life." She paused. "Not romantically. It will not be a man."

"I don't want a man," she said firmly, thinking about Stefan.

"Who does?" the woman said, and laughed a husky laugh.

Courtney smiled. Evelyn was impossible not to like. When she got home, she would add another web recommendation for the psychic, even if this session didn't go anywhere.

"The person who is coming into your life," Evelyn said slowly, dramatically, "will either be a woman or a child."

Courtney forced a shrug. "I doubt it will be a child."

Just last week, her doctor had finally said that something *was* wrong with her: she was suffering "premature ovarian failure." She would never have guessed that her estrogen level had fallen so low it was equivalent to the level of an eighty-year-old woman. It seemed impossible because she still had her periods, though in truth they were more commas than periods, lasting only a day or two with no cramps and no real flow. The doctor had no explanation for why she'd ended up in menopause at thirty-eight years old. Though she'd never have risked having a child again, it still hurt to know that this phase of being a woman was already over. Over before she'd even understood it—like most things in her life.

She was wearing her brand new estrogen patch on her hip. She wasn't sure if it was doing anything, though she realized it might be the reason she'd had the energy to come here tonight.

"It will not be your own child," Evelyn said, and gave Courtney a long look. "I'm sorry."

"Don't be," Courtney said flatly. Could Evelyn know what had happened with Joshua? Her questions about the past had made it seem like she did. But wasn't that the way these things worked? Psychics made statements that felt like insights, but were really so general that most people found a way to apply them to themselves. Still, she desperately wanted Evelyn Rose to be the real thing. She needed help.

The psychic talked for a while about the mystery person, even though Courtney was anxious to get to the real reason she was there. She didn't care about the possibility of a child coming into her life since she knew it couldn't be Michael. After that day in the co-op—and the twenty-four hours she'd spent weeping after she left—Courtney had promised herself that she would never try to see David's child again. Now if only her dreams would cooperate. Nearly every night, she dreamed of that little boy, always smiling, running toward her like he'd known her all his life.

The psychic admitted the mystery person was more likely to be a woman. And this woman will come from "far away." (Don't they always?) The mystery woman will be important in Courtney's life. (Ditto.) There will be trouble, something will happen that Courtney won't expect. (If Courtney already expected everything that would happen, it wouldn't be much of a mystery, would it?) And Courtney will be changed forever by knowing this mystery person. Her whole life will be different.

If only.

"I told you on the phone what I'm worried about," Courtney finally said. "Do you have an answer for me? Can you tell?"

The psychic paused for so long Courtney wondered if she was

daydreaming about her grocery list or what she planned to do tonight. Courtney watched the smoke from the candles as it rose in spirals before it disappeared.

Evelyn clasped her hands together and said, "It will all be over soon."

Without blinking, Courtney said, "Because I'm going to die?"

This was what she'd come to ask the psychic. The doctor had assured her that premature ovarian failure wasn't life-threatening; it didn't mean the rest of her body was failing, too. But she still felt like something serious was going wrong inside of her. Her heart had settled down a little, but she felt herself disconnecting from the earth, day by day, even hour by hour, and she just wanted someone to tell her how long she had. Before she died, she had to talk to David. She needed to hear him say, "I forgive you," even if she had to beg for the words.

"No, dear," the psychic said. "Because you're going to live."

Her smile was so gentle. If it was also a little patronizing, Courtney didn't notice. She wouldn't have cared anyway. If the psychic thought her fears were ridiculous, then maybe they really were.

When she got home, she put on her pajamas, flopped down on the couch, and turned on the TV; then she flipped the channel until she found *Law & Order: Criminal Intent*. The show was her obsession since she'd lost her job, but she'd seen every episode many times. It wasn't distracting enough to keep her from thinking about what the psychic had predicted. Was it possible that it was true? Her life wasn't over? She wasn't about to die? She recognized the feeling in her chest—hope—though it was something she hadn't felt in a long time. It scared her how much she wanted her life to change.

SIXTEEN

April 8

Dear Mother,

So it turns out that my first letter to you didn't actually count for my assignment. My psych doc didn't like that I wrote an imaginary conversation between me and you. (Yeah, I was stupid enough to tell him about that.) He shook his head and said that I "fell back on my habit of inventing reality" so I wouldn't have to talk about what happened to me. I promised him I would try harder, so here goes.

It was September, school had started a few weeks before, and I had just turned seventeen. Dad kept calling me "sweet seventeen," and though I shrugged like I was annoyed—I'd already had a year of being "sweet sixteen"—it was pretty close to true. I was a very innocent girl then. I'd spent the first three years of high school being quiet and getting straight As. I knew the popular kids considered me a dork, but I had two great friends: Leah, who was one of the smartest girls in our grade, and Kevin, who was so hilarious that I felt sure he was going to be a famous comedian someday. I also had friends in my youth group at church. You could say I was very sheltered, though of course I didn't know it then.

Because she will turn out to be important in the story, I should also mention Renee. I have known Renee since we sat in the same row in Mrs. Applegate's kindergarten class. She was my best friend for almost eleven years, but then in the middle of tenth grade, she stopped hanging out with me. She became one of the cool kids, probably because she'd grown up to be the prettiest girl in school. She looks a little like Angelina Jolie. Everyone says she could be a model if she wants, and I hope it's true. Her family is really poor. They could use the money.

The doc has asked me a bunch of times how I felt when Renee dropped me, though I've told him over and over that I was OK with it. I even told Renee, when she disinvited me to her tenth-grade party, that I understood. She was having the party while her mother was out of town and all the cool kids and wild kids would be there. None of them really knew me or liked me, and Renee desperately needed them to like her. She never said this, but I felt like I knew it, the same way I knew that she was afraid of a stuffed turtle in kindergarten.

Wait. I'm supposed to remind myself that what I just said about her being afraid of the turtle isn't reality. That's what my shrink said. It's a good example to show you how my stories used to work, though.

First I'll tell you what really happened. I was five years old, and I brought the stuffed turtle you gave me to class for show-and-tell. The teacher told me to pass the turtle around and let everybody see it. When the turtle was given to Renee, she looked into its eyes for a minute and then she threw it on the floor and said it was dumb.

Then I realized why she did it. She thought the turtle's eyes looked mean, which they kind of did if you didn't understand that the turtle was supposed to be thinking hard, because he was a very wise turtle. She was afraid of those eyes, I told myself, and then before I knew it, I had spun this fear into a bigger story where Renee wasn't the person who kicked people out of her way on the playground, but instead, a regular girl who didn't have a bicycle or very many toys and felt sad a lot, but who was pretending not to be sad or scared.

According to the shrink, if I'd only thought all of this might be true, it would be OK. But I was convinced it had to be true, and because I believed my story, I was friendlier to Renee, and she was friendlier to me, and pretty soon, she wasn't kicking people out of her way anymore. So the doc says it would have been understandable if I'd believed this particular story had changed reality, except that I never thought of it that way. I thought the story had always been the truth, and most people couldn't see it.

I don't see it anymore, either, but it's not the shrink's fault. This happened before I even met the doc. When Brad Jeffers called Kevin a "faggot," because Kevin is gay, I had no story to explain Brad's behavior. So instead I scratched his face until it bled and I got suspended from school, and that's how I ended up at the psychiatrist's office in the first place. It was my dad's idea. He didn't know what else to do for me.

But let's get back to before. Back to last September, when my teachers loved me and I got great grades and had two good friends and my goal was just to be a nice person and get into a top-ranked college. Though my shrink says this Little Miss Perfect phase couldn't have lasted forever (as opposed to those phases that do last forever, I guess—the doc is a good guy, but he's always saying weird things like this), I don't know if that's true. Even now when I see no reason to continue with my life, I still wish I knew how to get back to my stories. Sometimes I think if only I could see you, I would be transported back to where I used to be, and everything would make sense again. Other times, I think that girl was a fool who believed something even most preschoolers know is crap: that people are basically good.

My birthday, as you know, is September 14. That morning, Dad surprised me with a car: a 2002 Honda Accord, gray, manual transmission. I was already an experienced driver and I think Dad was tired of me borrowing his Ford Explorer. The Honda is important, because if I hadn't had it, I wouldn't have been able to go to the party that night. But it's not the car's fault. It took me away in the end, for which I will always be grateful to the car, even if it is just an object.

This is where I really wish I could stop. But it's OK, because you're not reading this, and even if you were, you could handle it, right? My dad can't, but you are different. You have your own crime. In my favorite story of you, you like sad books and dark movies. You have amnesia about the past, which is why you haven't contacted me, but you still feel the past's influence. You wear black, live in New York, and sit in coffee shops chatting with people you don't know. You are unafraid to talk about the worst parts of the world: the brutal murders and devastating earthquakes and all the broken children.

So, September 14. It was around 8:30 in the evening when my cell phone rang. Renee hadn't called me since the day after Thanksgiving, sophomore year, so of course I was very surprised when I heard her voice. She wished me a happy birthday, and asked what I was doing. I told her the truth: that I'd just settled down to watch a movie with my dad and the girls. "The girls," as my stepmother always calls them, are Natalie and Nicole, her daughters from a previous marriage, who are twenty and twenty-one, respectively, and who live in their own apartment near the strip mall, where they both work as hairstylists. Even though I've known Natalie and Nicole all my life, no one has ever thought it was strange that we didn't play together or act like real sisters. Part of it was that they were older than me, but mainly it was that they always had each other. It didn't help that they were gone on the weekends and most of the summer, visiting their real dad. My stepmother was always a little irritated that her free weekends were never actually free, because I was always there. I used to wish that she and my dad would have their own kid, so I wouldn't be the only one home all summer, and so I'd have a brother or sister who might want to hang out with me—but that doesn't matter now.

By the time I'd taken the phone into my room, Renee told me she had a surprise for me. "Ian wants you to come to his party tonight." She paused. "He thinks you're really cute."

Ian was one of the stars of the basketball team. Pretty much every girl in school had a crush on him, including Leah. I took some pride in being the exception, but I was obviously not as much of an exception as I thought. My heart was jumping out of my chest at the mere possibility that someone like him could notice me. "I don't believe it."

"He asked me to call and invite you."

"For real?"

"Yeah. It starts at 10:30. Are you coming or not?"

I said I'd think about it, and she said OK and hung up. I let out a long breath and went back into the living room, where my dad was sitting with the DVD paused. Natalie and Nicole were on the love seat, gossiping about some friend, waiting for the birthday cake that my stepmother was frosting. Chocolate with white icing, same as every year. Two of those chunky number candles: 1 and 7.

Back when Renee and I were friends, my stepmother used to say that Renee's family lived on the "wrong side of the tracks." We don't have any tracks in Summerland; we've never even had a train. Our idea of public transportation is the school bus, or someone with a car who doesn't mind letting other kids have a ride. But it's true that Renee's family lives on the other side of town, farther away from the river and nearer to the factories. Ian lives in our neighborhood, though, only five or six blocks away. I'd known him long before he became the school's personal god. His older brother Brett had taken Natalie to the senior dance. When Ian and I were kids, we used to splash each other in the neighborhood pool. I let him play with my cool yellow beach ball.

What if he really did like me? Even though I was a senior now, I'd never had a boyfriend. I'd never even been kissed. Leah and Kevin were in the same boat, so I didn't feel like a freak, but it did bother me. Leah and Kevin were both thin. My secret fear was that I was too fat for any boy to like.

I was five-five and I weighed 132 pounds. According to the health charts, I was normal. But I was heavier than most of the girls at school who had boyfriends, which wasn't hard to be: a lot of those girls were so skinny they looked like they'd never smelled a hamburger. Sometimes I tried to diet, but it never worked, partly because I liked food too much, but mainly because my stepmother got offended if everyone didn't eat huge helpings of whatever she cooked for dinner. But Natalie and Nicole were chunkier than me, and they'd always had boyfriends. And Leah and Kevin told me I was pretty all the time. My dad said I took after your side of the family, Mother, and since you were beautiful, I know this meant I couldn't be a downright woof-woof.

I felt like I'd woken up inside the plot of a movie. A very cute boy said I was cute—on my birthday. It was a truly magical development. I'd been invited to Ian's party. Of course I was going!

I told my dad, and he said fine. I think he was relieved that I had something to do for a change. My stepmother said something about Ian's father being too lazy to keep up his yard, but this was typical for her. She'd said Renee was "white trash" and Kevin was "strange," and Leah was the worst, because "she thinks she's so smart."

In case you're wondering, I did have a story that explained my step-mother. I actually worked with my shrink to separate what was true and what wasn't about her. We wrote it all down in a grid.

Story: She grew up so poor she had to eat Cream of Wheat for dinner every night. Truth: She was from a somewhat poor family, but the detail must have come from my own hatred of Cream of Wheat.

Story: Her first husband left her for his secretary. Truth: Her ex did get remarried awfully quickly, but I really have no idea why.

Story: She can't have any children with my dad for some biological reason. She's devastated by her infertility. Truth: She has never discussed this in my presence, but I still say it's probably true, as I know my dad wanted a son and yet they never had a kid. Unless my dad is the infertile one? (This possibility makes me so nervous I can't think about it. I bet you know why, Mother. You're the only one who could, right?)

Story: She's gotten quite old-looking in the last ten years, and she worries that my dad regrets marrying her. Truth: She's six years older than my dad and she looks it, she says so herself. But I've only sensed this worry. So maybe it isn't real. I don't know because I can't *know. My shrink emphasized this.*

Story: She wishes her daughters had done better in high school and gone to college. Truth: Again, I can't know, but I sure would wish this, if I were in her shoes.

You get the drift. The story went on and on, until I felt like my stepmother was doing her best considering her difficult circumstances, and so there was no reason to be upset with her. This was the conclusion of most of my stories, actually. Everyone was doing the best they could. People were basically good.

My dad turned off the DVD and went into the kitchen. I heard him tell my stepmother, "It's her birthday. She should be able to do what she wants."

Before I left, Nicole and Natalie insisted I change into the short black skirt and tight pink tank top they'd given me for my birthday. They also fixed my hair with one of the ceramic flat irons from the beauty salon. They pressured me into putting on the only shoes in my closet that I'd never worn because the black straps dug into my ankles and the heels made me feel wobbly. When they were done putting makeup on me, they said I looked like a girl instead of a geek for the first time in my life.

I was nervous until I got behind the wheel of the Honda. I was still so amazed that I had my very own car, with a stick shift, no less. Heading down the block, I gunned the engine and downshifted just to have more to do with my hands.

I got to the party at 10:06, according to the clock in the Honda. I left at 10:43. It was only thirty-seven minutes, but it changed my entire life.

Whenever I feel like a wuss because this keeps hurting so much, I think about Gracie. There were three other girls in the same position as me that night: Gracie, Megan, and Marcella. I didn't know any of them very well, but nobody knew Gracie. She was a quiet girl who was bused to school from her parents' farm, a twenty-mile ride each way. I wondered later how she got to Ian's party, and especially how she got home. I didn't see her there. She'd left by the time I arrived.

It was a few months later, December and already snowing, when Gracie came home from school and took an overdose of her mother's OxyContin.

Her family claimed they had no idea she was depressed. The whole senior class went to a special church service to pray for Gracie, even Ian and Renee and all those popular kids who should have spontaneously burst into flames for daring to sit in a pew and act like they cared. She did recover, but she never came back to school. The rumor is she's finishing the year in a psych hospital in St. Louis.

I scratched Brad's face and got suspended less than a week after Gracie took the overdose. My shrink says I did it for her. He also says that I'm still trying to do the same thing to myself that Gracie tried to do to herself, but just taking my time about it.

Like the song says, "Everybody hurts sometimes, everybody cries."

Blah, blah, blah.

I have to go down to face dinner, but first an interesting fact. You gave me a stuffed turtle, but did you know that female turtles lay their eggs and walk away? The babies don't grow up with their mothers. They never even meet them.

SEVENTEEN

Finding the "friendly" kidnapper's note in the backyard had made the police a little more relaxed about the investigation—at least so it seemed to David, who felt himself becoming, conversely, more agitated. Yes, it was good news, as his mother said, that they didn't think the kidnapper intended to harm Michael, but it was hardly a reason to believe their son *wouldn't be* harmed. What if the kidnapper was too unstable to act in accordance with her supposed intentions? If nothing else, what about the psychological trauma of keeping a child away from his family and his home? David couldn't understand why they weren't out looking for his son rather than spending more time questioning him and his wife. Detective Ingle said additional questioning was necessary because of the new assumption that the kidnapper was somehow connected to the family. New to him, perhaps, but infuriatingly not new to David, who'd been telling the police about Courtney since the moment they arrived.

The detective insisted that David and Kyra be questioned separately this time, and so she was upstairs in her study with one of the officers, while he was stuck talking to Ingle in the living room. David was leaning against the wall, and Ingle was sitting on the couch, twiddling his thumbs. Literally. The thumb motion was probably a nervous tic, but David found it extremely irritating. Their discussion had been going on for at least twenty minutes, and David was becoming frantic for Ingle to stop talking and *do something.*

At the moment the detective was stuck on one phrase from the note: "think of me as a babysitter." "It just doesn't sound like something your ex-wife would say, does it?"

"I have no idea," David said. He was thinking that the detective had even less of an idea. Less than no idea? Yes. The man had achieved the impossible. "The entire thing could have been some self-justifying lie for all I know."

Ingle cleared his throat. "Was your ex-wife in the habit of lying?"

"Are you joking? Even if she never lied before, she never kidnapped a child before, either. It's not relevant."

"That's right," the detective said, and gave David a meaningful glance. "She's never taken anyone's child, has she?" He emphasized his point by tapping his thumbs together before the twiddling began again.

This was so absurd that David would have laughed in other circumstances. "Surely you're not implying that whoever took my son must have done this before? That every kidnapper has always been a kidnapper?"

Before Ingle could come up with anything to defend that ridiculous position, the officer who'd been questioning Kyra came into the room. What followed was a veritable code of raised eyebrows and nods: the officer nodded, Ingle raised his eyebrows, the officer nodded, paused, and nodded again, Ingle nodded, the officer raised his eyebrows, and on and on, until finally the two men headed in the direction of the kitchen.

David was about to follow and ask what was going on when Kyra came down the stairs. She sat down on the white-and-blue love seat near the window. He assumed she wanted to talk, and he took a seat on the piano bench across from her. She looked so sad; he wished he could be next to her and comfort her, but the love seat was too associated with their little boy. In the evenings, the three of them usually snuggled there, talking and reading together. If only he could believe their son would be back in his usual place tonight, but as the hideous afternoon dragged on, he knew it was becoming less likely.

He heard the back door slam—either Ingle and the officer going out or the giant officer coming in. The giant had been in the backyard since the note was found, supposedly dusting for fingerprints. David wondered how long it could possibly take. More to the point, he wondered what Ingle had been getting at during his questioning. What was the man up to?

"It's as if he wants me to admit she didn't take him," David said. "It makes no sense."

He was talking more to himself than to Kyra, who was staring down at her hands. But then he heard his wife's soft voice, "Unless she didn't."

"Ingle has no way of knowing that," he said, more sharply than he intended. He let his shoulders relax and took a deep breath. "He told me they sent an officer by her house and she wasn't home. That's it. They haven't even talked to her yet."

Kyra raised her face and looked at him. "But why would she do it? There has to be a reason, doesn't there?"

He knew his wife deserved an answer, but he simply couldn't discuss all that. He mumbled some platitude about the difficulty of understanding why anyone does anything, and looked out the window. It was a perfect sunny day, which seemed so incongruous with his family's distress that it made him want to punch something. But he wasn't the kind of man who punched things. He felt out of control in a way he hadn't since he was a hormonally challenged teenager.

"Besides," he finally said, taking another breath. "It's not like there are any other suspects. You know they're wasting their time sending police to question everyone in my family. As if someone like Peggy or Eleanor would take our son."

Peggy was his former stepmother, who hadn't seen Michael in years, and Eleanor was a second cousin on his mother's side. Eleanor *was* a little crazy, but her craziness took the form of hoarding junk and telling everyone she was about to be famous for some accomplishment she never bothered to specify. She'd been over to the house two or three times, always with Sandra, and she sent Michael a birthday card every year, like most of David's relatives did. She had no reason to take Michael. As David had told the police countless times, no one he knew was capable of doing this other than his ex-wife.

"Maybe it's someone in my family." Kyra wrapped her arms around herself. "Have you thought of that?"

No, he hadn't thought of it, because it was so obviously false. David remembered going to Kyra's father's funeral; it was before Michael was born, maybe seven years ago? The service was attended by over a hundred people. David met old Callahans and middle-aged Callahans and a few baby Callahans. He helped Great Aunt Something-or-Other balance her plate of food. He had his foot stepped on by an overweight guy everyone called Uncle Grumpy. He shook hands with a cousin that had lost his leg in the first Gulf War. He listened to the bragging of another cousin who claimed to be the next Donald Trump. And he spent a lot of time with Kyra's stepmother, who cornered him not to talk about her loss but to discuss her beloved horses. He remembered because one of the horses was named Sandra. The other was Fletcher or Flicka, something horsey like that.

It was all normal enough, if not particularly pleasant, but what struck David was that *not one* of these people had come to their wedding, though Kyra had invited them all. Maybe they couldn't afford the trip, but why hadn't they sent a present, or at least a card? Even Ray and Peggy had sent a check for two hundred dollars, though Ray's note was so offensive that David would have been happier if he hadn't heard from his father. *Good luck. You can't say I didn't warn you.*

The sad fact was that the police didn't need to question Kyra's relatives, because none of them had ever shown the slightest interest in Michael or any other aspect of her life. Hell, half the people at that funeral couldn't even correctly pronounce her name. Her stepmother seemed to care more about her horses than about Kyra; her own mother had deserted the family when Kyra was a little kid, and her only sister had cut off contact with all the Callahans when Kyra was barely out of college. The only family Kyra had—apparently the only one she'd ever had—was the one she'd made with him and their beautiful son.

"No one would want to hurt you," he said gently. "I'm sure this isn't your fault."

He turned to the doorway because he could hear Ingle. The detective was barking orders to one of the other officers, but even the man's bark was too quiet for David to make out the words. "I think I should go see what they're—"

"Does it have to be either my fault or your fault?" Kyra said.

"Of course not." He rubbed his palm over his forehead, wondering where this had come from. "Whoever took him is responsible for this."

"But you said it's not my fault, as though if it *were* my family, it would be. So if it turns out to be Courtney, will it be your fault?"

She leaned forward and her hair fell over the side of her face. "Is that what you think?"

He said no, but before he could elaborate, Ingle walked in with the news that two new policemen had arrived. David heard their footsteps on the front porch. Ingle let them in, and a moment later, he announced that he and the original officers were leaving to follow up on leads. Finally.

"I'll call you as soon as I know anything." He handed David his card. "You can also call me if you have any questions or think of anything that's *relevant*."

David took the card and ignored the sarcasm. For the hundredth time, he wished they'd been assigned a different detective. But if Ingle found Michael, he would forgive the man anything. He would let the detective come over and twiddle his thumbs in their living room every day for the rest of their lives, if only he brought back their son.

When he turned away from Ingle, he saw that Kyra had slipped out of the room. He went upstairs and found her in their bedroom, sitting at the end of the queen-size bed. He thought about this morning, when he'd been distracted by a phone call while he was making the bed. He'd obviously done a poor job: one side of the pale yellow blanket was scraping the wood floor. His chest hurt remembering this. It was such a normal thing to do. Such a normal morning—until it wasn't.

"Honey." He sat down next to her and took her hand in his. "What's going on?"

"I keep reviewing all the things in my life that led to this moment. What I should have done differently. What I would do if only I could go back and have another chance."

He assumed she was feeling guilty again for taking her eyes off Michael when he was in the backyard. He tried to reassure her, but she cut him off.

"Why do you think I'm a good person?"

"Because you are. You're a wonderful mother, my best friend, and the woman I love."

"But you're only saying that because you think you know me."

"Uh-oh." He forced a smile. "Is this the scene in the movie when you tell me you're really an alien?"

He wanted to cheer her up, but he also wanted to put a stop to this, though he couldn't have said exactly what *this* was. Unfortunately, Kyra ignored his feeble attempt at humor. She looked into his eyes. "Do we really know each other, David? Do you think I know you?"

"Of course we know each other. Honey, we're under an enormous amount of stress. It's not the time to—"

"But there are things I haven't told you."

"Whatever they are, they won't change how I feel about you. Please don't worry about this now."

She squeezed his hand, but she acted like she hadn't heard him. "There are things I haven't shared with you," she said slowly, "and things you haven't shared with me. I could tell when we were talking about Courtney, how sure you are that she took him, that there's something you're not saying. I understand, but I can't help worrying what this means for us."

"I'm sorry," he said, looking away from her. "I just . . . I can't discuss this. I need to go downstairs. I have to find out what they're doing to find him." He exhaled. "If anything."

"It's all right." She nodded at the doorway. "Go on."

"I'm sorry," he said again, and he meant it. He was sorry for saying the word *fault*, which seemed to have started all this. Of course it wouldn't be Kyra's fault if someone from her nonexistent family had taken Michael. He would never blame his wife for what had happened today. And though it was, in a sense, his *fault* that Courtney had taken his son, he saw no point in dredging up the past. He'd told Ingle the same thing when the man had pushed him to talk about the specifics of Joshua's death—and he shrugged off the detective's claim that this was somehow ironic.

"My field is the history of labor," David had said.

"No interest in your own history?" Ingle said. "Don't you think that's even a little ironic?"

"Just find my ex-wife," David told him, and Ingle thankfully dropped the topic. Later, David realized his fists had been clenched so tightly during that part of the conversation that he still had marks on his palms.

EIGHTEEN

Courtney had spent a month and a half doing basically nothing but searching for a new job. She'd been aware that the economy was bad, but she hadn't really understood what this meant until she started getting rejection letters that included apologetic things like "We had hundreds of qualified applicants for this position." Hundreds of applicants? For a position as a technical writer at a tiny start-up company that paid less than half of what she was making before? And most of the companies didn't even bother to send rejection letters because, as one recruiter explained, "We get so many résumés that we simply can't respond to people we don't intend to interview." She forced herself to keep applying for any job she was remotely qualified for, even though she was incredibly discouraged. Her phone never rang.

Her phone did, however, play "Get Back" by her favorite rapper, Ludacris. She'd liked rap ever since college, when one of her professors had called hip-hop the future of poetry. "Get Back" was the ringtone she reserved for calls from people like Stefan, when he would call last year and tell her that the title of the painting didn't mean anything, why was she being so bourgeois about this? Or Jordan, a friend of hers from high school, who liked to call every month or so and brag about her three fabulous children and her house in the Hamptons and her husband, the brilliant surgeon. Or Courtney's mother, Liz, who'd inspired Courtney to download the ringtone in the first place because it was such a perfect fit: *Get back, mother-mother, you don't know me like that.*

The third word was not actually *mother-mother*, but close enough.

Liz used to call every few weeks, but now that she knew Courtney was unemployed, she called every evening, ostensibly to find out how the job search was going. Courtney knew better than to answer—and Luda warned her not to—but she kept picking up the phone, as if this time might be different. Admittedly, she was desperate to talk to someone after another day spent all alone. But she knew full well that one couldn't really talk to her mother. One could only listen as Liz described her day in excruciating detail.

Her mother always sounded so breathless; Courtney even interrupted once to ask if she'd been tested for asthma. "I'm just excited, my dear child! You would be, too, if you got out of your house and experienced the wonders of this world!"

Liz was a former hippie who had not only been at Woodstock but had also done some political thing in the sixties in Italy that Courtney had never really understood. David, her ex-husband, the graduate student historian, had listened to it and said Liz's role had been a lot less important than Liz seemed to believe. She still smoked pot occasionally and always had, as far back as Courtney could remember. And for the last few years she'd spent most of her days with her "life coach," a woman whose job it was to see that Courtney's mother "reached her potential." One of the only things Courtney remembered fondly about Stefan was that he'd said her mother's life coach was really a babysitter. "She keeps your mother busy and out of your father's hair," Stefan said. "What would you call that other than a babysitter?"

It was truer than Courtney had known at the time. Many of the activities her mother reported during these evening calls sounded exactly like something kids would do at camp. One day she went horseback riding out in Amish country. The next day she went to her finger-painting class designed to "free your inner child." She had another class called "writing your soul." She went on "adventure days" with other adults, exploring the woods or the shore. She also had what seemed like dozens of spiritual activities: from yoga to her sessions with her Buddhist counselor, who was helping her be more mindful and reflective.

Courtney couldn't imagine when Liz had time to reflect. Her mother was gone all day, Monday through Friday, as if this were a job. In reality, it was costing her father thousands and thousands of dollars, but he never complained. He'd retired a few years ago from the insurance company where he'd been executive vice president. Maybe he really did want her out of his hair.

One afternoon in the first week of May, her mother spent several hours pretending to be an actress. That wasn't how she put it, of course. It was yet another class, this one designed to help you "release the people who live within yourself." Courtney thought the whole thing was the definition of self-indulgent, but that wasn't what really bothered her. The class had taken place only a few miles from Courtney's house in Bucks County, which gave her mother a perfect excuse to drop by unannounced.

If only her doorbell had played the Ludacris rap she could have prepared herself. Instead, she went to the door in her black sweatpants and a gray T-shirt that was so stretched out it hung to her knees. Her coffee table was littered with Diet Coke cans and her yogurt cups from lunch and dinner the night before. Her bed pillow and blanket were on the couch, where she'd been lying down, watching a *Law & Order CI* marathon.

"You look awful," her mother said. Liz was dressed in tight white jeans and a paisley halter top. Courtney wondered if it was possible that after two facelifts, a tummy tuck, a butt lift, and continuous Botox, her sixty-seven-year-old mother actually looked better than she did.

Courtney stepped back to let her in. What choice did she have?

Her mother walked through her living room and dining room to the kitchen in the back of the row house. Courtney didn't bother to follow. She could hear her mother opening the refrigerator. A moment later, Liz was standing over her with a bottle of water.

"What's wrong with you?" she said.

Courtney was back on the couch, lying on her side with half her face hidden by her pillow. She'd only muted her TV. She could see Detective Goren tilt his head to face the suspect.

"Just tired," Courtney said.

Her mother went to the window and pulled up the blinds. "You need some light in here. It's depressing."

It was already seven o'clock. Courtney hated watching the sunset, but she didn't resist.

Her mother plopped down in the leather chair across from the couch and proceeded to tell Courtney all about the acting experience. Apparently, she'd discovered a young boy, an angry toddler, a slutty teenager, and a sarcastic old woman—all living inside herself. "The experience of letting them have a voice was simply amazing! You have to try this, Court. It's one of the most liberating experiences I've had in my life!"

Courtney nodded. Her mother was fond of the word *amazing*. And everything she enjoyed was "liberating," though Courtney was never sure what she was being liberated from.

By the time her mother was finished, Detective Goren and his partner had gotten the suspect to confess and another hour of the show had begun. Courtney recognized the new episode. It was about an angry chef who killed a woman, though she could no longer remember the motive.

"So you're just lying around feeling sorry for yourself, is that it?"

"More or less."

Her mother crossed her toned arms. "As the seventh Dalai Lama said, 'Who has magnificent self-confidence, and fears nothing that exists? The man who has attained to truth.'"

Courtney nodded again. It was much easier than asking questions, because then she and her mother would end up in an argument. When she was younger, she'd been willing, even eager, to fight with her mother, but for years she hadn't had the heart for it. Really, no one argued with Liz if they could help it. The woman had so much energy. Courtney felt exhausted just looking at her mother's excellent posture as she sat in the leather chair, guzzling down her water.

"Remember what the man says, Court." Her mother gesticulated with the empty water bottle to emphasize her point. " 'We either make ourselves miserable, or we make ourselves happy. The amount of work is the same.'"

"The man" was Carlos Castaneda. He was one of her mother's favorite writers; Courtney had heard this quote a hundred times. She nodded and said she had to go to the bathroom. As she walked upstairs, she thought, you can either go to the bathroom or put up with a full bladder. The amount of work is the same.

When she came back downstairs, her mother was sitting at her dining room table. Courtney's heart started pounding as she got closer and saw what Liz was up to.

"You know I don't like it when you do this." She hoped she sounded calmer than she felt. She reached up and closed the lid of the laptop. "My email is private, Mother."

"Amy Callahan." Her mother stood up, with one finger to her lips. "Callahan. Why do I know that name?"

Courtney thought about lying, but she knew her mother would remember soon enough. Liz had read about David and Kyra's marriage in the paper. She'd even ever so helpfully called Courtney to tell her all the details.

"Amy friended me on Facebook." Courtney forced a shrug. "She's some kind of long-lost relative of David's wife's."

"Really? Why on earth would she write to you?"

Courtney went back to lie on the couch. Her mother followed and sat down, but on the edge of the chair now. Her voice was even more breathless than usual. "I asked you a question. Why did she write to you?"

The truth was that Facebook had suggested Amy befriend Courtney, probably because Courtney and David still had enough college friends in common to fool the program into thinking they were connected. Amy sent a message that she was trying to reach David and his wife, but they'd ignored her friend requests so far. "They don't seem to use Facebook much," Amy said. Courtney wrote back with the truth. She said that though she'd been married to David, she had no connection with him now other than being friends with his mother. She also admitted that she'd met his wife and child only once. "Actually, the word *met* is too strong," she wrote, refusing to lie about even the smallest detail. "I've seen David's wife and son, but I haven't spoken to them."

She expected Amy Callahan to disappear then, but she didn't. Her new correspondent wrote back the next day, and the day after she wrote back using Courtney's personal email, not Facebook. And that was when it occurred to Courtney that Amy might be the *mysterious stranger* the psychic had predicted.

True, mysterious strangers arrive all the time on Facebook: people who want to friend you without even knowing you, to raise their number of friends. And Courtney had gotten several new friend requests since she'd become a fan of the Workplace Bullying Institute—her rather pathetic attempt to send a hint about Betty Jean to her former colleagues. But something was different about Amy Callahan. She was smart and funny and so honest about herself that Courtney couldn't help but look forward to her emails. Amy said she needed help, but when Courtney asked if she could do anything, Amy said she just needed a friend. "I don't feel like I belong in life right now, know what I mean?"

God, did Courtney know what she meant.

She tried to explain to her mother the way Facebook recommendations worked, but Liz interrupted, "Have you told David about this?"

"Are you serious?"

"Surely you've told your *real* mother."

It had been over a decade since Courtney had told Liz, during an argument, that Sandra treated her more like a mother than Liz ever had. The truth of the point had been made a hundred times over since then—most obviously because Courtney had said some stupid things to Sandra, too, but Sandra had never thrown them in her face like Liz was doing right now. Still, Courtney couldn't help feeling bad for hurting her mother's feelings. She tried to avoid even mentioning Sandra's name to Liz, and she was glad she could truthfully say that her former mother-in-law knew nothing about Amy. Actually, she hadn't told Sandra about any of it: not the cancer scare nor losing her job nor even the truth about why she broke up with Stefan last year. She still loved her ex-husband's mother, but she refused to be a burden on her again.

"I don't like it," Liz said slowly. "This person could be a serial killer for all you know." She was clicking her perfect nails on the arm of the chair. "People assume false identities constantly on the Internet. You're being naive."

"She's not a killer." Courtney exhaled. "I think she's very isolated. She lives in a little town in Missouri." Courtney thought about the way Amy talked about Philadelphia as if it were a glamorous big city *and* a place where everyone might know each other. It was oddly appealing, and made her seem younger than forty, the age on her Facebook profile. Another thing they had in common, as Courtney considered herself younger than thirty-eight, partly because most of her boyfriends had been at least five years younger than she was, but mainly because her life had stalled in her twenties rather than moving forward to maturity. She owned her house. That was her only card in the game of becoming an adult.

Liz frowned. "How much money have you given this person so far?"

"None, Mother. Everything isn't about money." Courtney laughed. "And I don't really have any money to give her, remember? I don't have a job."

"You know it would be easy for any criminal to find out about your father." She adjusted the strap on her halter top, though it didn't need adjusting. "How do you know this person isn't going to try to get to him through you?"

"I just know, okay? Trust me, she's a depressed woman, not some kind of blackmail mastermind."

"She's depressed? Does she need help?"

"I think so. I'm trying—"

"I'm talking about a professional." She paused and traced her right eyebrow. "That program you mentioned, Face Space, is for young people, isn't it?"

"Facebook. And no, it's obviously not only for young people. I'm on it."

"I read an article about this. It said that most people who try to make friends online are either too young to know better or very troubled. If this Amy person is in—"

"Thanks a lot." Courtney forced a laugh. "Since I'm not young, that makes me, what?"

"Laugh all you want. Surely you know that if this Amy is truly depressed, you may be in over your head with her."

"I'm exchanging emails with the woman, not moving in with her." She sighed. "Let it go, okay?"

"Fine. I just don't want you to feel responsible for the well-being of a stranger. It's hard enough when someone in your own family needs help, much less—"

"Really, could we drop this?"

"Think about what poor Ruth is going through with Mandy."

Courtney was in no mood to hear the story of her mother's new friend Ruth and her screwed-up daughter again. She rolled her eyes, and her mother's voice became louder, clearly irritated. "I know you've never been a mother, but would it kill you to sympathize with this woman?"

"That's enough," Courtney said, and stood up too quickly. She felt light-headed as she walked to the front door.

"I just meant that you've never been the mother of a teenager." Her mother's voice sounded whiny. "I can say that, can't I?"

"I'm feeling very tired," Courtney said. "I'm sorry." She opened the screen door and walked out on the front porch. It was almost dark, just a whisper of pink and orange was visible behind the trees. She looked up and down her block, but everything seemed slightly off, like she no longer belonged here, though she'd lived in the same house for years. This time of day always had that effect, and her mother's presence certainly didn't help.

Liz joined Courtney on the porch. "Fine, I'll leave. I didn't mean to upset you." She kissed her lightly on the cheek. "You might want to think about whether you're being too sensitive.

You let yourself get upset about the most trivial things, darling. I wish you would get in touch with your inner warrior."

"I'll think about it," Courtney said, and then she said good-bye and went back inside, shut the door behind her, and bolted the lock.

NINETEEN

May 9

Dear Mother,

Nicole is getting married. That's the big news from Summerland, Missouri, USA, Universe, Mind of God. You wouldn't believe how happy my stepmother is about this. As my dad told her, she seems happier than Nicole does, but he took it back when she frowned and said he didn't understand because he wasn't a mother. I'm not in the wedding, because Nicole already has Natalie and four good friends to be bridesmaids and because, honestly, no one knows if I'd be able to do it. I'm glad I don't have to try. Standing up for that long in the hot church sounds exhausting. I don't have to go to my graduation, either, which I'm very glad about. Principal Yager didn't seem to care when I handed back my invitation, but he and I haven't gotten along so well since that whole scratch-the-homophobe-and-get-suspended thing.

The second news here is about you. About a month ago, I started searching for you on the web. I'm not going to talk about what I've found yet—I don't want to jinx it—but I really think I'm getting somewhere. At least I can open my laptop and find something other than invitations to join groups on Facebook like "High School Students for Tax Reform" and "Christians Who Date But Wait."

Which reminds me, I have to tell you that I'm not a virgin anymore. Last December, I slept with some junior I barely knew in the parking lot of Burger King. It was after I hurt myself, when I was in what my shrink calls my "breakdown phase." I hope you're not a super Christian like my stepmother, because she would be very disappointed if she knew— disappointed for my future husband, that is, assuming I have one. Good men like to marry virgins, she always says, ignoring the fact that when my dad married her, she had two kids. I would be shocked if either of her daughters is a virgin, but hey, they'd probably be shocked to know I'm not. I've still never had a boyfriend, but I don't think anybody expects me to now that I don't even have any friends.

I hope it doesn't sound like I'm having a good old pity party here, because I'm really not. Today was a beautiful day in Summerland. I snuck out to the field by the woods after church and discovered the purple prairie clover was blooming and the two dogwood trees were bursting with white flowers. When I came home, I sat in the kitchen and ate a few bites of the most delicious banana frozen custard while I worked on a crossword puzzle. My dad and stepmother were over at Nicole and Natalie's apartment, having dinner and talking about the upcoming wedding. They didn't say one word about me refusing to go. It was an excellent day.

So, why ruin it by telling you the rest of the story of my seventeenth birthday? Because I figured something out this week that's important. Now that I actually have some hope for the future because of my search for you, I really don't want to die. I say that because I'm starting to worry I might die, like the doctor said. Not my psych doc, who continues to believe in me, though it's been months, but the other doc who stitched up my little finger after I cut it on the top of a tuna can. "It would have stopped bleeding on its own if you weren't sick," he said. Then the death threat, and a mean look, and a question: "Do you realize what you're doing, young lady?"

Well, no, of course I don't. I mean, I'm only seventeen and I'm pretty messed up. Why'd you become a doctor if you hate sick people? Are you trying to be the world's most craptacular asshole?

Sorry about the cursing. I hardly ever curse, but I just can't imagine saying something like that to a sick teenager. And like I said, I no longer have the stories so I can't say the poor doc just found out that his wife is sleeping with her trainer, or his mother has cancer, or his son has autism. I don't know the man at all. I no longer pretend to know anything other than what happened. The impulse to know why is gone, leaving a gaping hole in my understanding of life.

And it all happened on September 14. So finally, I'm just going to blurt it out and be done with it. Sorry it's taken so long. That is, I will be sorry, if you end up reading this, which I really hope you do.

I went to Ian's party. When I walked in, the music was cranked up so loud it felt like Lil Wayne's voice was vibrating in my head. There were dozens of people there, which surprised me, but I'd never been to one of these popular kid parties before. Many of the guys were in the kitchen. I was so nervous when I caught a glimpse of Ian standing by the refrigerator that I walked the other way, down the hall. I was wishing I'd asked Renee if I could come with her. It was weird being alone when everybody else was talking to someone.

I walked past a few bedrooms and a bathroom before I got to a large den, probably Ian's father's office. His dad worked at home doing some kind of stock market thing. My stepmother was always asking me if they'd lost a lot of money when the market crashed. How would I know? All of the furniture had been pushed against the wall, but the floor lamps had been adjusted so the center of the room was flooded with light. Four or five people had their cell phones out and two kids had expensive-looking digital cameras. They were all taking pictures of the girl standing in the center.

It was Marcella Alvarez, a junior, who was relatively new in town— meaning she'd lived here for a few years, rather than all her life like the rest of us. She was smiling and striking poses, pursing her lips, letting her

T-shirt fall down to expose her shoulders, hiking up her shorts to expose her thighs. It reminded me of those fashion shoots in movies, except that Marcella was on her crutches, as always, and it took her longer to change positions.

I wanted to walk the other way, but I just stood there, staring at this bizarre scene. The very same kids who were taking pictures of Marcella now had called her a moron all last year. She is actually smarter than most of them, but she has cerebral palsy. I couldn't imagine what had happened over the summer to change her into a popular girl. If that's what she was. She certainly seemed comfortable letting them do this to her. She was laughing at everything. It didn't occur to me that she might have been drinking. I was so stupidly innocent that I'd never even seen a drunk person except on TV. And Marcella's family went to the same church my family did. She was in youth group with me. She'd signed the same "no alcohol, no drugs, no sex" pledge I had.

One of the people using a digital camera was Jon Rubitch, whose face, according to Kevin, should be the icon for stupidity. He was whistling and egging on Marcella, but so was everybody else, including Devon Wheeler, the other person with a fancy digital camera, who was like the queen of the popular girls. A lot of the geek/dork population found Devon scary, but she sounded so friendly: "Oh my god, Marcella, you look really pretty. Hold it just like that, k?"

The thing is, Marcella is pretty. I've always thought so, I just didn't think people like Jon Rubitch and Devon Wheeler could see past her disability. But it wasn't their fault—according to me, anyway. A long time ago, I had made up stories that explained why they were mean: Jon must have accidentally killed someone, a little brother or a little sister most likely, and Devon had been raped by her Uncle Timmy. She liked to brag about Uncle Timmy because he drove her around in his BMW. Why would a grown-up call himself Timmy unless he was some kind of perv?

I was still in the doorway when Renee came up behind me. "What are you doing here?"

I turned around and there was my former best friend. She looked amazing, as always. She was wearing a white tube top and jeans, and her long black hair was so shiny it twinkled. "Um, you invited me?"

"I told you to come at 10:30. It's not even 10:15!"

"I'm sorry." She was right. I was so excited I'd forgotten what time she said as soon as I hung up. "Oh well. Everyone else seems to have come early, you know?"

She pushed past me and went over to Devon. They whispered back and forth for a minute. Then Devon turned to Marcella, "Time to go home now."

"But you said—"

"Even Cinderella had to leave at midnight," Devon said. All of the people in the room laughed hysterically. I was totally confused.

Marcella started to walk out of the room. When she came up to me, I asked her if she was all right.

"Yeah." Her eyes were looking down at her crutches. "I don't know what I did wrong."

She smelled like alcohol, but I said, "It's not your fault." I was sure of that, even though I didn't understand what was going on.

She disappeared down the hall. I don't know what happened to her after that. I guess she left the party.

I was still thinking about Marcella when Devon came over to me, took my hand, and pulled me into the room. I'd never even spoken to her before. I was surprised how soft her hand felt, like the skin of a baby.

The lights were too bright. I wanted to get away from her, but she asked me if I wanted some water, and before I could say yes or no, she handed me a plastic cup of what was definitely not water. I took one sip and spit it out. Of course everyone thought that was hilarious. I could feel my cheeks get hot.

"It's your turn to be our model," Devon said, smiling. Her teeth had been capped. They were big and so white. "Are you ready?"

"I don't want to," I said, and turned to leave.

The next thing I knew, a sophomore girl named Angel grabbed my wrist. Jon grabbed my other arm. They pulled me into the center of the room.

For a split second, I thought of yelling for Ian to help me. Since he liked me, right? Oh the stupidity, it burns.

I was thrashing and trying to get away when Devon picked up her camera. I yelled at her to stop and told them I would have them all arrested for assault. "Holding me against my will is illegal!"

Devon looked at Renee, who laughed. "She won't do it. She's a total baby who cries all the time about her mommy leaving."

It's not true, Mother. Up until that night, I'd cried about you only a dozen or so times in my entire life. Unfortunately, a few of those times had been with Renee, who was, after all, my best friend for ten years. Even more unfortunately, I started crying then. I looked at Renee and mouthed, "Please," but she turned her face to Devon.

Devon took pictures of my face, my shirt, my waist, and lots of pictures of my thighs. I felt sure that every inch of cellulite was being photo-documented, and I cursed the short black skirt and myself for wearing it. I thought about my stepmother saying, "Look how cute," and wondered how she could like these slutty clothes and at the same time hold her Virgins First policy. But mostly I thought about Renee. When they finally let me go after pronouncing me "lame" and "no fun," I moved to the doorway, but then I turned around and walked straight over to her. I had to know.

She didn't answer. I repeated the question. My voice was becoming loud. "Why did you do this to me?"

"Shut up," she hissed.

"Tell me why!"

When Jon and Devon decided to go to the kitchen for more alcohol, the rest of the room filed out after them. Everyone except Renee and me.

"OK, fine." She exhaled loudly. "Devon told us each to pick some-one. I picked you."

Of course Devon had put her up to it, I already knew that. And Renee must have picked me because she knew I was the one person who wouldn't try to retaliate against her in any way. So picking me would be safe. Mean but safe.

"I guess I understand," I said. It sounds crazy, but I was really trying to. "It makes sense in a sad kind of way, but you're better than that, you know?"

"Oh god, not this again!" She burst out laughing. "You've always been so pathetic with your make-believe reasons why everyone does everything. As if a retard like you would have any idea." She flipped her hair over her shoulder. "You want to know why I did it? Because it's fun to screw with losers. There's your big why, moron."

She didn't give me a chance to speak before she left the room, but it didn't matter. I had nothing else to say. When I got home, I told my dad that I'd left early because the party was boring. Then I waited until he and my stepmother were asleep and slipped out onto the patio. I sat on the lounge chair in my bathrobe all night, listening to the crickets and staring at the moon. The annoying yellow bug light on our neighbor's back porch made me wonder if invisible insects were climbing up the lounge chair legs and burrowing in my skin. But I wouldn't say I was worried about it. For the first time in my life, it was like I had no feelings.

By noon the next day, half the school had linked to the Facebook page with a total of eighty-nine photographs of Gracie, Marcella, Megan, and me. The caption was "EPIC FAIL. These losers think Ian wants THEM."

The page was taken down when someone's mother complained, but not before all the comments, over three hundred the one time I dared to look. Most were of the short LMAO variety, but there was a lot of really ugly stuff, too. I guess I was lucky in a way. Most of the comments didn't single me out, and those that did weren't nearly as horrible as what they said about the other girls:

She's a little chunky, but I'd do her.

Vomiting a little bit in my mouth over all of 'em but not as much over the last one.

On Monday when I went back to school, several kids came up to me and whispered that I didn't belong there. But none of the other girls belonged there, either. That's what I kept saying. When no one would *listen . . . I guess you could say I went crazy. It seems as good a word as any for what happened. I just couldn't accept the world becoming what it had always been.*

Maybe I'm still crazy, I'm not sure, but at least I'm not hopeless anymore. For the first time in a long time, I want to get up in the morning. Searching for you has given me something to do and something I really want, a goal, *as the doc always says I need, though he means the usual stuff like getting into a good college. I haven't told him what I'm up to, and not only because I have a feeling he'd disapprove. I can be really superstitious, and now that I'm getting closer, I'm afraid to do anything that might mess up my chances of being lucky enough to actually find you.*

I do have one more thing I want to say. It's not about what happened at school, but about all those stories I made up about you. I never told anybody how the stories ended, not even the doc, though I'm sure he'd think it means something that all the stories ended pretty much the same way.

You would get over your amnesia or escape from the cabin in Canada or be finished with your rehabilitation in Florida, and then you would hurry to a train station. You would get on board and sit down in a window seat, clutching your ticket in your hand. I could always see the ticket so clearly: it would be light blue and stamped in black, Summerland, Missouri. *Sometimes I could see your face, at least the way I remember it from when you brought me the turtle and puzzle when I was four. Most of the time I just saw your long brown hair.*

I know it sounds weird that you always took a train, when we don't have a train station in this town or even any track. I never really understood why I kept imagining it that way, because I knew it was impossible. But that's how the stories always ended. That's how you came back to me.

TWENTY

Courtney's mother had insisted that they meet in the city. It was the second week of June, a Wednesday, and Liz had a dance class in the afternoon, but she claimed she had something very important to discuss first. Courtney tried, "Just tell me," but her mother said it couldn't be handled on the phone. "You won't believe me if I don't give you the evidence."

A few hours later, they were settled on a bench at Washington Square Park, which was right around the corner from the dance studio. Courtney was wearing her usual baggy jeans and a T-shirt; her mother was in leggings and a white silk shirt with pearl buttons. Liz was sitting up straight, watching a group of kids throwing Frisbees, while Courtney was hunched over, staring at a death certificate her mother had forced into her hands. The woman's name was Harmony Meers. She'd died in a car accident in California in 1996.

"Who is she?"

"The real Amy Callahan."

"That's impossible," Courtney mumbled, but she was nervously twisting the ends of her hair, knowing Liz had hired a private investigator. The last time Liz had done this, when Courtney was dating a man her mother didn't trust, it turned out that the man was not only married but also behind on his child support payments from another marriage, unemployed, and recently bankrupt. He'd told Courtney he was single, of course, but he'd also bragged about being part of a team that had created Flash Player.

"Amy Callahan changed her name when she moved to California." Liz opened up a thin brown envelope and handed Courtney the investigator's report. "It's all explained here. And before you ask, he assured me that David's wife doesn't have any other relatives named Amy. This has to be the person your correspondent is pretending to be."

Though she and Amy had been corresponding for only about two months, they'd gotten so close that simply seeing Amy Callahan's name on the top of the first page made Courtney tear up, as if someone she actually knew had died. Thankfully she was wearing sunglasses, so her mother couldn't tell her she was being silly.

All of the important facts were in the summary. Amy Callahan had left Kansas City for Los Angeles in 1995, and changed her name to Harmony Williams. A few months later, she had changed her last name again after she married a man named Glenn Meers. When a truck broadsided her car, she'd been married for only a few weeks, and her husband obviously didn't know her very well. The investigator had tracked down Meers, who admitted he'd never tried to contact any of his wife's relatives after her death. Meers had been in and out of prison for years on drug charges. Maybe that explained his lack of interest in his wife's past. The investigator had also tried to contact Amy's family back in Missouri. He found only a stepmother, who complained that neither Amy nor her sister had visited her after her husband died. She hung up without asking why a private investigator was calling about her stepdaughter.

The report included two driver's license photos: one of Harmony Meers and the other of Amy Callahan. There was no denying they were the same person, though Harmony looked like a hollowed-out shell of Amy, who'd been positively pretty.

Courtney sat back for a minute. It was just hitting her that the graceful, cautious woman she'd seen at the co-op was the same person whose sister had died years ago. She was surprised by how sad she felt for David's wife.

"It says there are seventeen pages, but you only gave me the first four," she finally said, looking at her mother. "Where's the rest?"

Liz shrugged. "I didn't bring it because it wasn't relevant. It was primarily about Amy Callahan's failed attempts at a singing career. I suppose that's why she chose the name Harmony, though it seems to push it a bit much."

Courtney scrutinized her mother. She didn't seem like she was lying, but if she was, it had to be because of David. "Did the investigator also talk to Kyra?"

Liz shook her head. "I told him to find out what he could without discussing this with David's family."

"She may not even know what happened."

"I'm confident she does. It would be quite easy to discover using Amy's social security number."

"But it says right on the first page that she changed her social security number."

"I don't believe that's legal," her mother said, which seemed ridiculous under the circumstances. Before Courtney could object though, Liz clapped her hands together. "In any case, David's wife is obviously estranged from her sister if she hasn't tried to look for her at least as hard as I did. She's had years to do so, if she wished to. And it's hardly your business, is it?"

Courtney vaguely remembered Sandra mentioning something about Kyra being estranged from her family. This was a long time ago, right before Michael was born, when Sandra was talking about helping them as much as she could with the new baby. But her mother was right. None of this was her business.

Liz turned to face her. "I would think it would be obvious why I insisted on keeping David's family out of this. I was trying to spare you the embarrassment, in case this turned out to be a scam, as I suspected."

Courtney didn't say anything, but she was thinking it couldn't be a scam. The writing in Amy's emails was nothing like some Nigerian money request.

I'm listening to Ravel's "Piano Concerto for the Left Hand," which Ravel wrote for another musician who lost his right arm in World War I. It reminds me of what my shrink always says: you can lose what feels like everything and still find your way back to yourself.

Even if her name wasn't Amy, she wasn't pulling some kind of scam. It wasn't possible.

"I hope you didn't share any of our personal business with this identity thief," Liz said. " Your father would be mortified."

"I never mentioned Dad at all."

She reached over and pushed back Courtney's sunglasses. "But you did mention me?"

My mother called for the fifth time this week. I know she still feels guilty about the way she treated me after my son died, but I wish I could convince her that I've never been angry about that. She's always trying to help me with something I don't need help with. She thinks that will make us close again, ignoring the fact that we were never close.

"Not really," Courtney said, and adjusted her sunglasses. She was thinking about all the private things about her own life that she'd told Amy or whoever she was.

Normally, she wasn't the kind of person who shared anything about herself with strangers. In fact, she'd often lost the chance to be friends with people when she wouldn't reciprocate their confessions. With Amy though, it was different, and it wasn't just that Courtney had too much free time. Yes, she'd written to Amy at least two times a day, often three or more, but if she hadn't felt sure that Amy was the mysterious person who was going to change her life, she wouldn't have opened up to her. She'd trusted a total stranger because of the vague prediction of a psychic. And she didn't even believe in psychics. She was such a fool.

A man and his collie walked by. He was probably twenty-five, but Liz elbowed Courtney in the ribs. "See the kind of person you'd meet if you lived in Center City?"

Courtney slid the investigator's report into her purse. "Right. Because everyone who lives downtown knows each other."

Liz ignored the sarcasm. "Do you want to get lunch? There's a great Indian restaurant down on—"

"I'm not very hungry." Courtney stood up.

Liz stood, too. "I was only trying to protect you, darling."

Courtney let her mother give her a hug, because she knew Liz was trying to help. Her mother couldn't know how much this hurt. Even Courtney wasn't sure why it hurt so much.

Before they said good-bye, Liz made her promise not to contact "Amy" again. "I'll delete her emails and block her address," Courtney said, and tried not to be annoyed when her mother acted surprised that she knew how to block an email address.

When she got home, the first thing she saw on her computer was a note from Amy, asking how her meeting with her mother had gone. *I hope she didn't depress you.* Courtney did as she promised; she deleted all the emails and blocked the address. She walked away from the laptop, but not fifteen minutes later, she sat back down again and undid the block. She had to know who had been doing this.

Amy was online, too; her Gmail address was visible, green.

She'd never instant-messaged Amy before, but as soon as she said hello, Amy wrote, *you're back. How was it?*

> **me:** What's your name?
> **Amy:** good idea to do chat
> **Amy:** what?
> **me:** I know you're not Amy Callahan. Tell me your real name.
> **Amy:** It's Hannah. I'm sorry.
> **Amy:** How did you find out?

Courtney was both surprised and depressed by how quickly this person had relented. She'd been hoping against hope that, despite the evidence, the woman she'd been writing was trustworthy.

> **me:** Save the apology. My mother hired a private investigator . . . Just tell me the reason for the pretense. I think you owe me that much.
> **Amy:** wow, a private investigator. I never thought of that. Did your Mother find Amy Callahan?
> **me:** Do you think this is a joke?
> **Amy:** please don't be mad. I can explain. I didn't mean to lie.
> **me:** Of course you didn't. You just needed money.
> **Amy:** $$? No. I had to deactivate my real facebook page because of something that happened at school. It's a long story.
> **me:** At school??
> **me:** How old are you?
> **Amy:** OK, I'm only 17, but I'll be 18 in a few months. And I'm not in school now. I graduated, so it doesn't matter anymore.
> **Amy:** I wanted to tell you before, but I was afraid you wouldn't want to keeping emailing. ☹
> **Amy:** I thought you would think I was too young to be your friend. But I'm really not. I mean, you know it's true, right?

Amy: I didn't want to lose you. You've helped me feel a lot less alone.

Amy: are you still there?

Courtney had dropped her face into her hands. She was reeling from the fact that she'd told some teenager about being bullied at work, about the end of her relationship with Stefan, even about her premature ovarian failure. And about Joshua. This seventeen-year-old knew more about how her baby died than most of her friends did.

me: So you needed a new Facebook identity? That's your claim?

Amy: It's true.

me: I don't believe it. Why did you pretend to contact my ex and his wife then?

Amy: I wasn't exactly pretending. I was thinking I would try to friend them, but first I wanted to know what they were like. That's why I tried to contact people on their friend lists. To find out.

me: Why me? I'm not on their friend lists.

Amy: I know. Facebook recommended you. I already told you that.

Courtney thought the last sentence was laughable, given how much this person had lied to her.

me: I have no idea why you're doing this, but it's cruel. Has it ever occurred to you how Kyra might feel about a stranger using her sister's name?

Amy: I had a good reason.

Courtney saw that Amy was typing. She was typing, too. She went back and forth, trying to explain how much this could have hurt David's wife, but she deleted all that and decided to wait. If this person really was seventeen, she might have done this for a relatively innocent reason.

Whatever it was, it was going to be long. While Amy kept typing and typing, Courtney thought about the psychic. She started biting her thumbnail when she remembered that Evelyn Rose had only said the stranger would change her life, not that the change would be good.

> **Amy:** I was trying to find Amy Callahan because she's my mother. I took her name because I thought anyone who knew her would write me back and maybe tell me where she is. Kyra is my mom's sister, though my stepmother and my dad acted like it was killing them to admit it. When I first saw her on facebook, I mentioned her at dinner and it was like I said I was going to be buddies with Osama bin Laden. I never had the nerve to write her, but now I don't have to. Your mom's private investigator knows where Amy Callahan is, right? So this is really cool. Meeting you has been so lucky for me.

Courtney's nail was bleeding but she couldn't stop tearing it as she read what Amy had written. Even though this person had lied to her constantly, Courtney had a bad feeling this was the truth. It fit so well with a vague sense of longing that was always present in the girl's emails. It even explained Amy's fascination with all things mother-related, including Courtney's tense relationship with Liz.

Of course she knew what was coming next.

> **Amy:** I've imagined her so many places, you have no idea. So where is she?

She sucked her nail and typed with one hand as she tried to figure out what to do.

> **me:** What's your phone number? The landline I mean.
> **Amy:** It's 816-2. Wait. This seems weird. Why didn't you ask for my cell?

Later, she would realize that she could have simply said *I want to google that number to make sure you're who you say you are.* But at that moment, her heart was beating so hard she couldn't think of anything other than the truth. She wanted to call the girl's parents. She wanted to let them tell her about her mother. Amy or Hannah or whoever she was, the person she'd been emailing for weeks, was depressed. Courtney was positive about that in the way only a fellow depression sufferer can be. She was so over her head. She felt as if Liz was right in the room, warning her not to take responsibility for a stranger's life.

> **Amy:** You told me you never use a landline anymore. This doesn't make sense.
> **me:** All right, give me your cell number.

At least she could talk to the girl that way, try to soften the blow. But instead of her number, Hannah typed, *What state does my mother live in?* When Courtney didn't answer, she repeated the question.

> **me:** Tell me your number and we'll talk about it.
> **Amy:** What state?

The cursor was blinking.

> **Amy:** It's only one word.

She had just decided to lie, but before she could type *California—*

Amy: She's dead, isn't she?

me: hold on

Amy: That's why you don't want to tell me on chat. Oh my God.

Courtney felt awful, but there was nothing she could say to make this easier. Hannah didn't give her a chance anyway. Before she could type something soothing—she had no idea what—Amy's daughter had signed off.

For the next hour or so, she paced her apartment, trying to figure out what to do next. If only she knew the girl's phone number or at least her last name. Hannah's emails told her nothing she didn't already know: the location of the teenager's IP address was in the northwest part of Missouri. There was no way to find her.

She'd just made up her mind to contact Kyra, via Sandra, when she heard the tone that announced she had mail.

Hi Courtney,

I wanted to let you know I'm OK. I never knew my mom. It was a shock, that's all. I put a lot of energy into finding her, or at least wishing I would, so it was hard to hear. But having a mom doesn't solve everything, as you know.

There's one other thing I haven't told you. When I first found Kyra on facebook, my dad told me that Kyra has always known my mom had a daughter. She even knows where I live. I don't know why she's never visited or sent me a card, but that's why I haven't reached out to her and my uncle yet.

I really am sorry I lied so much to you. You came along in my messed up life when I needed a friend so badly. I'm so thankful that you wrote me back the first time. Honestly, I spent a lot of time in the last month hoping that when I found my mother, she would be as cool and nice and funny as you are. I hope that doesn't sound pathetic.

I just found out this morning that my dad and stepmother are dragging me on their vacation to Colorado against my will, so I'm going to be offline for the next two weeks. We're going on some wilderness adventure. Ugh! I have two little half brothers that I'll be stuck in the backseat with. I can't stand them, but as you always say, such is life.

Talk to you soon I hope.
Hannah

Courtney would have been very skeptical about Hannah's vacation claim if the girl hadn't mentioned two half brothers in the backseat. It sounded like such a teenage thing to say, at least from what she could remember of being that age. She herself had only one brother, and he was so much older that they had never gone on vacations together, much less in a car, but if they had, she would have said the same thing.

At the time she was too upset to consider the fact that she'd told Hannah about her feelings for her annoyingly successful brother Christopher, the film producer. She'd also told Hannah about Liz's wilderness adventures in New Mexico. She'd even told Hannah about a few of the long vacations she'd been forced to go on with her parents when she was a teenager.

Courtney wasn't thinking about how well Hannah knew her, making it easy for the girl to construct a lie that she would believe. But even if she had seen through the lie immediately, what could she have done differently? She didn't know how to get hold of Hannah's parents. The girl's aunt didn't have any relationship with Hannah, nor did she seem to want one.

It was a little shocking to Courtney that David's "perfect" wife had not only ignored her sister but also rejected her niece. It made her wonder what Kyra was really like. Not that it was any of her business, but she couldn't help worrying what this meant for Michael. She wanted the little boy who looked so much like Joshua to have a good mother, a nice home, everything.

She wrote back to Hannah within minutes of receiving the girl's email. *Please don't disappear. I'm going to worry until I hear that you are back from Colorado.* At the end of the email, she added, *Your aunt has no idea what she's missing out on, not having you in her life.*

TWENTY-ONE

In the middle of Kyra's junior year in college, her sister mentioned that she'd missed a period. Amy figured it was just a product of her crazy life, working all night and traveling with the band, and, Kyra thought, thinner and more hyper than she'd ever been—though definitely not on drugs. Kyra had spied on her for months after Zach said her sister was using; she was sure about this. But when Amy started throwing up whenever she smelled hamburgers or bacon or basically anything greasy, she peed on a stick and discovered the depressing truth. She'd been so careful with birth control, but as Kyra, the math major, knew, birth control only has a high probability of working. Someone has to be part of that unlucky three percent.

Kyra made the phone call and set up the appointment. She offered to go, but Amy said she wanted to do this alone. It was scheduled for Wednesday, and Kyra skipped her philosophy class to take care of her sister when she got home. When Amy walked into the apartment a few hours later, Kyra was sitting on the wooden chair by the bookshelves she and Amy had made from concrete blocks and pine boards. She had a pamphlet in her lap about the *abortion experience* that she'd been trying and failing to comprehend.

Her sister threw her coat on the kitchen cabinet and plopped down on the wicker chair by the window and arranged her ever-present blue blanket on her knees. She joked that she'd turned into Linus, but the truth was she was always cold now that she was so thin.

"I went to the address you gave me at ten on the dot, like you told me," Amy said. She pushed her hair behind her ears, but one side fell out again when she looked down at her hands. "They got me on the table, you know, ready to go." She pulled the blanket up so that everything but her face and blond hair disappeared into the blue cloud. "I hope you're not mad, sis. I just couldn't do it."

Kyra was so relieved—and so surprised she was relieved—that she couldn't find her voice. Until that moment, she hadn't realized how much she'd hated being the one pushing her sister to get an abortion. When she was ten years old she'd marched with the anti-abortion crowd in St. Louis on the anniversary of Roe versus Wade. Amy was there, too; the whole Catholic grade school was there; but Kyra had really believed in the cause. She'd made her own sign using her stepmother's red and black magic markers: "What If **Your** Mother Had Chosen Abortion?" By the time she was in high school, she wasn't quite as confident that abortion was wrong, but she still thought it should be used only as a last resort. If the idea of having one herself was horrifying, the idea of her sister having one was almost as bad.

Amy being way too immature to be a mother wasn't a good enough reason to qualify for a last resort, but Amy not knowing who the father was or even seeming to understand why knowing the father's identity was important—that did qualify. A child needs a father, as Kyra had told her sister over and over. And when she recovered her ability to speak, she said it again while Amy and her blanket slumped down in the wicker chair.

"I get it," Amy said, rubbing her thumb against her forehead. "And I do know who the father is." She looked out the window though there was really nothing to see. It was a gloomy day in February: dreary and drizzling and threatening to ice up that night. "It's Zach," she said softly. "Who else?"

The question seemed strange. In the last few months, Amy had slept with Peanut and possibly Tim, in addition to having a one-night stand with some guy she'd met when the band was on the road. And these were only the ones Kyra knew about it.

She took a breath. "Are you sure?"

Her sister nodded.

Kyra put the useless pamphlet down. "Then you have to tell him."

"I knew you'd say that, so I stopped at a pay phone outside the clinic." She was still rubbing her forehead, like she had a headache. "He's looking for an apartment for us right now."

"Good," Kyra said, but she leaned forward and covered her face with her hands. A moment later, she felt Amy's arms around her. "Naturally, I told him I'm not moving anywhere without my sister."

"You and Zach should stay here. It's two bedrooms, perfect for a baby. I'll move to a studio apartment closer to school." She looked up at Amy, kneeling in front of her. "Please don't argue with me."

Of course Amy tried to persuade her anyway, but for once it didn't work. By the middle of March, Kyra had moved out and Zach had moved in. Zach was predictably ecstatic. He cut back his school schedule and got a full-time job selling medical supplies to support them. A good thing, too, because when Amy was four and a half months pregnant and definitely showing, Peanut dropped her from his band. "People don't come to clubs to see that," Peanut said, pointing at her stomach, and proving what Kyra had always thought: Peanut was a total lowlife.

Zach pressured Amy to marry him, but she kept saying no—until Kyra told her sister that she had no choice. Zach's new job had health insurance and a 401(k). It was the responsible thing to do. Amy reluctantly agreed, and Kyra served as a witness at their wedding in the courthouse. She would never forget how unhappy her sister looked that day.

To say the pregnancy was uneventful, though true on some level, would be to ignore how it must have felt to be Amy. She was alone in the apartment most of the time, with no school or band to distract her as her twenty-one-year-old body underwent the strange, necessary metamorphosis to accommodate a new life. Zach adored her, but it clearly wasn't enough, though he remained confident that her sister would come around sooner or later. He never understood that Amy couldn't seem to find a way to love him, no matter how hard she tried.

Kyra thought it was a serious flaw in her sister, that Amy failed to recognize how great Zach was. But she truly believed Amy was trying, until the hot afternoon when Amy was eight months pregnant, and she found out otherwise.

Zach was working nine to five at the medical supply company, and Kyra had been working all summer, too, as an actuarial clerk. It was a paid internship, but the only thing she'd learned was that she most definitely did not want to be an actuary when she graduated. By the middle of August, she was so sick of running programs of meaningless numbers and formulas that she decided to take the afternoon off, telling her supervisor that she was coming down with something. It wasn't a lie. She was coming down with extreme ennui.

It was 97 degrees, according to the sign at the bank across

from her office, and so humid that the leaves on the trees looked as droopy as Kyra felt. She thought about going to the mall and wandering around in the air-conditioning, but then she remembered her sister and how miserable she must be. Amy and Zach's apartment had a window AC unit, but half the time the blower didn't come on. The landlord was supposed to have replaced it weeks ago.

As Kyra climbed the stairs, she could hear music coming from inside the apartment, but when she knocked, Amy didn't answer. She knocked again, harder, and when Amy still didn't answer, she reached for the knob. Amy had left the door unlocked, as usual. Kyra said, "It's me," as she walked in. She could hear water running in the kitchen. The radio was playing, too, a Nirvana song. No wonder Amy hadn't heard.

When she walked into the kitchen, she saw her sister awkwardly kneeling on a chair, which had been pushed over to the sink. Amy's head was as close to the sink as she could get, given her huge baby bump. It was a ridiculous way to wash her hair, but that was what she was doing. Or, more precisely, that was what *some man* was doing for her. One of his hands was holding the nozzle of the spray hose, the other was pulling up sections of Amy's hair, which had become much thicker since she got pregnant. She was always complaining that it was itchy, especially in the heat.

The first thing Kyra noticed was that the man looked old. He had gray hair and a graying beard and lines around his eyes and mouth. Some people probably considered him distinguished, and he was definitely well-off, judging by a very expensive-looking watch that was lying on the card table that served as Amy's kitchen table, next to a briefcase that also looked expensive. But he was old enough to be their father. Literally. Their real father was forty-four. For all Kyra knew, this guy was older than their father.

He was wearing Amy's goofy cow apron over pin-striped pants, a white oxford shirt, and a burgundy tie. The cow apron had been a gift from Zach for her birthday. Amy was wearing nothing but her stretchy black shorts. Her large breasts were hanging down, touching the edge of the sink.

At some point Kyra must have made a noise. She felt like her throat was too tight to let any sound escape, but suddenly, both Amy and the man were looking in her direction. Or maybe they just looked over because the radio had switched to a woman talking about the mayor, and the strange man had finished rinsing Amy's hair and turned the water off.

Amy walked over without bothering to wring out her hair or grab a towel. When she was standing right in front of Kyra, she pulled her wet hair off her neck with one hand. She sounded furious. "What are you doing here?"

Kyra tried not to stare at her sister's belly, but it was right there, between them, enormous and pink and glistening, with a strange line down the middle that made Kyra think of the indentation of a peach.

"I don't know," Kyra said. She was so shocked that for a moment, she honestly couldn't remember. Then she said softly, reminding herself, "I was going to take you to the mall. Buy more booties."

The booties were a joke between them. Their stepmother had sent eight pairs of crocheted booties for the baby, and she was reportedly working on another pair or two; their father wasn't sure how many more were coming. Amy and Kyra knew she loved to crochet, but why not a blanket or a hat or a sweater? Why only booties? Amy said it was her obsession with feet, which wasn't a joke: the woman had more socks and shoes than anybody in their town. From the calves up, their stepmother wore strictly polyester from Venture or Kmart; from the ankles down, she could have been featured in *Glamour* magazine.

The man walked over. He handed Amy her towel and her white robe, and introduced himself as Gregory Todd. Or was it Todd Gregory? He made some comment about people reversing his name, but Kyra wasn't listening. She was staring at the ring on his left hand.

"This is my sister," Amy said.

"Oh, yes, I've heard so much about you, Kyra," he said far too pleasantly. She hated everything about him, but she hated his insouciance most of all.

After a moment or two, when no one had spoken, Gregory or Todd or whoever he was said, "I should go." Kyra stood on the right side of the doorway, sweating, as the man took off the apron and put on his watch. Amy walked with him into the hall. They kissed for a very long minute. He whispered something in her ear and she laughed.

When Amy returned, she went into her bedroom without saying a word. After a minute, Kyra remembered how to move and followed her. Amy was lying on the side of the bed closest to the air conditioner, which was working, at least. The bedroom was actually a little chilly.

"What's going on?" She heard her voice becoming squeaky, hysterical. "Why was that man in our apartment?"

Of course it wasn't her apartment anymore, but that was only because she'd given it to Zach and Amy and their baby. Not to Amy and this *stranger*.

"You're not going to say anything?" Kyra stomped over to the bed and looked down at her. The robe barely tied around her sister's huge waist. "You're going to cheat on your husband with some guy you barely know and not even try to justify yourself?"

"He's not a guy I barely know," Amy said. She lowered her eyes. "I've been in love with Gregory for almost a year."

A year? *A year?* How on earth was that possible when Kyra had never heard the man's name before? She thought back to the week of her sophomore finals, when Amy had broken up with Zach and Kyra had gone to his apartment, to comfort him. Had Amy already known this guy then?

Without being questioned, Amy explained that they'd met one night last fall, when the band was playing on the Plaza. So the answer was no: she did not know Gregory when she broke up with Zach. And Gregory was not the father of her child, she emphasized that, though Kyra hadn't thought to wonder about it yet.

"He's not happy with his wife," Amy said.

Kyra rolled her eyes and snickered. "Oh, of course."

"I don't care if you believe it. It's true. His wife is awful to him, but he can't leave because he has three kids." She smiled. "I've met them. They liked me; I could tell. It's nothing like Marie."

Marie was their stepmother. Meaning Amy was already pretending she was some kind of stepmother to this guy's kids? After meeting them in secret somewhere, what, once or twice?

"You're delusional," Kyra snapped. "What is this guy for you? A father figure?"

"So what if he is? It's not like I ever had a father who loved me."

"Neither did I, but I'm not—"

"Think what you want about me. I don't care. When I'm with him, I'm happy. He doesn't want me to be perfect or special. He likes me as I am, just Amy."

Just Amy? What did that even mean? The whole situation was so bizarre and overwhelming that Kyra slumped down on the bed, but on the other side, as far as possible from her sister. Amy was lying very still. Her wet hair was soaking the pillowcase. The air conditioner was only a foot or so from her bare legs. Her feet looked puffy and red and cold.

"You have to tell Zach," Kyra finally said. She was looking at a pile of his T-shirts sitting on top of the dresser. She knew how devastated he would be. Where would he move? How would he and Amy deal with sharing child care?

Amy didn't respond.

"I'm serious. If you don't tell him, I will."

"Don't you think it's a little strange," Amy said, "that you're the younger sister, but you're always telling me what to do? It's like you think you're my mom."

Kyra could have said a hundred things to defend herself. Since they'd moved to Kansas City, Amy had done one irresponsible thing after another. What was she supposed to do? Just sit back and watch her sister ruin her life? The truth was that this was hardly the way she'd imagined college would be. She was always being forced to drop whatever she was doing to deal with yet another problem of Amy's. Her own problems, such that they were, never got any attention. Compared to her sister's drug use, pregnancy, marriage, and now affair, how could it matter that Kyra was afraid some of the people in her math study group didn't like her? How could her feeling that life was passing her by possibly be important, when her sister was living like she was speeding down the road, about to crash into a wall?

Amy turned to her side and used her hands to push herself up to a sitting position. She leaned closer and made her voice sound like a child's. "Mommy, don't you like me anymore?"

"Cut it out," hissed Kyra.

Her sister shook her head like a wet dog, and a water droplet from her thick hair hit Kyra in the face. "Have you ever been in love, Mommy?"

Kyra felt her cheeks burning. "Stop it, Amy."

Amy put her hand on her abdomen. Kyra could tell the baby was kicking. But it didn't stop her sister. "Of course you haven't," Amy said flatly. "You're too busy looking down on screwups like me to have time to fall in love with anyone."

Kyra stood up, but before she could leave the room, Amy said, "You know what I told Gregory?"

"I don't care." She refused to turn around, but she couldn't help walking more slowly.

"I told him about the worst day in my life." Somehow, Amy had gotten to a standing position. Kyra could hear her breathing heavily as she came up behind her. "Want to know what it was?"

"No."

"Come on, sure you do."

Kyra was wearing a sundress. Amy's cold hand on her bare shoulder made her jump. She spun around. "I already know, okay? It's the day Mom left. You've been telling me about this all my life, like I wasn't even there."

"No. It's the day you moved out of this apartment."

"Oh bull." She shook off Amy's hand. "You wanted to live with Zach!"

"No, I didn't. He wanted me to and you wanted me to, but I just wanted to be with you. Like the Callahan Child Care Company, the two of us, taking care of the baby."

Kyra remembered Amy saying that she wouldn't live anywhere without her sister, but she refused to think about that now. It had nothing to do with what was happening with this married man. It changed the focus and turned the whole thing into a guilt trip.

Amy heaved herself over to the couch, and Kyra leaned against the wall and stared at her. They were both silent for a while. At some point, Kyra sat down on the dusty floor and said, "This is why you didn't want to marry Zach."

"Yeah." She paused. "Why did you push that so hard? It can't be just insurance."

Amy was right. Though the insurance was a perfectly good reason on its own, it wasn't her only concern. "It will probably sound dumb to you, but it was Father Tom. Remember him, from church?"

"Sure I remember him."

Kyra picked at a piece of rubber hanging off the heel of her sandals and thought about when Father Tom had suggested Amy might be an angel. It seemed like a million years ago. She wondered what Father Tom would say if he could see them now and sighed. "I thought about that lecture he gave us on teenage pregnancy and giving birth to a bastard. I just didn't want your baby to be a bastard." She sat up straighter. "I'm sorry if that seems stupid."

"It doesn't seem stupid."

"So you do want the baby, at least?"

"Oh for God's sake. Someday you'll realize that a pregnant woman this far along wants her baby more than she's ever wanted anything." She patted her stomach and her voice grew soft. "I don't care how bad the timing is. I love this little person more than I've ever loved anyone."

Kyra looked closely at her sister and realized it was true. After months of Amy being strangely disconnected from the life growing inside of her, she'd finally fallen in love with the baby.

Maybe that was why, before Zach came home that night, Kyra had softened enough to agree not to say anything to him about Gregory. Amy had to promise not to see the man again; Kyra insisted on that first. Amy had to promise that she would try to give her innocent baby a normal life.

A few weeks later, on September 14 at 11:17 AM, the baby was born. She was gorgeous, with a tiny tuft of blond hair and light blond, almost invisible eyebrows, pink cheeks and startling blue eyes, and a plump little mouth and perfectly shaped little head. Not one mark on her, as Amy said, laughing that she'd finally done something right by pushing out her baby so efficiently. Both Kyra and Zach fell in love with the little girl the first time they held her, in the delivery room. Naturally, Kyra was in the delivery room, too. Her sister had said she needed her there, and that was all Kyra had needed to hear.

The fact that Amy got a huge bouquet of roses in the hospital, without a card, should have alerted Kyra to the fact that Amy had broken her promise, but they were all too happy about the baby. Amy named her Hannah, which she said meant "grace" or "favored one."

"You are my favorite," Kyra whispered in Hannah's little ear, so intricate it looked funny sprouting from the side of such a tiny head. She put her finger in the baby's hand and Hannah grasped it tightly. It was only a reflex, but it felt like Hannah was holding on to her for support or even protection. Zach noticed it, too. He said to Amy, "Our baby likes your sister."

"Of course she does," Amy said. She was still in the hospital bed, waiting for the doctor to say they could go home. She looked tired, but she was smiling. "Hannah's going to be smart. She knows her auntie will be her best friend."

Part Three

TWENTY-TWO

Michael had been sitting on the side of the road for a long time. He'd watched as the shadow from the sun had moved across the empty parking lot of the restaurant and past the Out of Business sign and onto the brown field. At one point, he'd unhooked his seat belt to lock the doors, though he knew it wouldn't help that much, since the windows were unrolled. The rest of the time he'd spent arranging the toy cars in rows along the seat next to him, practicing his six times tables, and most of all, wishing that April would stop being sick.

When she finally said she was going to call for help, he felt like he could breathe better, like a breeze had blown into the car, though the air was just as still as before. "My mommy and daddy will help," he said.

"I'm sure they would," April said. She was lying down on the front seat. All he could see was her skinny hand, thrown against the passenger headrest. "But I'm going to call somebody else."

He wanted to tell her that his parents would help better than anybody, but she was already sitting up, stumbling out of the car, and walking in the ditch next to the road. He could hear her voice rising and falling, but not the words. When she got back in the car, she turned on the engine. She didn't speak at all as she made a U-turn and headed back down the road they'd come from.

"I don't want to go back on the boat," Michael said.

"We're not," April said. "We're going to a motel."

"I want to go home."

"I know, buddy," she said, but she kept driving in the same direction. "I'm really sorry, but I promised I would do this."

She said she was sorry again when she came out of the motel office holding a big black plastic key. "We got stuck with room 13," she said. "It's the only one they had."

"Thirteen isn't really unlucky," Michael said. His parents had taught him the word *superstition*, but he couldn't remember it right then.

April took his hand and they walked on the crumbly black pavement toward the room. "I bet you don't even believe in Santa Claus, do you?"

He didn't, but he wasn't about to say so. After this boy named Drew started crying at his second kindergarten, he'd decided not to tell anyone else that Santa Claus was only a story.

April opened the door with the plastic key and told him to go to the bathroom. When he came out, she said she had to go. He looked around the room while he was waiting for her. There were two beds with green and gold bedspreads, a dresser, and a big TV bolted to the wall. He didn't want to be in bed while it was light outside, so he sat down on the only chair, over by the window. The cushion felt sticky against his bare legs. The heavy curtains smelled bad when he pulled them back to look at all the big trucks in the parking lot.

He watched a truck pull out and another one pull in, and April was still in the bathroom. When she came out, she looked really pale again, but when he asked her if she was feeling sick, she told him not to worry.

"It's going to be okay." She pushed her lips into a smile. "We'll get something to eat, and then wait here, like I promised."

There was a hamburger place right across the parking lot, so they just walked there. April told the clerk they wanted their food to go. "This way we can watch TV while we eat," she said, looking down at Michael. "Does that sound fun?"

He nodded, though it didn't really sound fun. He liked to eat dinner at the big table at home. Sometimes Mommy turned off the overhead light and used the little lamp instead. She called this "intimate dining." He kept forgetting what *intimate* meant, but he liked the word.

April asked him what he wanted. When he couldn't decide, she ordered a cheeseburger, a chicken sandwich, two orders of fries, and two chocolate milkshakes. They went back to the room, and she told him he should pick what to watch on TV. He picked a show about antiques, because he knew it wouldn't be violent and give him nightmares.

"Do you watch this with your parents?" April said. She'd finished her milkshake so fast that Michael was surprised she didn't have an ice-cream headache. Her face was a lot less pale though. Now she was lying on her stomach, holding herself up on her elbows, chewing one French fry really slowly.

"No," Michael said. He'd washed his hands and he was sitting on the sticky chair, eating the cheeseburger. He didn't like it very much, but he was hungry and it was the only thing that wasn't fried. "I saw it with Grandma."

It was last year when he and Daddy were at Grandma's apartment. Grandma had turned on the TV while his dad went to the drugstore to fill a prescription for her. Michael liked the show because it was about a clock that was taller than a person. But when Daddy came in, he said, "You know we don't let him watch television." Grandma said, "It's PBS," but she turned off the show, and Michael never got to find out how much it would cost to buy that gigantic clock.

April looked at him. "Your dad's mom is nice, isn't she?"

Michael nodded. His grandmother played Sorry and Uno with him. She had soft cheeks and arms. She smelled like flowers.

"What about your other grandmother?"

He didn't know, but he was distracted by a bigger problem. He'd forgotten to take off the pickle from his cheeseburger. He hated pickles. They were so slimy and wiggly, and now he'd just swallowed one.

"You've never met her, have you?"

He took a drink of the milkshake, but it didn't help.

"Have you ever asked your mom where her mother is?"

He hadn't, but he didn't care. He could still feel the pickle, like a worm sliding down his throat.

"Do you think she doesn't want to tell you for some reason?"

This time April paused, waiting for the answer. He could feel her eyes on him. He was so mad about all these questions and the pickle that he forgot to use his indoor voice. "Stop it! I don't like this!"

"Sorry, buddy." April sounded like she meant it, but now that Michael had gotten upset, he couldn't seem to calm himself down. He was mad about the pickle and the grandmother he didn't have and the grandmother he did have and hardly ever got to see. He was mad about the bad-tasting cheeseburger and the smelly curtains and the ugly room and the whole awful day. Except the part on the boat, which he still liked, but he wasn't thinking about that. He was thinking about a book his mommy used to read to him when he was little, *Alexander and the Terrible, Horrible, No Good, Very Bad Day*. He was already starting to cry, but when he heard himself sputter out the word *Mommy*, he began to hiccup and cry so hard his chest hurt.

April tried to gather him in her arms, but he slapped her away. "I don't want you! I want my mommy!"

He didn't mean to make her cry, too, but when he realized he had, he couldn't stay mad anymore. She'd cried a bunch of times that day, but she'd never sounded this sad. He'd never seen a grown-up sobbing before, and it made him feel bigger and older—and really afraid.

He stood up and went to where she was sitting on the bed. There were French fries all over the floor. He could feel them being squished under his feet. She was doubled over with the empty box upside down in her hand. He said her name and patted her arm. When she finally looked up, he was so relieved that he crawled into her lap.

After a while, she sat up straight and shook her head. "This dump is definitely not utopia." She smiled. "Come on, buddy. I've got a surprise for you."

He was glad that April was happier and he wanted to leave the hotel, but he was nervous, too. She took out a piece of paper from her purse; she said she had to write to someone first. He went to the bathroom again, and by the time he came out, she was finished with the letter. When he asked her where they were going, she said, "Someplace we belong."

TWENTY-THREE

Though David hadn't asked for her help or even seemed to want it, Sandra had ended up driving to Mt. Airy when she left Courtney's. Of course. Her son's house wasn't as chaotic as she'd expected. Yes, there was a police car out front, but the back-yard wasn't surrounded by yellow tape and the front door wasn't blocked by an armed guard and the only person who came when she rang the bell was her frantic son. David said the detective in charge and his team had left a while ago to investigate leads. The two officers that remained were milling about the kitchen, drinking coffee and talking about some guy named Freddy. David frowned as he told her that Freddy, whoever he was, had nothing to do with Michael's disappearance. Sandra sympathized with her son's frustration, though she understood why the police were talking of everyday things. It was the same reason that some nurses told more jokes when they were working in the ICU: the greater the stress, the greater the need to be reminded of all of life's ordinary stuff.

She'd stopped at a deli on the way over, but she couldn't persuade David to eat. "I'm busy, Mom," he said when she asked him to sit down for a minute. In a way it was true; he was busy pacing the dining room, cracking his knuckles, running his hands through his hair, and eavesdropping on the two officers, as if any minute they would have to stop gossiping and reveal Michael's whereabouts. She wished she knew what to do for him, but she headed upstairs with the bag of food, hoping to be more successful with her daughter-in-law. David said she was in their bedroom, but when Sandra didn't find her there, she went down the hall. She peeked into Michael's room and there was Kyra, all elbows and knees and endearingly big feet, curled up sadly on her little boy's bed.

Though Sandra had never really gotten along with her own mother-in-law, she'd had high hopes that she and David's second wife would be friends. She'd liked Kyra from the beginning, when she proved to be David's first girlfriend who could help in the kitchen rather than standing in Sandra's way, pretending not to know what to do next—or, in Courtney's case, actually not knowing. Kyra didn't pride herself on being "intellectual" like Courtney (or David, for that matter), but she was smart enough to have a job in math, which had been Sandra's worst subject in her nursing program. Best of all, she wasn't *troubled*. She didn't require constant propping up, and she was way too strong to need or want to be rescued.

By the time Kyra and David were married, Sandra felt like her hopes were being realized. She and Kyra talked on the phone at least once a week, and they did a lot of girl-type things together, from shopping trips at the King of Prussia mall to getting their hair colored at Sandra's favorite beauty salon and going to a spray-on tan place before David and Kyra's trip to the shore. It didn't always work out perfectly—Kyra thought her blond highlights made her look like she was trying too hard; Sandra's spray-on tan was a streaky orange disaster that everyone kidded her about at the nursing home—but it was fun. Even shoe shopping was fun, Kyra had to admit, though she hated her size 10½ feet so much that she'd always ordered shoes from a catalog.

When her relationship with her daughter-in-law suddenly stalled less than a year into the marriage, Sandra felt both hurt and embarrassed that she cared so much. It took her a long time to decide to ask her son if she'd done something to upset Kyra, but David just laughed. "No, Mom. If you were any nicer, she would leave me and move in with you." Sandra could tell he meant it, but she also knew something had changed. However, over time, she adjusted to the reality that she wouldn't be spending as much time alone with her daughter-in-law. Indeed, after a while, she let herself forget what her relationship with Kyra had been like.

Kyra's eyes were closed, but she wasn't asleep. When Sandra walked in, she sat up and thanked her for coming. Her voice was hoarse, like she'd been yelling, or more likely, crying, all day.

Sandra eased herself down next to Kyra. Her right knee was stiff and achy. It seemed like some joint or another was always rebelling these days. "He's going to be all right," Sandra said. "He's going to be home very soon."

"How do you know?" Kyra's eyes had brightened, and Sandra felt bad that she didn't have new information from the police or some real evidence.

"I can feel it," she said firmly. It was the same sensation she had when a patient was about to turn a corner, except in this case, she would not allow herself to believe otherwise. Her grandson would be home. What would happen after that was another story. David and Kyra were already so nervous about Michael's safety. She honestly couldn't imagine how they would recover from this.

After a moment, she remembered the bag of food clutched in her hand. "Do you think you can eat something?"

Her daughter-in-law nodded, but when Sandra handed her

the vegetable and cheese hoagie, Kyra set it in her lap without even unwrapping the foil. Instead, she stared at the corkboard wall across from them, covered with stuff Michael had cut out from magazines. Like most five-year-old boys, he liked robots and trains and dinosaurs, but he'd also hung up a photo of a pyramid and an odd one of a giant paper clip. Right in the center was a picture of a group of little kids standing next to a fire truck that had been taken on a field trip at one of the schools Kyra and David had sent him to last year. Sandra assumed Michael had hung it there because he missed being in school. True, he never said he wanted to be with other kids, but he was such a sensitive little thing. He rarely said anything that could upset his parents.

David had been the same way at Michael's age. It was something Sandra was still capable of feeling guilty about: how her son, from the time he was so small he could barely reach the light switch, had tiptoed around Ray's and her feelings. Somehow the poor kid must have sensed that his family was as wobbly as the sloppiest block tower: the kind the unruly boys made, while little David himself was laying row after row of foundation for *his* towers. Of course in Michael's case, it had to be different, since Kyra and David had a good marriage, unlike her and Ray. In fact, Sandra sometimes thought her son and his wife were too well matched, if such a thing were possible. Neither one of them would ever dream of doing something with Michael that was the least bit risky. Honestly, she was stunned that they'd let the little boy go into his (fenced) backyard by himself this morning. It might have been a sign that they were finally loosening up, which was just painfully ironic under the circumstances.

David had already told her that Kyra blamed herself, so she wasn't surprised when her daughter-in-law said it was all her fault. Sandra told her it wasn't true. Kids played outside all the time and nothing happened. It was the most normal thing in the world. Her reassurances didn't seem to make any difference though. Kyra was still upset, and finally she whispered, "I need to talk to Father Polano."

Father Polano was a friend of Sandra's. They'd met a long time ago, when his church flooded and Sandra had volunteered to help with the cleanup and restoration project. He'd been very surprised that she'd signed up to help, given that she didn't live in his parish and wasn't even Catholic. She told him the truth: she liked the stained-glass windows. She drove by Sacred Heart every day on the way to work and the sight of the sun shining on the intricate designs of colored glass never failed to lift her mood.

"Can you ask him to come here?" Kyra said. "I know it's an imposition, but I can't do it on the phone and I don't want to leave in case . . ."

Sandra knew her daughter-in-law had been raised Catholic, which was why she'd introduced Kyra to Father Polano in the first place. Michael was fighting meningitis, and Sandra had wanted her daughter-in-law to have someone good to pray with in the hospital. But Kyra and David were decidedly not religious. They never went to church, not on Easter or Christmas, not even to get married. Sandra had been a bit shocked that their wedding ceremony had made little mention of God and used no passages from the Bible, not even the obvious ones from Ruth or first Corinthians. Their ceremony was held at Valley Forge Park rather than a chapel; David thought it would be more relaxed that way. It was a beautiful spot, but Sandra didn't remember it being all that relaxing. The park had so many rules. No throwing rice because rice expands when birds eat it and can hurt them. No birdseed in lieu of rice, for some reason she couldn't remember. No flower petals, because they'd have to be raked up later by the park crew. No photos taken near the historical buildings; she had no idea why. No alcohol, period. But at least it was nothing like his first wedding, which the superstitious part of Sandra couldn't help but see as a good sign.

"I have something I need to confess," Kyra said. "Something important."

Sandra could hear David talking to one of the policemen, but it was clear from how clipped his voice sounded that the situation downstairs was unchanged. "Sweetheart, you can wait on that until Michael comes home. Now why don't you open that vegetable and—"

"But I have to confess or he won't come home!"

Working at the nursing home, Sandra had learned how intolerable it was for her patients and their families to feel completely powerless. She figured Kyra was just doing what most people did: choosing guilt because it meant there was something she could do to help. But when Kyra added, "I think I know who took him," Sandra sat up straight. If her daughter-in-law knew, why hadn't she told the police?

She was about to ask that question when Kyra jumped up and started crying. As she wandered back and forth, her hands were shaking and her face had turned a sickly shade of white. Before Sandra could make her knee work well enough to stand, David was in the room, too. Kyra's crying wasn't loud, but he must have been listening for it. He took her in his arms and said he was there and it would be all right; they just had to hold on. His voice was always so gentle when he was talking to his wife. Sandra loved that about him.

"I need to talk to your mom," Kyra said, sniffing. "I'll be down in a little while."

Her son walked away with his shoulders hunched forward, more than a little defeated, though Sandra felt sure that neither he nor Kyra would think he had any right to be hurt. Somehow their generation had gotten past the assumption that wives had to cultivate their husbands' nurturing instincts. It was a lot better than the old days, when men like Ray expected to be applauded for every single thing they did at home; still, she couldn't help feeling sorry for David. She remembered when she used to call him Prince Charming. Even as a boy, he'd been the type of person who needed to feel like he could protect the people he loved.

Kyra had already closed the door behind him when Sandra said, "I can call Father Polano for you. But if you really think you know who took Michael, you have to tell the police."

"I have." Kyra looked surprised. "I told them I thought it was my sister, Amy."

Sandra had forgotten Kyra even had a sibling. Her daughter-in-law basically never talked about her family; she'd only mentioned her father once, when she and David were planning a trip to his funeral. It was David who'd told Sandra about an older sister, but a very long time ago. By the time they got married, he was used to Kyra's estrangement from everyone she grew up with.

Was it possible that Kyra's sister had really taken Michael? It fit the facts, at least the ones David had shared with Sandra: the kidnapper was a woman; the kidnapper said she loved Michael and felt like she was part of his family. But David hadn't mentioned anything about the police investigating Kyra's sister. Maybe he was so sure Courtney had done it that he'd dismissed any other possibility. Or had Kyra only told the police what she suspected when he wasn't there? If she was trying to keep David from knowing some secret—oh, how Sandra hoped she wasn't—it would certainly explain why she'd sent him back downstairs.

Sandra looked closely at her daughter-in-law. Her eyes were lined with red and her hands were twisted together like she was praying. All of a sudden Sandra's stomach lurched into her throat. She could feel her heart pounding painfully in her wrists and her knees, but she waited until she could breathe again, until her voice wouldn't give her away. "Do you think your sister would hurt Michael?"

"No," Kyra said. "No, absolutely not. I never thought that, not even then."

Sandra wasn't sure what the last sentence meant, but she didn't care. Her whole body was relaxing again. He would be all right. Of course he was all right; he had to be.

"Amy is trying to punish me," Kyra continued. "This is why I need to talk to Father Polano. The punishment won't stop until someone forgives me."

Her voice was oddly calm, matter of fact even, though what she was saying sounded nutty. Sandra seriously doubted that being punished by a sister played any part in Catholic dogma; nevertheless, she took out her cell phone. She didn't have Father Polano's number with her, but she got the number of the church from information. Unfortunately, after a recording giving the times for Mass, an answering machine picked up. She left a brief message, but she told Kyra she really doubted that anyone would listen to it until morning.

"I can't wait that long." Tears were rolling down her cheeks. "I need him back."

Sandra put her arm around her. "God isn't keeping Michael away to punish you, sweetheart. Haven't you asked Him to forgive you?"

"A million times."

"Then I'm sure He already has."

"You don't know what I did," Kyra said miserably. "I don't know if anyone can forgive this."

"Well I'll try my best," Sandra said. "So you can tell me if you think it will help."

She meant it; still, she was very surprised when Kyra seized on it as the solution she'd been waiting for. Her daughter-in-law grabbed her hand. "I remember David told me that you'll forgive anyone. So if I tell you what happened, you can forgive me?"

Sandra promised she would, but she was a little distracted by the part about David. The inflection in Kyra's voice—forgive *anyone*—made it pretty obvious that her son had meant this as a criticism. She wished this were more of a surprise. Just a few days ago, she'd found herself tearing up when she heard "You Are So Beautiful" on the oldies station, remembering when David was a little boy and he used to sing that to her. She was so sure back then that taking care of a young child would be the hardest part of being a mom.

Kyra insisted that they go to her office to talk about whatever it was. Sandra followed, though she was so tired her bones ached. She hoped it wouldn't take too long, not because she wanted to sleep—she knew she wouldn't be able to sleep until the police found Michael and brought him home, safe and sound—but because she didn't like the idea of being shut up here with Kyra while David was roaming around downstairs by himself. It would be getting dark soon. No parent would want to face the night with a child gone, but for David . . . well, it was hard for Sandra to imagine how her son was going to get through this.

TWENTY-FOUR

Each Christmas for the last twelve years, Kyra had received a greeting card from Terri Barnes. The annual slap in the face always included a holiday letter written in Terri's small, cramped handwriting as well as a photograph of Zach and Terri and the three girls sitting on a couch: first solid blue, then, a few years later, green with flowers, then, two years ago, black leather. Though the cards never found their way up to the mantel of the Winters' fireplace and the letters were so cheerily vague as to be useless, each picture was carefully placed in an accordion file that Kyra kept locked in her desk, a file she thought of simply as *Amy*.

If Zach had only been her sister's ex, she would have told David the truth. She could even have told her husband the more important truth that Zach had been her own first love. She imagined David looking quizzically at the latest photograph of Zach, who'd turned into a thick-waisted, balding, incredibly ordinary-looking man. But she knew David wouldn't laugh and say *that guy?* He never teased Kyra about anything that could conceivably hurt her feelings. Only if he knew she didn't care would he tease her: about her knowledge of wine, for example. Or her habit of wearing the same ratty robe every morning. Or her insistence that they keep one clock unchanged all year, despite daylight savings time, so they would always know the "real" time and understand why they didn't feel as awake or as tired as the other clocks said they should.

It was inconceivable that David would make fun of her if he knew the truth about Zach, yet he might do something far worse. He might judge her. He might analyze her complicated motives and decide that the one selfish instinct had hopelessly tainted what she'd done. In other words, he might confirm her worst fear that it was her own fault that she'd lost her sister, that what she'd done to Amy truly was unforgivable.

On some level she knew that telling her mother-in-law what had happened was unlikely to change anything, that this was magical thinking, completely contrary to the logic at the center of all her working life, but she was too far gone to care. All day, she'd felt like the punishment she'd been dreading for years had finally arrived, and though she knew she deserved it, she also knew she could not survive this way much longer. It was almost Michael's bedtime. He had to come home soon if she was to continue to breathe, and live.

She sat down at her desk, and Sandra took a seat across from her, in the big white rocker, the one Kyra had used to nurse Michael. Neither woman spoke as Kyra opened the locked desk drawer and took out the accordion file. She pushed aside the record of all the fruitless searching for Amy she'd done over the years: from receipts and printouts from "people locator" sites on the Internet to Xerox copies from when she used to go to the library and scour phone books from all over the country for an Amy (or A) Callahan and then call every number she hadn't already called. The first photo was a little blurry—they must have upgraded the camera

before they took the rest—but she handed it over to Sandra, pointing at the five-year-old on the end of the couch. "This is Hannah,
my sister's daughter," she said. "Hannah," she repeated, because it
was such a relief simply being able to say the child's name after so
many years of only thinking it.

Kyra heard her mother-in-law take a breath. She could tell
Sandra was nervous all of a sudden, but it didn't occur to her that
David's mother could be afraid that the next thing Kyra would say
was that this child had died. Kyra assumed Sandra was reacting to
the same thing she saw in Hannah at this age. Michael's age. "She
looks like my baby, doesn't she?"

Sandra nodded. After a pause, Kyra thrust the rest of the photographs into her mother-in-law's hands—the record of Hannah
from five to seventeen. Sandra went through them all slowly. "A
pretty girl," Sandra said, handing the pictures back. "Is she . . .
all right?"

"As far as I know. Her parents haven't let me see her since she
was four years old." Kyra lowered her eyes. "Even then, I only got
a half hour. Long enough to give her a few toys."

She smiled at the memory of how happy Hannah was with
everything Kyra brought, but especially the stuffed turtle. The
little girl had kissed the turtle's shell and eyes and mouth and
then clutched it to her chest as though she was afraid someone
would take it. The turtle was still in her arms when Kyra reluctantly hugged her good-bye. Zach had agreed to let her visit only
because it had been almost a year and she'd broken him down
with her begs and pleas and promises not to ask in the future. Of
course she ended up breaking that promise many times, but he
never relented again, not on any of Hannah's birthdays nor any of
the holidays, not even when Kyra was about to leave for the East
Coast, and her new job, when Hannah was seven. After that, she
stopped asking.

"Aunts have no legal rights to visitation," she said flatly. "It's completely up to the parents. They can say no for any reason whatsoever." Sandra probably knew this already, but back then, Kyra hadn't. Kyra had been young and impulsive and desperate. She'd had to learn the hard way, when Zach had her arrested for taking three-year-old Hannah to the filthy house where Amy was living, hoping if Amy just saw her daughter, she would start visiting the little girl again, and stop destroying herself.

"I'm sure you've missed her," her mother-in-law said gently. "Do you know why your sister didn't want you to see her daughter?"

The question was eminently reasonable, given that Kyra hadn't mentioned that by Hannah's parents, she meant Zach and his second wife. Not Amy. It was reasonable, and yet it hit Kyra hard. She felt like she could hear her sister thanking her for agreeing to help with Hannah while her band was on the road, thanking her for taking Hannah to the pediatrician for a checkup, thanking her for everything she did for the baby after she moved out. And Amy talking to little Hannah: "You're going to have such fun with Auntie, my sweet. Your auntie loves you so much, and I adore your auntie!"

After a moment she recovered enough to mutter that she wasn't talking about her sister. "Amy had left town by then." Kyra felt her eyes burn as she remembered the last time she saw her. She was wearing black stretch pants and a torn-up jacket advertising something or other. Her skin was gray and her eyes were so dull. As she spoke, Kyra could see spittle in the corner of her lips. *You'll never see me again.*

Her mother-in-law had to be confused, but she didn't push for an explanation. She lifted her glasses and rubbed the bridge of her nose, then folded her hands back in her lap. Kyra knew she had to get on with it; she had to tell Sandra everything, but it was as if her rational mind had deserted her, as if she'd kept the past to herself for so long, she'd lost the ability to make sense of it.

"I don't know how to do this," she finally admitted.

Sandra suggested she simply start talking. "Tell me about a day here and a night there, an argument or little snippet of talk, some song that was on the radio. You can just tell me whatever is in your head, honey."

The first thing she thought of was the night Amy went back to work, when Hannah was two and a half months old. Her sister's absence from the local clubs had been noticed and an agent had tracked her down; an agent had actually called her, begging her to be the singer for one of his biggest bands. The money was three times what it had been with Peanut's band, and the agent felt sure he could get Amy a record deal. She would only have to travel occasionally. It would help their little family financially, which was very important now that they had to supply Hannah with diapers and formula and clothes and so on.

Amy was nervous about leaving Hannah, and she'd asked Kyra to come over that night. The baby was asleep when Kyra arrived, so she and Zach decided to study. She was taking hard classes for her senior year, and he was taking two science courses and work-ing full-time. After about an hour, Zach stood up and said he was starving. "I'm going to heat up the ravioli from last night," he said. "Want some?"

"Sure." She stood up. "I'll help." There wasn't much to do. While Zach watched the ravioli spinning in the microwave, Kyra put two placemats, forks, and paper towels folded into napkins on the kitchen card table. She poured them each a glass of iced tea. Then she sat at the wobbly table and waited until Zach brought in the steaming bowls of ravioli.

"I think I'm losing weight," he said. "Not as fast as Amy, but look at this." He pulled on the waistband of his jeans and it was true: there was at least three inches between his jeans and his (unfortunately still beautiful) stomach. He sat down and picked up his fork. "Note to self: remember to eat more often."

They talked about their classes for several minutes. At some point Zach said, "Did Amy tell you some local rich guy has agreed to be the sponsor of the band? Her agent worked out the contract. It's really cool. The guy puts in money for equipment and ads and everything the band needs, and he gets back a percentage of the future profits."

"What's his name?" she said, though part of her already knew. Or at least, she felt like the bite of ravioli she'd just swallowed had turned into a rock as it made its way down her esophagus.

"Gregory Todd. He's the president of a PR firm downtown. It's great because he has a lot of media contacts, too. "

Kyra said "cool" or "great" or something positive. But she couldn't control her face, and Zach was looking right at her.

"What?"

"I think I heard the baby." She stood up and rushed down the hall despite Zach's insistence that he hadn't heard anything.

She opened the door as quietly as possible, but the old hinges squeaked and poor Hannah woke up anyway. Kyra picked her up and sat down in the used rocking chair she'd found at a thrift shop. As she rocked the warm baby back and forth, she thought about when this had been her room, not even a year ago. The curtains on the window were still the blue ones she and Amy had made when they first arrived in Kansas City, before they'd started college, a lifetime ago.

Hannah was making her sucking sound, but Amy had said not to feed her. She'd had a full bottle of formula right before Amy left, and spit up half of it. Kyra walked over to the crib and held the baby in one arm while she felt around for one of Hannah's pacifiers. As soon as she stuck it in Hannah's mouth, the infant closed her eyes, but Kyra took her back to the rocking chair. She sniffed back tears and held Hannah close while the baby slept. She was so worried about what was going to happen to Amy and Zach and especially to her little niece, who didn't deserve any of this.

For the first and only time in her life, she wished she were the kind of person who could put out a hit on somebody. There had recently been a news story about some woman who'd paid a criminal a hundred and fifty dollars to kill her husband. Kyra had only about sixty dollars to her name, but if she budgeted carefully, she could save a hundred and fifty by the end of the month. If only she weren't so morally opposed to murder, she could get rid of Gregory Todd once and for all.

Her stupid morals were causing so much trouble. She couldn't even tell Zach who Gregory was because she wasn't positive it was the ethical thing to do. Of course she wasn't positive that it *wasn't* the ethical thing to do, either. She felt so guilty when Zach slipped into the room. He left the door open a crack; from the hallway light, she could see him smiling at his sleeping daughter. It was the same whole-face smile he'd always given to Amy. He seemed so trusting and young, too young to suspect or even understand what his wife was doing, though he was five years older than Amy.

That semester Kyra happened to be taking the only literature course that was required for her bachelor's degree. She'd waited until her senior year because she hated writing papers, but she'd discovered that she actually loved reading classic novels. They'd just finished *Anna Karenina*, which she would forever after think of as *Amy Karenina*.

"Amy ended up telling Zach about the affair herself," Kyra said, looking down at her hands. "Just like Anna."

"Who?" Sandra said.

"It's not important." Kyra was already thinking about that winter morning when Amy told her what she'd done. They were walking in the park by the Art Museum. It was the middle of February and very cold, but five-month-old Hannah was bundled up in her pink snowsuit and surrounded by blankets in the stroller. It was snowing, and Amy wanted Hannah to see how beautiful it was. And she wanted to get away from Zach, who hadn't moved from the bed since her confession.

"He must be in shock," Kyra said. She wasn't as angry with her sister as she'd expected to be. In fact, she felt like a weight had been lifted now that Amy had done the right thing.

"Yeah, I think so," Amy said. She was wearing her old peacoat and one of Zach's stocking caps, but she looked really pretty, as always. "I hope that's why he's so against the idea of separating."

"He is?" Kyra could feel a snowflake melting on her eyelash. She loved the smell of snow, and the way her footsteps echoed in the silence that fell over everything.

"He'll get used to it. I just need to give him time." After a moment, Amy smiled. "Gregory has decided to leave his wife."

"Really?"

She nodded. "He's staying in a suite at Crown Center. I'm going to take a bus over there with Hannah, so the three of us can have brunch together." She took Hannah out of the stroller and picked up the diaper bag. "Could you take this back to the apartment for me?" she said, nodding at the stroller.

The snow was coming down harder, but Amy had on her boots—Kyra checked. She'd be safe walking to the bus with Hannah. Kyra grabbed the handle and pushed the stroller out of her sister's way. "Where should I tell Zach you are?"

"Tell him the truth. I'm moving in with Gregory."

"Oh, Amy."

"I'm happier than I've ever been in my life, sis. Please be happy for me."

It took Kyra only a minute before she reached out and hugged her. If Amy really was happy, then maybe this was the right thing. Of course she shouldn't have married Zach, but an unplanned pregnancy could happen to anyone. And though the Church taught that divorce was wrong, it had been a long time since Kyra believed everything the Church taught. What if this relationship was what her sister had been looking for since she dropped out of college? What if Amy could finally settle down and be fine? Love worked in mysterious ways, or so Kyra had heard. She herself had almost no knowledge of love. The closest she'd ever come was Zach, and sure, this was hurting him, which made her feel awful, but her sister had to come first.

"At least he's rich," Kyra finally said, pulling away from her sister.

"I know!" Amy said, and they both laughed. Amy adjusted Hannah so the baby could look over her shoulder. Before they walked away, Kyra kissed Hannah on the chin. The baby was smiling her best toothless grin. She always loved being outside, especially when it was cloudy, because the sun in her eyes made her squirm and get fussy. Kyra wondered whether Hannah would grow up to be a winter person, like her aunt.

She was so deeply in this memory that she felt like the wetness on her checks was snow. But then she heard Sandra's warm voice. "'Course you miss that baby, sweetheart. Especially right now."

Kyra was crying for Hannah and Michael, but she was also crying for that Amy, who was so happy. Happier than she'd ever been in her life, she said—and much, much happier than she'd ever be again.

Unfortunately, Zach didn't get used to it. Though he couldn't stop Amy from leaving, he told Kyra that he did not want that "asshole" Gregory Todd raising his daughter. He decided to fight Amy for custody of Hannah. The first shock was when, almost immediately, temporary custody was awarded to him, primarily because he was still in the so-called "marital home," but also because the judge made no secret of disapproving of Amy's affair with a married man. Amy got two weekends a month with her baby. Her lawyer said it seemed punitive, but it was only for a few months, until the real case could be heard.

Of course a few months in a baby's life is an eternity. Amy had always been a physical person and she slapped her own face, hard, when she realized she had no choice but to go along with the court. The only thing that made her feel better was her sister's promise that she would watch over the baby. Zach had never blamed Kyra for any of this, and he was glad for the help. When Kyra wasn't with Zach, she was usually at Amy's, consoling her sister, who had moved into a condo with Gregory, except it turned out that Gregory was only "in the process" of leaving his wife. It was all so confusing that Kyra couldn't keep up with her feelings—or her classes. In the future whenever she applied for a job, they would invariably ask what happened at the end of her senior year. "Family crisis," she'd say, knowing they wouldn't press for what she meant. It was a good thing, because though she knew every detail intimately, she would not have been able to give them a simple summary. The job interviewer would expect to hear something concise such as "my brother got sick," or "my family's farm failed." If she said "my sister's heart was broken" that would be close, but *heartbroken* made it sound like Amy was innocent. She wasn't of course. None of them were innocent, including, unfortunately, Kyra.

The judge had ordered an evaluation by a psychologist. After Amy was finished with her evaluation, she felt like she'd done a near perfect job representing herself as a good mother. She'd even baked cinnamon cookies when Ms. Jenkins came to the condo the first time. "She liked me," Amy said. "She told me she'd wanted to be a musician when she was young." But she liked Zach, too. He said so, and Kyra knew it was true after her own meeting with Wendy Jenkins, at the beginning of June.

The psychologist had asked to meet with her because Kyra was the only member of Hannah's extended family. Predictably, Amy and Kyra's father had shown no real interest in the child, and Zach's parents, though they whined constantly for pictures, had visited the baby only once, for a few hours.

They met in Wendy's office, which was filled with toys. Wendy was wearing khaki pants and a loose-fitting blouse that she hadn't bothered to tuck in. Kyra felt stiff and ridiculous in her only suit, the one she'd bought for her job interviews. She'd just graduated; she was starting at an insurance company next week. She still didn't want to be an actuary, but there were no other jobs she could find in Kansas City.

Of course she began by emphasizing how much Amy loved her daughter. She said, "Amy would do anything for Hannah." She also said that Amy deserved to have her daughter more often. "She's a good mother." She even told Wendy Jenkins about the Callahan Child Care Company. "Amy's always been great with kids."

"Tell me what kind of person your sister is. The first four words that come to mind."

Kyra answered quickly so it wouldn't look like she was editing her response. "Loving, generous, spontaneous, and talented." She paused. "And patient. I should have put that in instead of 'talented.' Amy is so patient. That's part of why she's really good with kids."

"Do you know her boyfriend, Gregory?" Wendy said.

"Not really," Kyra said. "He's usually not around when I'm there." She paused and decided she had to say it, no matter how hard it was to get the words out of her mouth. "But from what I've seen, he's a great guy. I'm sure he would be very good with Hannah."

Wendy wrote something down. Kyra hoped it wasn't "sister is clearly a liar."

"How long have you known Zach?" Wendy said.

"A long time. Since he and Amy first started dating."

"Tell me what kind of person he is."

"But you've already met with him."

"Yes, of course. But I'd like your perspective. Just four words, as before."

She couldn't answer as quickly this time. She wasn't sure

why, but summarizing Zach in four words was really hard. And she didn't want his description to be better than Amy's. But she couldn't bring herself to use negative words to describe a really good person like Zach. She felt like Wendy was setting a trap for her, and she wasn't sure how to get out.

In the end, she decided to just use versions of the Amy words, weakening them if possible. Instead of "loving" she used "nice," for "generous" she said "warm," for "spontaneous" she had to go with the opposite, but she only said "cautious" rather than her first thought, "responsible." Finally, for "talented" she used "smart," as that was Zach's real talent. He was smart: at least smart enough that Kyra never questioned her assumption that he had to be smart or she wouldn't be in love with him.

Her crush had returned with a vengeance after Amy left—and turned into love one night in April, when she was spending the night on the couch, as she often did on the weekends to help with child care. She was almost asleep when Zach suddenly knelt down on the floor and kissed her. He kissed her again and again and she kissed him back and soon they were stumbling into the bedroom together. After it was over, he apologized, but she told him she was very glad it had happened. Since then, they'd slept together a dozen times, though they didn't act like boyfriend and girlfriend during the day. Kyra didn't mind. She assumed that Zach was being careful. Of course he would worry that someone could find out about his own affair, which could hurt his custody case. And she could tell by the way he touched her that he was falling in love, too. As soon as the custody hearing was over, they would be able to show how they felt.

Wendy Jenkins was looking at Kyra, staring really. Had she said something wrong? Kyra felt herself blushing, but she always blushed when someone stared at her. She often thought that if she were ever questioned for a crime, the police would decide she was guilty merely because her cheeks would be bright pink.

Kyra couldn't take it anymore. "Are we finished?" she said, and sat up straighter. She hoped she sounded professional, like the insurance clerk she was soon to be.

"I'm sorry," the woman said. "I was thinking about what a unique prospective you have about this." She smiled. "You know both of the parents very well, and even though one is your sister, I can tell you're striving to be objective. That's very unusual."

"Thank you," Kyra said. "I majored in math. I hope I learned how to separate my feelings from the facts."

"Then tell me this, if you had to choose Zach or Amy to be the primary caretaker for little Hannah, which one would you choose?"

"I wouldn't. I think Hannah deserves to have both of them in her life."

"Certainly joint custody is desirable whenever possible. The court has been very clear about that. Since both Zach and Amy seem to be fit parents, I see no reason why they wouldn't be given joint legal custody, which simply means that both of them can be involved in decisions in Hannah's life. And joint physical custody makes sense as well. However, the bulk of physical custody is usually given to one parent, especially in the case of a child Hannah's age. This parent we call the 'residential custodian,' and the other parent is the 'non-primary custodian.'" She paused. "So my question still stands. Which one would you choose to be the primary caretaker?"

For the rest of her life, Kyra would remember this moment. Of course she had no idea how important her answer would become, how it would sway Wendy Jenkins's recommendation, which would turn out to be the sole criterion the second, less-conservative judge would use to decide her sister's fate. Even so, she took it very seriously. She tried to consider only what was best for Hannah.

Did she have dreams of being in a family with Zach and the

baby she adored? She would have said no and meant it, but deep down, she already felt that they were acting like a family. They shopped together, cooked together, played with the baby together, even sang Hannah a lullaby that Kyra had invented for the little girl to the melody of "Row, Row, Row Your Boat." *Go, go, go to sleep, my sweet little one / happily, happily, happily, happily, you have all our love.* Neither Zach nor Kyra could carry a tune, but that just made it better. They were so much more alike than he and Amy ever were.

But did she think that if Zach no longer had custody of Hannah, her relationship with him would suffer? Not at the time, but later, she thought some part of her must have been worried about this—and she prayed that part had had no role in answering the psychologist's question.

She wanted to be objective. She wanted to be fair. Oh, she wanted so many things. She wanted Amy to be happy again. She wanted her sister to be stable, and normal, and a much better mother than their own mother had been. And she wanted Zach to love her. She was so desperate for him to look at her the way he'd looked at Amy. She thought she would never need another thing if only she could go to sleep each night snuggled up to Zachary Barnes.

She was barely twenty-two years old. She had no idea what would be best for Hannah forever, but for now, it seemed clear that Zach was the better parent. Amy traveled with her band at least one week a month. And her obsession with Gregory hadn't diminished despite all his broken promises to leave his wife. Whenever she wasn't talking about Hannah, she was talking about him: when he was coming over, when he didn't show up, when he acted like he loved her, when he seemed like he was losing interest. She had so many problems, and Zach just didn't.

Kyra couched her answer in those terms. Only for now. And the psychologist nodded. Kyra hoped that nod meant that custody orders weren't hard to change. She hoped that maybe by the time Hannah was two, they could switch it and Amy could have her for a year or so. By then, Amy and Gregory's relationship might have settled down. Or Amy would have a new guy who wouldn't put her through the emotional hell of dealing with his marriage.

It was a little over a month later when the judge ruled against her sister. Kyra would always remember that day, July 12, as one of the worst of her life. Though Amy knew what Kyra had told Wendy Jenkins—it was all in the report, unfortunately—she didn't scream or call her sister a betrayer. In fact, she said "it's not your fault" so many times that Kyra knew she was trying to convince herself of that.

Zach had to be happy with the results, but Kyra hadn't had a chance to talk to him. She stayed with her sister, who took to her bed when Gregory claimed he had to be with his family that evening, for a barbecue. It was the first of many gigs Amy would cancel for emotional reasons. By the time Amy finally fell asleep, it was after midnight, and Kyra was exhausted from trying to calm her down. But she still rushed over to Zach's apartment to spend the night. She had her own key, so she wasn't worried about waking Hannah. She hoped Zach might be awake, but if he wasn't, she planned to wake him. Or perhaps she would just slip into his bed. She hadn't decided.

When she got there, she discovered how right she'd been about Zach being careful during the custody case, afraid that if anyone knew he had a girlfriend, it would affect the outcome. He was so cautious that he hadn't even told her that he'd fallen in love with Terri, the woman who babysat Hannah during the day, while he and Kyra were at work.

Though Zach and Terri were only sitting on the couch together, holding hands, she instantly knew she'd been a fool. Indeed, she was so full of self-loathing that she almost threw up. Zach said something vaguely apologetic, but she couldn't find her

TWENTY-FIVE

All evening, David kept thinking he heard Michael's voice coming from the backyard. Again and again he'd headed outside, clutching his flashlight though it wasn't yet dusk, to look for his son. He walked the perimeter of the fence and checked the latch on the gate; he stared into his wife's tomato garden and pushed back the bushes behind the green ash tree. When he came back inside, he was too depressed to care that neither of the police officers would look him in the eye; he didn't even care when he overheard the taller one whisper, "He's losing it." But now, standing alone in the hall outside his wife's study, he wondered if it could be true; if he was, in fact, *losing it.* How else to explain his sudden conviction that his wife would not have fallen apart if his mother hadn't told her Courtney's version of that night?

Kyra had been holed up with Sandra for almost an hour—and crying for what seemed like a very long time. Thanks to the strange acoustics of their old house, the sound could be heard all the way in the kitchen, where the two officers were still stationed by the coffee machine. When the older one suggested that David might want to check on his wife, he'd headed for the stairs, relieved to have an excuse. But when he opened the door of the study, what he witnessed made him back out quickly without making a sound. To say he was surprised to see Kyra curled up on his mother's lap was an understatement. His wife was a very reserved person. Though she was openly affectionate with their son and with David himself, with everyone else, including Sandra, her embraces had always been a bit formal. Yet there she was lying in his mother's arms, with her face buried in Sandra's neck, sobbing like a desolate child.

On some level he was aware that Kyra's odd behavior didn't have to mean that Sandra had told her, but his mind was unable to hold on to this. Now it seemed obvious why Kyra had wanted to be alone with his mother. Earlier, when she'd said *there are things you haven't shared with me*, David had refused to discuss it. But Sandra wouldn't refuse. Sandra would tell Kyra the truth, for Kyra's sake but also because she'd think that David would be better off if his wife could help him with his "unresolved feelings" about the past.

He wondered why he didn't feel furious with his mother, why he didn't feel anything but more panicked. Kyra's crying seemed to be quieting down, but the idea of being there when she came out, full of questions—no, he couldn't bear it, not while his son was missing. He turned down the hall and rushed to the nearest bathroom, the only place where he knew he could be alone until he figured out what was happening to him. The nearest bathroom was Michael's, and his son's white terry cloth robe was still lying in a heap on the rug from the child's morning bath. David picked it up and clutched it against his chest as he crouched down on his knees.

He thought about his conversation with Detective Ingle earlier. The man had kept coming back to Courtney's possible motive, even though David had already explained that his ex-wife hated him. Wasn't that enough of a motive?

She'd taken his son because she was trying to hurt him, obviously. It was the same reason she'd befriended his mother. The same reason she must have told Sandra about the phone calls that night and anything else she thought would make him look bad. Admittedly, he couldn't explain why she'd waited until now to take Michael, but even when he was married to her, he couldn't have explained most of what she did. She'd told him she was unstable on, what, their third date? Actually, the descriptions she'd used for herself were *hypersensitive* and *a drama queen*.

At the time, he'd just felt bad for her. She was upset about an argument she'd had with her family at Thanksgiving, but also upset that she kept "overreacting" to things. They'd ended up having a long talk about what it means to overreact. David had tried to convince her that women were often belittled for their intense feelings, while guys were celebrated for theirs. He wasn't being politically correct—or trying to get her into bed—he believed this. One of the things he hated most about his father was how Ray liked to say women were "crazy bitches who got upset over nothing." This from a man who treated his own attacks of self-pity as the deepest expressions of sadness since Tolstoy.

David would never have used the phrase *drama queen*. Then and now, he thought it was sexist. But after they were married, when she was about four months pregnant, he found himself wondering if some of Courtney's reactions were in fact overreactions, just as she'd said. She'd talked her parents into paying for a cell phone service for herself and David so she could reach him anytime. This was the mid-nineties; no one he knew had a cell yet, and he heard his share of comments about his wife having him on a very short leash. But that wasn't what bothered him. Courtney had said the phones were necessary in case something went wrong with her or the baby. Fair enough, except that her definition of "something wrong" was nothing like his. He tried to remain sympathetic no matter how often she called, even when she interrupted his historiography lecture because she was hysterical about a form rejection letter she received for a story she'd written. He reminded himself of what his mother had said about first pregnancies being very hard, especially if the woman was sick. And Courtney had moved away from all her friends and her family. He just needed to be more patient.

Joshua was due on July 30, but he was born early, on July 8. Though it was summer, David was in the middle of teaching three classes at a local community college, tutoring five high school students to take the SAT, and writing revisions for a long, complex paper on the role of economic causality in historical theories of work. Luckily, his mother came up to help with the infant, though that caused some problems, too. Courtney called at least once a day to complain that Sandra was driving her crazy. He tried to be sympathetic, though his mother's only real crime seemed to be that Joshua was so much easier when she was taking care of him. The one time he hinted that the baby might be picking up on how tense Courtney was, she snapped, "Are you're saying I'm a bad mother?" "No," he said quickly. "I'm just saying you and I are new at this." He kept his voice gentle, though his jaw felt tight. Most of the time when Courtney called, she would end up apologizing, but he didn't feel like hanging on, waiting for her mood to change. He had ninety-two tests to grade before the end of the week. He was so stressed that it was hard not to be jealous of his grad school friends who didn't have colicky babies and upset wives and ninety-two students waiting for grades, friends who did nothing but study all day and hang out at bars most nights.

All of it—the classes, the tutoring, and the revisions—was over by the beginning of August. He had a full month off before the fall semester began, which was a good thing, as his mother had to go home and back to work. She promised to come up again as soon as she could, but in the meantime, they would be on their own.

After only a day and a half, they were already overwhelmed.

Joshua was cuter than any baby David had ever seen, so cute it seemed impossible that David had had anything to do with creating him, yet he was exhausting to take care of, primarily because he seemed to hate sleeping. Because he was three weeks premature, he was born very small, only 5 pounds and 2 ounces. David assumed that had to be part of the reason he woke up every hour and a half all night long, screaming to be fed. Courtney was breastfeeding, not because she wanted to, as she frequently admitted, but because she was afraid the pediatrician, and especially her mother, Liz, would disapprove if she didn't. David wasn't sure why she refused to try pumping milk so he could handle one of the nightly feedings. She also wouldn't discuss why she'd decided to stop waking Joshie during his long afternoon naps, though Sandra had told them they needed to do this until the baby learned to save his longest continuous sleeping period for the nights. David suspected that she was too exhausted to think straight, but it was becoming a vicious cycle. The more tired Courtney was, the more reluctant she became to listen to suggestions, much less let him make any of the decisions. So he did the only thing he could think of. He changed diapers when she told him to, grabbed another spit-up cloth if she snapped her fingers and pointed at her shoulder, took Joshie for walks when she yelled that the crying was driving her insane. Whatever she wanted.

Just getting through each hour was so challenging that he had no time to reflect, no time to see how bad everything was becoming until Labor Day weekend, when his mother came for a visit and Courtney fell apart. It was Sunday morning, and Sandra had kept the baby in the living room with her the night before. Somehow his mother had gotten Courtney to agree to express milk and to let Joshie have water if the milk ran out before morning. "He's not going to starve," Sandra said, which seemed true. He was almost two months old and still quite small, but the pediatrician said he was healthy and gaining weight on schedule. Courtney even called him "chubby" sometimes, though she frowned when Sandra cooed over his "fat little toes." To play it safe, David stuck to calling the baby "my little guy" or just "Joshie."

Sandra had managed to keep the baby from crying and waking them until nearly seven in the morning, meaning Courtney should have been more rested than she'd been in weeks. But when Sandra was out getting bagels, after Joshua went down for his morning nap, Courtney slumped down on a bar stool and said, "I think I hate your mother."

He sensed that she wanted to fight with him, but he was in such a good mood he refused to take the bait. He took Courtney's hand and kissed it. "I know," he said, lightly, teasingly. "How dare she think if she lets us sleep and buys us bagels, we'll forget what a villain she is?"

When Courtney grabbed her hand back, he knew the fight was inevitable, but he was still stunned when she screamed that he never listened and picked up his coffee cup and threw it against the kitchen wall. Of course the crash woke Joshua, and she shot David a look full of resentment before she stomped off to pick up the baby. He managed to get the coffee off the wall before Sandra came home from the store, but the cup had broken into too many shards to salvage. It was his favorite mug, given to him by his mentor, Professor Vinton: *History does not repeat itself, historians merely repeat each other.*

Sandra had to leave that afternoon. Courtney held herself together until his mother drove off, but then she started pacing around the apartment, talking about the impossibility of love, the "philosophical hopelessness" of love, the stupidity of believing in love—and how he didn't love her, how he'd never loved her, how no one did. He told her over and over it wasn't true, but he knew he wasn't as convincing as usual. He didn't even feel like himself now that he knew she was capable of throwing a coffee cup. This new version of Courtney bore too much resemblance to the angry father he'd spent his childhood placating. He was counting the hours until Tuesday, when the fall semester would begin and he could escape from the whole mess.

The first day of grad school was long, with an afternoon department meeting he couldn't miss, but he rushed home as soon as it was over, surprised by how much he missed Joshua. Courtney seemed fine, though she wasn't talking very much. She didn't call him on the cell on Wednesday, and he was grateful for the calm, but then he came home to find her scrubbing the cabinet over the oven, where they stored their spices. In and of itself, this was strange—as his mother's raised eyebrows made clear every time she visited, Courtney and David weren't very motivated house cleaners—but what alarmed him was the condition of their baby. Joshua was sitting in his bouncy chair with a diaper that clearly hadn't been changed all day. He was screaming his head off, and Courtney was acting like she couldn't hear it. When he asked her what she was doing, she shook her head and babbled something about spilling the basil.

He changed Joshua's diaper and dragged them both to the emergency room, where the doctors gave Joshua a bottle of formula and pronounced Courtney "a little dehydrated" and "obviously sleep deprived." For that, they charged him over a thousand dollars, but at least they gave her a prescription for a strong sedative that enabled her to sleep through the night. Of course that meant David had to get up with Joshua and give him formula when necessary, but it was worth it when Courtney woke up the next morning more like her old self than she'd been in a very long time. She finally told him what had happened over the weekend. Even though Sandra was there, taking care of Joshua, she hadn't been able to sleep all night. In fact, she hadn't slept at all for the last *four days*. But now she was fine, and very apologetic. She decided to keep taking the sedatives, though it meant she had to wean Joshua. David would handle all the nightly feedings, which sounded worse than it turned out to be. Within just a few nights, Joshua had moved from waking up every hour and a half to every four hours. Courtney joked that their baby knew better than to lose sleep for a mere bottle.

For a while after that, nearly a month, their lives were almost like he'd hoped they'd be when Courtney first told him she was pregnant. While he was studying and teaching, she was taking care of the baby, and in the evening, they had dinner together, nothing elaborate, usually rice or beans with a little cheese or chicken, whatever they could make quickly. As Joshua started crying less, they started talking again: mostly about the state of affairs in Babyville, but also about history and poetry and interesting (or stupid) things that had happened during the day. They found themselves holding hands again, while Joshua was in his swing or on a blanket under his jungle gym. If they still went to sleep on opposite sides of the bed, by morning they were usually curled up against each other. They even had sex a few times, and at the beginning of October, they spent a whole, crazy day in a cheap motel while Sandra was taking care of Joshua. They felt a little guilty for telling David's mother that they were going to a history conference, but even the guilt was kind of fun. It made them feel like they were mischievous kids getting away with something, instead of what they were: the only two people from their college graduating class—according to the alumni newsletter anyway— who'd already started a family.

When things started to go badly again, David initially blamed himself. The semester wasn't going very well. Professor Vinton was unhappy with the revisions David had done over the summer to the paper they both hoped could be published. The disapproval of his mentor made him deeply insecure about his ability to do scholarship; still, when he realized his mood was bringing down Courtney's, he worked hard to get over it, or at least hide it. He tried so hard to make her happy again, but it didn't make any difference. Within days, they were right back to where they'd been. His wife was utterly miserable and he had no idea what to do for her.

At some point he did think to ask if she was still taking her sedatives, though he wasn't surprised that the question irritated her. "You heard the doctor say they're addictive," she said. "I can't keep taking them forever."

They were picking up the dishes from the table. Courtney was upset that Joshua had gone to sleep later than usual. David was tired, but she looked exhausted. She had deep circles under her eyes and her normally pink face looked wan and depleted. He felt his heart clutch when he noticed she was wearing his college sweatshirt, the one he'd given her junior year, when they realized they were in love and she wanted to have it to sleep in when he couldn't be there. "I'm just worried, Court," he said softly. "I don't want anything to happen to you."

"Really? It seems like the main thing you want is for me to keep my mouth shut."

And just like that, his warm feeling for her disappeared. This had happened so often he was no longer surprised. He stared at her blankly, thinking *if only you would.*

By three and a half months, Joshie's colic and constant crying had become a thing of the past. He was still underweight, in the bottom ten percent on the pediatrician's growth chart, but he continued to be healthy and he seemed so happy. His days were spent rolling on the floor, sucking his toes, raising his big head, cooing and gurgling and giggling and laughing. David's love for him was so natural and uncomplicated. If Courtney had done anything to indicate that she couldn't take care of him, anything even vaguely reminiscent of that night when she was cleaning out the spices, he would have stepped in. But every night when he got home, the baby was well fed, dressed neatly, and blissfully unaware that his mother was revving herself up to bitch about something else.

Of course David never said that she was bitching. That he'd

allowed himself to even think the word disturbed him, but what else could you call her aimless complaining that seemed to be a gross overreaction to everything from their next-door neighbor's daughter, a cute kid who had apparently made an innocent remark about the short-lived rash on Joshua's cheeks, to Courtney's brother, who had given them an expensive high chair, not to be nice, according to Courtney, but to "throw his success in my face." Absolutely anyone was capable of upsetting her: David of course, but also her mother, his mother, his friends from grad school, their friends from college, the editors of every literary magazine to whom she submitted her writing, the clerk at the post office, even a newscaster on television. The sole exception was Joshua, whom she always saw as perfect, if slightly pitiable, because, according to her, "He was born to a mess of a mother and a father who doesn't care."

David really did try. He even pushed her to go to a therapist, though he'd hated his own brief experience with a psychologist when his parents were divorcing, which was supposed to help him deal with his feelings but instead had merely confirmed his teenage belief that the best way to handle an emotional problem was to think about something else. Predictably, Courtney refused to consider seeing someone, but she also accused him of having turned into the very thing he hated. "So you think I need a shrink now, David? What are you going to do next time I cry? Call me a crazy bitch?"

He felt deeply betrayed that she'd used his memory of his father against him. Though he didn't argue with her, he wondered how much more of this he could take. He thought of himself as the kind of guy who would never leave his wife, but he didn't see how he could keep letting her treat him like this, day after day. He was determined not to be his father, but he also didn't want to be in the position of his mother, who'd taken far too much abuse in her marriage. There was such a thing as too much patience.

But still, he kept on trying for another miserable week. She was always angry when he was home, which was bad enough, but the phone calls were becoming intolerable. He was back to tutoring again, gone a lot more than he wanted to be, but he had no choice: they were out of money. She interrupted him at least two or three times a day to tell him about some problem. Most of them didn't seem serious, and the ones that did only served to remind him how manipulative Courtney could be. On Thursday night, when he was leading a study group, she told him the rain was coming through the ceiling and flooding the apartment. He'd rushed home to find a small wet spot, not even a puddle. On Sunday, while he was helping a high school student with grammar, she told him that something was wrong with the oven, something dangerous. He'd rushed home to find she just needed to light the pilot. And then on Tuesday evening, after he'd decided he was not going to rush home, no matter what (even though he wished he could be there because it was Joshie's four-month birthday), she told him the baby was sick. He'd hurried back faster than usual only to discover that his son was fine. No fever, no vomiting, not even a runny nose. When he confronted her, she said, "He seemed like he was getting sick." She didn't even apologize.

Unfortunately, on that Tuesday evening, he'd rushed out of the seminar taught by Professor Vinton. Though he'd been deeply apologetic the next day, he wasn't entirely surprised when the professor suggested they meet at a local pizza parlor that night, to discuss "your progress in the program." It was an ominous request, as two of his friends in the department confirmed. Professor Vinton was notorious for using off-campus locations for delivering bad news. Supposedly, the professor thought it made it easier for the student to hear bad news away from school; it undoubtedly made it easier for him to escape if the student reacted badly.

David called Courtney around noon to tell her he was having dinner with his advisor. She said, "Fine," and she really did seem fine about it. But around five o'clock, she called to say that she needed him to come home early tonight. "I'm not feeling very well," she said.

"Do you seriously expect me to believe you're sick? After what you—"

"Okay, I'm not sick," she began. "It's just—"

"I don't have a choice. I have to go to this dinner. It will probably determine my future in the program."

"And of course your future is more important than me," she said—and hung up.

He hoped that was the last of it. He was nervous enough about this meeting without adding unnecessary stress. But when she called again, at 6:52, he'd just arrived at the restaurant. He was outside, rubbing his hands together because he'd forgotten his gloves, planning how to defend the latest version of his paper and make the case that he had the ability and commitment to cut it in the profession. He was so tense that he answered the phone without thinking.

"You have to come home," she said. No *hello*, no *I hope you're all right*, no *I understand how important this is*.

"I told you, I can't."

"But I really need your help."

"I'll leave as early as I can. That's all I can promise."

"I'm not doing very well, David. I'm serious."

"Well neither am I." He exhaled. "I wish you could see that this is our future, too. I have to support our family."

"No you don't. My father would be happy to—"

"Not this again. I've told you, I refuse to sponge off your father."

He saw Professor Vinton opening the glass door of the pizza parlor. He recognized the prof's trademark Cossack hat, which he wore from October to April, even if it wasn't particularly cold. "Got to keep the brain warm," Vinton would say, and chuckle like he hadn't said it a hundred times.

"We can talk about this later," he said quickly. "I have to go."

"Please, David, I'm so tired. I didn't want to tell you before, but I haven't been able to get another—"

Vinton was standing at the hostess desk. Waiting. David could not be late. He repeated that he would be home as soon as he could and said good-bye.

They were just sitting down when the phone rang again, but this time, David hit the ringer mute button. Vinton took off his hat and gently set it on the placemat in front of the empty chair next to him. He moved his menu over, too, without looking at it. "Shall we follow tradition?"

David nodded. He'd learned last year that most of the history faculty always ordered the same pizza. It wasn't a joke, though the newbies always assumed it had to be.

When Professor Vinton told the waitress, "Spinach and olive pizza and a pitcher of beer," she shot David a smile. She was pretty, but it didn't matter. Despite everything that had gone wrong in his marriage, he had no interest in other women.

After she left, the professor said he had some news. Did he say *good* news? "I was going to tell you this yesterday after class, but when you had to leave, I decided it would be better this way. I got a call from Bloomington. Your paper has been accepted."

David was so taken aback that he could only mumble, "Really?"

"They remarked on the strength of the last passage," said the professor, which was a nod to the work David had done in revisions.

David started gushing his appreciation for all Vinton's help, but the professor waved him away. "Everyone in the department knows you're serious. I told them when you applied that you're a star in the making." He grinned. "And you know I always like to be right."

The pizza arrived and David ate two slices, all he could manage given that he couldn't feel his stomach. His legs were gone, too. It was as if the rewiring of his brain to accept this had taken all the blood from his body. He did drink, because Professor Vinton encouraged him to. They finished the first pitcher, and David briefly wondered if he should get going, but then the professor ordered another one. When the room started to look fuzzy, less familiar, David switched to water. Vinton had walked to the pizza parlor, but he had to drive home.

They stayed until 10:47: almost four hours of talking history with the historian he admired most. It would have been heaven even if Professor Vinton hadn't kept emphasizing how well David was doing. How he belonged there. How Vinton was looking forward to working with him, and eventually, supervising his dissertation.

David found it simply incredible that this brilliant professor respected him. *I'll respect you when you act like a man*, his father had said, when David cried. *I'll respect you when you've worked for a living*—when David was eleven and brought home another perfect report card. *I'll respect you when you have kids and you show me what a better father you'll be*—if David dared to complain about his father calling him a sissy, a girl, a mama's boy, a weakling, or a crybaby.

And Professor Vinton wasn't just an intellectual heavyweight. He'd been a boxer in college, and he owned three motorcycles. He could probably beat up Ray without breaking a sweat. Yes, David knew this was a dumb thing to be thinking, but he didn't care. Sitting at this table, he felt more accepted as a man than he ever had in his life.

When they stood up to leave, David was in an expansive and wildly optimistic mood. He didn't feel the cold as he walked to his car. The streets around the university looked cleaner and brighter and bursting with possibility. As he drove by stately houses, he imagined them filled with people who were looking forward to the future as much as he was—now that he knew he was a *star in the making*. Somehow he'd have to live up to it, but for now, it was just so incredibly, impossibly cool.

He was out on the highway, almost back to the apartment

complex, when he remembered his phone was off. He thought about turning it on, but he didn't see the point of listening to all Courtney's messages telling him to come home when he was going there anyway.

Later, he would force himself to listen to those messages over and over, though the pain was unbearable. It was the least he could do, now that it was too late to do anything.

I took a cab to a doctor weeks ago, but he wouldn't give me any pills. I never sleep anymore. I lie there and listen to you but I never drift off, no matter how hard I try. Do you have any idea what that's like?

I don't want to be like this, David. Please help me. I don't know what to do.

Something bad is happening. I'm seeing things, baby. I know they're not there, but I'm so scared. Even if you don't care about me, please come home for Joshie's sake.

I just have to sleep or I'm going to die!

He kept the messages on his cell phone until the phone service deleted them. Even years later, he had most of them memorized. For as long as he lived, he would never forget the desperation in his ex-wife's voice.

He was still crouched on the floor in Michael's bathroom when he heard a noise and felt something banging against his head. "David? Are you there? Can I talk to you?"

It was his mother. She was knocking on the bathroom door, which he happened to be leaning against. He was still holding Michael's little robe, but it was damp with sweat.

She sounded a little apprehensive. He wondered if she was afraid to tell him what she'd told Kyra, and reveal the fact that she'd stayed in contact with his ex-wife all these years. But he wasn't upset with his mother. He didn't even care what Courtney had told Sandra about that night. What he was afraid of was more solid and intractable; it made the air feel so heavy in his lungs that when he stood up, he was dizzy from it.

He opened the door and looked into his mother's kind, weary eyes. "You're right," he said softly. "She didn't take him."

Without his anger, he wasn't sure how to think about Courtney, but he was sure she hadn't done this. There was no motive, just like the detective said. Courtney didn't blame him for that night. He remembered when the doctor said Joshua couldn't be revived, how she'd grabbed a blade from an ER cart. *I killed my baby!* She'd fought hard against the police who tried to stop her. The sound of her weeping and wailing as they took her away was something David would have given anything to escape. *I want to die! I can't go on without him!*

"Aw, honey." Sandra's voice was so soft, he could barely hear her. "My poor, poor boy."

She was looking at him, and then she had her arms around him. She was holding him tightly, as though he were six years old and her arms could protect him from the mean kids who teased him for being a bookish kid, from his mean father who teased him for being skinny and weak. Her cheek was against his neck. It felt softer than he remembered; the skin was looser and thinner, like the fabric of a favorite shirt worn a million times.

The next thing he knew, his wife was there. She'd come up behind him and put her arms around him, too. He could tell something had happened, some news about Michael, but they were waiting to tell him because he was obviously *losing it.*

For so many years, he'd been afraid that if he ever let himself cry, the pain would destroy him. Now he was crying hard, maybe as hard as Kyra had been crying when he saw her sitting in Sandra's lap, but the two women he loved best in the world were holding him up, telling him over and over that it would be all right, as though it really could be this time.

TWENTY-SIX

It was almost ten o'clock, and Courtney was sitting at the bar of the Ocean Nights Motel, trying to ignore the lowlife seated next to her. She'd already pointed to her laptop and muttered "busy" when he asked if she wanted a drink. A few minutes later, when the bartender set a margarita down perilously close to her MacBook, she knew that the lowlife had bought her a drink anyway. "All work and no play makes Jack go out of business," he said, chuckling before he'd finished his stupid joke. "Jack Daniels, get it?"

She didn't bother to point out that margaritas wouldn't help "Jack" much either, given that they weren't made of whiskey. At least they usually weren't. Who knew at a dump like this? The sign out front said that Ocean Nights had an on-site restaurant, upgraded rooms, air-conditioning and free Wi-Fi. The only part that turned out to be true was the free Wi-Fi, which, weirdly, was available only in the bar. The on-site restaurant was a hamburger shack across the parking lot, and the air-conditioning was "temporarily" out of commission, meaning the margarita she didn't want was already sweating through the napkin. Worst of all was room 13, which the front desk clerk had let Courtney see, after Courtney had given her forty dollars for the privilege. It was decorated in a nauseating shade of green and so filthy it was probably a health hazard. The clerk frowned when Courtney said that if it was upgraded a little more, it might be able to cut it as a prison cell.

Courtney had been on her way back from a disappointing job fair in Newark when Hannah called. She was glad to hear from her, and glad that the girl was on the East Coast—until Hannah told her what she'd done. Then she had to pull off the interstate or risk plowing into some innocent commuter.

"You have to bring him back to his family." She hoped she sounded firm, but she was having trouble catching her breath. "Right now!" She punched on her warning lights, knowing it wasn't safe to be sitting on the shoulder of the road in this traffic. There were notices up and down the interstate that these "breakdown lanes" were to be used only for emergencies. She hoped the highway patrol didn't stop to help her, or she'd end up with a ticket.

"But I'm feeling really sick," Hannah said. "I don't think I can drive."

"I'm going to call David and Kyra to pick him up. I'll call you after I talk—"

"Please don't tell them yet. You come, okay? By yourself. You can take him back."

"I have to call them," she said, twisting a lock of her hair. "I have to tell them where he is and that he's all right."

"But they'll have me arrested! I might have to go to jail. Courtney, I'm begging you. If you promise not to tell them, I promise I'll wait in the motel down the street. Please. I'm not doing so great here. I really need your help."

Courtney wondered if it was possible that David and his wife would really have their own niece arrested. It sounded unlikely, but what if it wasn't? Oh God.

Hannah was still talking. She had such a sweet voice; it was hard not to want to do whatever she asked. And Courtney wasn't actually very far from the shore town where Hannah and Michael were. She could probably be there in less than an hour. If only her heart would stop pounding; if only she could breathe slowly and make a decision. Finally, when she saw a patrol car pass by on the other side of the interstate—and realized her location might be being radioed in right now—she said okay. "Text me the name of the hotel. When I get there, we'll figure something out."

But when she got to Ocean Nights, Hannah wasn't there. Courtney tried to call her repeatedly, but the calls went straight to voice mail. Luckily, Hannah had left her a note. It was lying on the bed in room 13, and tucked underneath was a picture of Michael and a gaunt-looking girl with enormous eyes, standing on the deck of a boat. In the note, Hannah explained that she'd forgotten her phone charger and her phone was dead. But she said she was feeling much better and she'd decided it was time to take the little boy home.

Courtney was immensely relieved that Hannah was doing the right thing—and that she could call Sandra now and tell her what was happening. She was dialing her cell phone before the annoyed clerk had even escorted her out of room 13. The conversation turned out to be less difficult than she expected. Somehow her former mother-in-law already knew who Hannah was, and she didn't sound all that surprised that Hannah had taken Michael, though of course she was mystified that Courtney was the person telling her this.

"I met her on the Internet," Courtney said. "It's a long story." She waited a moment. "But I had nothing to do with . . ."

"I know you didn't," said Sandra.

"She's very sorry for all this. She told me she didn't intend to scare her aunt and uncle."

Courtney didn't share with Sandra the other things Hannah said. The girl was very upset with Kyra for not bothering to inform Hannah or her father that Amy Callahan had died. This was why she'd decided to come to Philadelphia while her father and stepmother were in Colorado, on their annual trip to visit her stepmother's family, and one of her stepsisters was on her honeymoon. Her plan was to confront her aunt and uncle, but in a nice way. She even bought toys for their child, so they'd let her in and listen to her. But then she saw Michael standing alone in his backyard, and he looked so much like her that she knew it was true: he really was her cousin, and the first person she'd ever seen who was related to her mother. Before she had time to think about the consequences, she'd talked him into spending the day with her.

"She didn't mean any harm," Courtney said. "She's only seventeen and a little impulsive, but she's a good person."

"This is such a relief," Sandra said. It was the third or fourth time she'd said this, but her voice still sounded a little tight and airless, as if her feelings hadn't caught up with her words.

Courtney's head throbbed as she thought about what her former mother-in-law and David and his wife had been through. She couldn't help feeling that if she hadn't told Hannah that her mother was dead, none of this would have happened.

"One other thing." Courtney rubbed her left temple. "I hope the police won't have to get involved . . . With Hannah, I mean. I think that's a very bad idea." She paused. "She may be afraid to drive up to the house if she sees a police car. Could you stress this to David and his wife?"

Sandra said she would. Then she said, "Thank you, Pumpkin. You have done so much for us with this phone call. David is going to be so grateful."

Sandra always called her "pumpkin," because she had red hair, but she smiled hearing it this time. And the part about David—it would be great if it turned out to be true. If only her ex-husband would see her as a decent person. A wrecked-up mess maybe, especially now, when she'd torn off every nail on her left hand on the drive to the Ocean Nights, but at heart, not that bad.

The lowlife next to her at this bar, now, *he* was a bad person. First, he kept bugging her while she was trying not to panic as she kept thinking about Hannah's note; then he ordered her a drink she didn't want; and now he was telling her how uptight she was after she'd ordered another Diet Coke.

"I can't deal with this." She scooted her stool as far away from him as she could go without crowding the gray-haired woman on the other side. "Please, I have to do something."

If only she hadn't canceled her phone Internet service when she lost her job. If only there was someplace else with Wi-Fi around, a normal place like Starbucks or McDonald's. The Wi-Fi connection here was slow of course, but she'd finally loaded Amy/Hannah's Facebook page. Amy's friend list had always been hidden; Courtney had originally liked that, because it meant no one would know that she'd friended Amy. But now her wall was hidden, too. There was nothing except her name and her profile picture: a sea turtle.

"I'm not going to leave you alone until you drink that margarita," the creep said. "A pretty gal like you deserves to have some fun."

A pretty gal like you? The guy was older than she was, but he couldn't be more than fifty. The last person who'd called her a "pretty gal" was her grandfather.

He was clearly drunk, and probably a regular at the fabulous Ocean Nights bar. On a normal day, when Courtney wasn't stressed beyond belief by the fact that she might have just told Sandra something that wasn't true, it would be bad enough. But this was no normal day. She was going to have to break into Hannah's Facebook account. Of course she wasn't some hacker mastermind, but she didn't need to be. In one of her emails, Hannah had said something about her password, some hint. Unfortunately, Courtney no longer had those emails, but she might be able to remember what Hannah had said if this jerk next to her would just shut up.

"You gotta tell me why you won't drink it," he said. "Come on, I bought it just for you."

She got out her ChapStick and bathed her lips. This was why she hated bars. If you didn't drink, you were treated like there was something seriously wrong with you. Which there was, actually, but she wasn't about to tell this stranger the truth about why she hadn't touched alcohol in almost fifteen years, since the night her baby died.

Joshua had been asleep in his crib when she took out the bottle of scotch. The doctor had told her she couldn't have any more pills, and she hadn't slept for seventy-two hours. Not for one minute. She had a terrible ache inside her skull. Her eyes felt like they were bleeding. She thought if she didn't sleep soon, her brain would explode. So she sat at the kitchen table and quickly downed one shot after another, until the noises finally stopped. The noises were part of her "postpartum psychosis," according to the doctors at the hospital, but whatever the cause, they were unbearable. Tiny noises, like papers being blown across a room. A buzzing that seemed so real, like a bee had flown into her ear, and she dug into her ear canal until it bled, trying to get it out.

She didn't remember bringing Joshua into bed with her, but the police said she'd passed out and rolled on top of him. Her own body had killed her baby. *You should never take a child into bed with you when you've been drinking!* The officer told her this as if there would be more children in Courtney's future: happy, healthy children who would be saved if only she understood.

She put her ChapStick back in her pocket. Her hands were

trembling, but she wrapped them under her knees and forced herself to concentrate on the present. If only she could figure out Hannah's password, she could find out if there was somewhere else the girl might have decided to go.

The first time she'd read Hannah's note, she thought it was clear that Hannah was taking Michael back to David and Kyra: *He's been crying and I think he needs to be with someone who loves him. Don't worry, we'll be home soon.* But something was off. Why would Hannah say "someone who loves him" rather than "his family"? And would she really have considered her aunt's house *home*, given how mad she was at Kyra?

The lowlife was still watching her. "Don't tell me you're in AA."

"I am," she said, wondering why she didn't think of this before.

"Why are you in a bar, then?"

He sounded whiny, but he looked a little suspicious. When she didn't offer any explanation, he stood up so quickly that he stumbled, and rushed away like she was an AA counselor about to perform an intervention on him.

Without his constant prattle, it didn't take her long to remember what Hannah had said about her password. It was when they were just getting to know each other; Courtney had mentioned that she'd forgotten her password again, that she was so paranoid about privacy that she always used some impossible to remember combinations of letters and numbers. Hannah wrote back that her password was only six letters, and it was easy to remember because it was a word. *I'm a really superstitious person. I know it probably sounds weird, but I really believe if I type this word enough, it will bring me luck.*

Unfortunately, it wasn't much of a hint. A lot of the obvious choices—*luck, lucky, happy*—weren't six letters. She tried *Hannah;* then she tried *turtle.* When those didn't work, she just sat there, staring at the screen, because she knew if she kept putting in the wrong password, the account would lock up.

The bar was noisier than before, but at least no one was bothering her. She didn't notice that the bartender was annoyed with her for taking up space with her laptop and drinking only Diet Coke. She watched the cursor blinking for what felt like a long time—and then she felt stupid, because the answer was so obvious. *Of course* Hannah's password was the word *Mother*. And the girl had capitalized it because it was a tic with her, even when it wasn't grammatically correct. *Are you going to see your Mother today?* She treated the word like it stood for something sacred: the good Mother who would never leave you, who would never hurt you, who would even protect you from the devastating truth that you were never good enough to be a mother yourself.

Sandra was the only person Courtney had ever met who came close to the kind of mother Hannah was dreaming of. Only Sandra had been willing, when Courtney came out of the hospital, to stand with her as she faced the blighted ruin of her life. And now, oh God, she had stupidly given Sandra and David false hope that the little boy was on his way home. Because, as it turned out, Hannah was not driving to Mt. Airy. In fact, she'd planned this part of her trip before she left Missouri. Why she hadn't mentioned it on the phone, Courtney had no idea. But she knew exactly why the girl had taken Michael with her, even if her original kidnapping of him had been an impulse. And she knew why she'd said they were going home, though after reading all the messages, she felt almost positive that Hannah was setting herself up for another crushing blow.

Since Courtney had found out that "Amy" was really just a teenager, she'd been forced to rethink everything about their brief, intense relationship. In retrospect, there were so many signs that the person writing those emails was very young. Courtney felt a little foolish, but what bothered her more was the sense that she'd failed to be responsible. "Amy" had frequently alluded to something traumatic that had happened to her last year. She was vague about the details, but she often talked about going to a "shrink," and she clearly needed one: *A few months ago, I took a kitchen knife and cut my wrists. I hope you're not shocked. I guess I just couldn't take being me anymore.* Courtney had thought she was doing a good thing by reassuring her that she wasn't shocked. How could she be, given what she'd tried to do to herself after Joshua died? However, knowing that a seventeen-year-old girl had done something like this was very different and yes, shocking—and Courtney couldn't shake the feeling that she should have known. If only she'd been the adult for a change and protected this kid. If only she hadn't made it so much worse by killing the girl's dream of finding her mother.

She wrote down the address where Hannah was going, put ten dollars on the bar, and headed out to the parking lot. She threw her laptop in the backseat and climbed into her car. Her jaw was aching but she couldn't stop grinding her teeth. She was dreading calling Sandra again: dashing their hopes, having to explain all the things she'd left out the first time about why Hannah had done this, but mainly she was worried about Hannah and David's son. She desperately wanted to believe the two of them were all right, that the little boy was safe with Hannah, but how could she be sure when Hannah might not be safe with herself?

TWENTY-SEVEN

By the time Kyra and David discovered where their son was going, the police had been gone for hours. Detective Ingle had called off the investigation after Kyra had twisted the truth to get him to believe that her niece had contacted them and Michael was absolutely fine. She had to promise to bring Hannah by the station tomorrow. "I'm going to have a talk with her about what she did," the detective said. "Make sure she understands she'll be in serious trouble if she ever pulls another stunt like this." Kyra mumbled agreement, whatever it took to get him off the phone. Then she sat down with her husband and his mother, and they waited and waited until Courtney called for the second time, with the depressing news that Hannah was not bringing Michael home.

Now they were on the Pennsylvania Turnpike heading west, still at the beginning of the 180-mile trip to Maryland. David had insisted on driving, though he was just as exhausted as she was. But, as he said, Kyra had had a very rough night. She'd had multiple blows, one after another: discovering that Hannah, the first child she'd loved, had taken her baby; hearing that Hannah was very angry with her, and then hearing the reason—because Kyra hadn't told Hannah that her mother had died.

Over the years Kyra had had many sleepless nights, worrying that something might have happened to her sister, but every time she screwed up her courage to look in the social security database of deaths, she'd come away able to breathe again because Amy wasn't there. Of course it had occurred to her that Amy had gotten married and changed her last name, and she'd often wondered if Amy might have changed her first name, too, to make it impossible for Kyra to find her, but it had never crossed her mind that Amy had changed her social security number. In her entire life, Kyra had never done anything illegal other than take Hannah to Amy, but that was back when she was young and dumb and incapable of believing that her friend Zach would actually have her arrested.

She'd been wrong about Zach, and apparently, she'd been wrong about David's ex-wife. Sandra had told them how much Courtney had done to help. She'd broken into Hannah's Facebook account and figured out where the girl was taking Michael. Another shock for Kyra, as it was the last place she would have expected to be driving. The one place she would never have voluntarily gone, if her niece hadn't forced her to.

It was after midnight, the highway was almost empty, and David was making good time. Courtney would be there first, because she'd had a head start, but they would all be there by three or three thirty at the latest. Courtney had told Sandra that she was going for Hannah sake's, that Hannah had confided in her about some problems she was having. Kyra had barely thought to wonder why Hannah was involved with David's ex-wife or even to worry about her niece. She was focused on Michael, but she was also haunted by the news about her sister. All those years of thinking that Amy was punishing her, feeling that *this* was the worst thing that could happen, and yet the truth had turned out to be far, far worse. It was shocking and yet brutally ordinary. The reason she hadn't seen Amy wasn't some intricate grudge played out over time. For Amy, time had ended in 1996, the year that she died.

David was trying to distract her by talking about the historical significance of the region in Maryland where they were going, only about ten miles north of the site of the Battle of Antietam, the bloodiest battle of the Civil War. He went on about the significance of this battle for a while before he said, "This isn't helping, is it?"

"I'm sorry." She reached for his hand. Even in her grief, she was touched by how hard he was trying. He had to be very confused. She'd only managed to give him the basic facts about her sister and her niece, yet she felt sure now that he wouldn't condemn her once he heard the whole story. He'd already told her that she'd been right: he did have things he needed to share with her, too. But none of it would change how they felt about each other; she knew that now. Of course it wouldn't.

"I think you should go to sleep," David said, gently rubbing her thumb with his. "If you can."

Kyra looked out the window. A train was going by; it looked ghostly in the light from the moon. She closed her eyes, sure she wouldn't be able to sleep, but then she did. In her dream, Michael was in the front yard, holding a bright orange ball, throwing it up and down. She was standing in the doorway, watching her son and smiling. But when the ball bounced into the street and Michael started after it, she realized she couldn't move her legs. She couldn't make her mouth form the words though her mind was screaming them: *Michael, stop!*

She startled awake. David was shaking her shoulder.

"You were whimpering, honey."

She blinked as her eyes adjusted to the familiar sight of the green lights on the Subaru's dashboard. "It was just a dream," she said, and exhaled.

Her shoulder belt was cutting into her neck, so she sat up straighter and peered out the window. All around them was a vast emptiness. She assumed it was farmland, though she felt like they'd driven off the edge of the world. "Where are we?"

"On 81. About halfway there."

"Are you sure you don't want me to drive?"

"I don't mind. It's much easier that sitting at home, doing nothing. Every mile I drive is bringing him closer."

"Unless he's not there," she said, before she could stop herself. They'd already discussed this. Sandra was spending the night at the house, downstairs, with both the living room and the porch lights on, in case Hannah changed her mind, though Courtney had said it was unlikely.

"Let's not worry about that yet," David said, and she quickly agreed. She knew what would happen if they didn't find Michael tonight. The police would have to broadcast Hannah's description and license plate to every law enforcement organization across the country. Whatever it took, no matter what happened to her niece.

He urged her to go back to sleep, and she closed her eyes, but her mind wouldn't cooperate. It was so painful, thinking of Hannah being arrested for the same thing Kyra had been arrested for, though it wasn't really the same. Hannah had apparently taken Michael on an impulse, while Kyra had planned it all out. Kyra had taken Hannah because she had to save Amy.

Her sister had been on a path of self-destruction for almost two years at that point. Gregory Todd was long gone. He'd left because he was a heartless jerk who said Amy was too depressing to be around after she lost custody of her baby. She'd been fired from her band for missing gigs; she'd had to move out of her condo. She moved in with Kyra for a while, but after they had yet another argument about what Kyra had said to Wendy Jenkins, she left one afternoon while Kyra was at work. Since then she'd drifted from one place to another, until she finally landed at what she called the "peace house," which was actually a house full of addicts. Kyra was afraid that this might be the last stop, that her sister might not make it if she couldn't somehow pull herself back from the abyss. She'd decided to take Amy's daughter to show her sister that she did have another life, that Hannah was worth whatever it took to get herself clean.

It was a Saturday afternoon in October, a beautiful Indian summer day; however, that didn't mean Zach and Terri were going to agree to let her take Hannah to Amy's or even to a movie or the mall. They used to let her go anywhere with her niece; she'd even taken Hannah to her apartment to spend the night, but all that had changed two months ago, after they participated in a program at Terri's church called "divorce-busting boot camp," and Zach had ended up telling his wife that he and Kyra had slept together. Kyra had been stunned, and she didn't feel any better when Zach insisted that Terri wouldn't hold it against her. Instead, she felt like a fool for having ever believed that this guy was smart.

That Saturday, her plan was to get Zach alone and beg him to let her take Hannah out for a few hours, just this once. It worked, but before she made it out the door with her niece, Terri found out. She was obviously angry, but she only said, "You have to bring her back in fifteen minutes." Kyra nodded. She assumed Zach would tell Terri it was okay when the fifteen minutes were over, and she headed off with Hannah to the bus stop.

Hannah liked the bus ride, and the little girl didn't seem afraid as Kyra carried her down the street in the crime-ridden neighborhood. But Kyra was very afraid. Every corner had a drug dealer and guys kept stepping out of the shadows to leer at her and say "Hey, baby" and "What you up to?" She ignored them all and picked up her pace. She'd been to the peace house before, but never with Hannah. She felt so much more vulnerable, knowing she had to protect her niece.

Of course Amy must have been surprised to see her daughter, but she didn't show it. She led them into the back room she shared with some pinched-face woman named Bonnie. The room had nothing but two mattresses, a microwave, and a few crushed boxes. Bonnie was sitting on one of the mattresses, shooting up, and Kyra turned around so that Hannah couldn't watch.

They talked of nothing for several minutes, and Amy didn't even really look at the little girl. Her voice was flat; Kyra wondered if she was coming down from her high. Her pupils were still dilated, but everything about her seemed slow, like she barely had the energy to stand up. After a while, Hannah was complaining that she wanted to get down, but Kyra couldn't let her. The place was too filthy. The toddler was squirming when Kyra said, "She's getting heavy," as casually as she could manage, as if Hannah were just some kid they were taking care of for the Callahan Child Care Company. "Want to take her for a few minutes?"

Kyra felt sure that if only Amy held Hannah, she would remember how the little girl felt and how she smelled and how her hair felt brushing against your lips—and what a gift it was to be able to know these things about a child you loved.

"Sure," Amy said. Bonnie had flopped over, but Kyra had reassured herself that the woman wasn't dead because her chest was still moving. The two sisters were essentially alone in the room. There was one window, and Kyra was watching the light splay across the floor, all too aware that she couldn't stay very long or she would have to walk back to the bus in the dark.

Hannah let Amy take her, and it was just as Kyra hoped. Amy held her close and took a deep breath, inhaling the sweet smell. "Oh, my baby girl," Amy said. "You've gotten so big." She smiled. "How did that happen?"

"I'm three!" Hannah smiled, too, and held up three fingers.

"I know you are." Amy kissed the little girl and patted her bottom. "She's already potty trained?" she said to Kyra, and she sounded upset. Kyra wasn't sure why this particular detail bothered her sister. It wasn't nearly as important as all the other things Amy had missed out on during the ten months she hadn't visited her daughter: from Hannah's birthday to her first full sentence to her obsession with her tricycle, which she loved so much she tried to drag it to bed with her.

"She basically did it herself," Kyra said. Terri was a big believer in independence, at least when it came to little Hannah. Her own daughters were still held in her lap and carried all over the house, though they were six and seven.

When Amy just stood there without saying anything, the child started to get fussy. Still, Amy might have tried to engage Hannah again if the little girl hadn't held her arms out and said, "Mommy, hold me"—to Kyra.

"She knows I'm not her mother," Kyra said quickly. "It's just pretend." Kyra had reminded the little girl over and over that she was her aunt, but Hannah kept calling her "Mommy." Another reason that Terri was furious with Kyra, but Kyra thought Terri deserved most of the blame herself. Hannah could sense the woman was not her mother—and someone had to be.

"She wants you," Amy said, handing her back. "She doesn't even know who I am."

Amy sounded so sorry for herself. It was infuriating. "What do you expect? The poor kid hasn't seen you since—"

"She's better off."

"No, she isn't. God, Amy, were we better off with Dad and Marie? Because that's what you're saying about your daughter. Terri's her stepmother, but you're her mother. She needs you in her life, and you know it!"

Amy shrugged. "Too bad you didn't think of that before, huh?"

Though this usually made Kyra back off, it wasn't going to

work this time. Not when she'd brought Hannah with her, even though she knew Terri would be so angry that she probably wouldn't be allowed to take her niece out of the house again for another two months.

"This isn't about me," she said. "It's about you and Hannah." She grabbed her sister's skinny arm. "Don't you see what's going to happen if you keep living like this? You're going to die, Amy, and this little girl is going to grow up without her mommy."

Kyra could hear the word echoing from when she and Amy were little: *Mommy, Mommy, Mommy.* She had tears standing in her eyes, but she was surprised to see that Amy did, too.

Bonnie was groaning on the mattress. Hannah said, "Go home now! Bus?" Kyra told Hannah "a few more minutes," and promised the little girl they would get ice-cream cones when they left. Then she looked into her sister's eyes. "I want you to come with us." She shifted Hannah's weight onto her other arm. "I have it all arranged. There's a rehab place only a few blocks from my apartment. Once you get clean, we can go back to court, try to get custody or at least a lot more visitation. It will be like you wanted it to be. Just me and you, taking care of your daughter."

Amy smiled then, a real smile. After a moment, she put her arms around Kyra and Hannah. The hug was real, too, and so much like the old Amy that Kyra was positive she was about to agree to do it, to go with them and enter rehab. They were both crying, and Amy whispered, "Sis, thank you for—"

Before she could finish her sentence, the police were shouting, banging on the front door. The sound was so loud that Hannah screamed and covered her ears. Kyra was terrified; she wondered if Amy would be arrested with all the other addicts and prayed her sister wouldn't be. The police did take about half the people in the house to jail, including Amy, but they let them all out a few hours later. Only Kyra had to stay.

Kyra would never be sure who called the police, but even if it was Terri, it was still Zach's fault for not stopping his wife. And it was her own fault for keeping Zach up to date on where Amy was living, because he always acted like he was a friend, like he was worried about Amy, too.

She got off with only a night in jail, a small fine, and community service, but she lost everything that mattered to her. She was not allowed to see Hannah again for a full year, and after one brief visit, she was never allowed to come back. And she never had another chance to save Amy. Her sister ended up leaving Kansas City only a few weeks later—after Terri told her that Kyra had been sleeping with Zach during the custody battle.

"I would never have picked any man over you," Amy said, laughing bitterly. "To think that I loved you more than anyone in the world."

Her jacket was ripped at the shoulder and so dirty it looked like Amy had found it in the garbage; her cheeks were hollowed out, and her skin was as gray as the late afternoon November sky. But it was her eyes that Kyra would never forget. They were so hopeless. And yet Amy was still feigning a laugh when she spit out, "You'll never see me again," and turned to walk away.

She begged her sister to stop, but when Amy didn't, Kyra felt like her heart was breaking. She knew her sister meant it when she said she'd never see her again, and she was horribly afraid that it might turn out to be true.

For years after, she tortured herself with daydreams of the life she and her sister could have had if only she'd picked Amy that day instead of Zach. The only thought that comforted her—but then she wouldn't have moved to Philadelphia, and she wouldn't have met her husband and had their son—also made her feel guilty. It was as if her family's very existence relied on the collapse of her sister's.

"We're almost there," David said. "About twenty more minutes."

She'd been staring out the window, but she hadn't really seen anything. Now she was surprised to realize they were back in civilization. They were driving by a huge shopping mall. In the dark, it looked strangely frightening rising up in the middle of the immense empty parking lot.

He gently rested his hand on the back of her neck. "Are you ready for this?"

"I'll have to be." It wasn't really an answer, but it was the only one she had. If her son was at Vivian's house, then she would have to be at Vivian's house, no matter how she felt about it.

All night, she'd refused to spend one minute thinking about her mother. She didn't even intend to speak to her if she could help it.

When Vivian had found her email address last year, Kyra had been surprised, yet she knew she shouldn't have been. She'd joined all the social networking sites looking for Amy, and though she'd quit participating when the disappointment became too much for her, she'd left up a profile with basic information, in hopes that someday Amy would come looking for her. Instead she'd ended up with her mother, whose breezy, self-centered emails were all too similar to the postcards when they were kids. Kyra deleted them without responding and hoped her mother would get the hint. She felt sure that Vivian hadn't changed, but even if she had, it was too late from Kyra's perspective. The woman couldn't just decide to be a mother or a grandmother when it suited her. That wasn't the way it worked. You had to be a mother when you didn't want to; that was how you earned the right to be one when you did.

She sat up straighter and forced herself to concentrate on the street signs, but it didn't help. She was back there again, remembering that hot afternoon when her mother left. When Amy let go of Kyra's hand and ran down the block to catch up with Vivian's car, Kyra was standing on the walkway, staying put, as she'd been told to do. But she was pulling on the corners of her eyes, straining in the bright sunlight to see what was going on. All she could see was an empty street. No cars, no grown-ups, no kids. No one but herself.

Their father wasn't home. She'd never been alone like this, the only person in the yard, no one in the house. After a while, her stomach was doing flip-flops, and her head felt too light, like it might melt all over the walkway pavement, but there was no one to tell. She felt like she'd been discarded, like she was a bag of old clothes waiting for the Salvation Army truck. She felt like she needed to cry, but her eyes didn't remember how.

It was only a few minutes, maybe even less, but her seven-year-old self couldn't have suffered more if she'd woken up alone on the moon. Or maybe it was just that she was already learning what it meant to be left by your mother and feeling a pain so new to her that she didn't know the word for it yet: *loneliness*.

She never forgot that feeling and she never forgave her mother for what she did. But she also never forgot the relief of that moment when all her squinting and blinking in the July sun finally paid off, and she saw her sister, wailing and clearly miserable, but nevertheless, walking back to her.

TWENTY-EIGHT

After they left the motel, April drove for a long time, but Michael didn't mind because she was talking and laughing her Christmas bell laugh. She even offered to tell him three good secrets if he promised not to be mad that she hadn't told him before. He wanted to know the secrets, but he told April he couldn't promise. His mother had read him a book about being sad and happy and excited and a bunch of other feelings he couldn't remember. "Mad is a feeling," he said. "You can't make yourself not be mad."

"All right," she said, and sighed. "I have to tell you anyway before we get there. One, my name is really Hannah, not April. Two, I'm your cousin. And three, we're going to see your other grandmother, the one you don't know. I met her when she friended me on Facebook. Actually, she didn't friend me, because she thought I was somebody else named Amy Callahan." Hannah laughed. "I wonder why. Anyway, she was really glad when I told her who I was, and so last week when I got some awful news, I called her. She felt so bad for me that she told me to come to her house, so she could help me handle this. So that's where we're going—to meet your grandma. What do you think of that?"

He wasn't sure what she meant by *that*: the last secret, or all of them? He didn't like that she'd told him a different name. It felt like a lie, and that made him sort of nervous. Also, he was a little confused by what *cousin* meant. He knew it was someone in your family, but he wasn't sure exactly how. He did like the idea of having two grandmas to play Sorry and Uno with, and two grandmas to make him root beer floats. Best of all, when this grandma called his parents to tell them he was there, they would come right over, since they never let him stay at Grandma's house without them. Even when he said he really wanted to, they said it wasn't a good idea.

They were out of New Jersey and through Delaware and into Maryland, and Hannah was still talking. "Sorry I'm so wired, buddy. I've been knocking back Red Bulls, the sweetened kind, so I'll have the energy to make it. Now I can't seem to shut up."

"It's okay," Michael said. He knew her drink was called Red Bull, because he'd read the label on the shiny can. He figured it was some kind of milk, since a bull was a cow. He had no idea what *wired* was, but he liked listening to her. She was so happy and she kept making him laugh by saying goofy things about the other cars and trucks and places they went by.

But after a lot more driving and talking, she made a wrong turn and got lost. They had to stop at a Food Mart for directions, but when she didn't understand the directions, she got lost again. Finally she pulled into a truck stop and she wrote everything down and got back on the right road, but by then she wasn't talking at all. He didn't mind. It was really late, way past his bedtime, and his eyes kept closing. Even though he hadn't counted the things he was sure of yet, he wanted to go to sleep, fast, so he could wake up and not have to ride anymore in this car.

He woke up a few times, but only for a minute or two when Hannah honked the horn or a loud truck went by. Then he woke up for good when the car stopped in front of a house with a giant lightbulb above the door that was so bright, he could feel the light right through his eyelids.

"Hey, buddy," Hannah said. Her voice was soft. She'd taken off her seat belt and she was looking at him. Michael was rubbing his eyes. "You want to go meet Grandma?"

He nodded. She got out and opened his door. It was warm and sticky outside, but there was a breeze that left goose bumps on his bare legs.

The house was almost as small as a playhouse, without a front porch or any steps—just a big square of concrete to climb up to the door. The driveway was made of dirt and there were tree limbs lying all over the front yard, like someone cut them down and forgot to put them on the curb for the mulch truck. But the house was yellow, which he liked, and the shutters were blue, his favorite color.

When they got to the concrete stair, Hannah held his hand and pulled him up. She leaned down and kissed him on the cheek. "I'm really stressed out," she said. "I'm so glad you're with me right now."

She rang the doorbell and then she rang it again when nothing happened. She started knocking on the door and banging on it with her fist.

"She has to be home. I told her I'd be here tonight." Hannah flipped out her cell phone with the blue and white clouds. "It's 2:07. She said she'd be home by midnight at the latest."

He didn't know what to say. When Daddy was late, it was because a student needed help. And Grandma, the one he knew, was only late when a sick person got sicker. And Mommy was hardly ever late unless her haircut took too long, or a doctor made her sit in the waiting room *forever*.

Hannah helped him back down off the concrete block. She sat down on the hood of the car and started typing on her phone. "I'm sending her a text. Once she knows we're here, she'll come. Don't worry."

Michael was looking at those blue shutters on the big front window. The paint was chipping off, and underneath was a gray color. He wondered why paint did that, when it never chipped off clothes or hands.

"Want to get back in the car?" Hannah said. When he didn't answer, she said, "You can walk around if you want. Just stay in the front yard, where it's light."

The yard was easy to see, but it had all those tree limbs that he could fall over. And it might have mosquitoes that would make him sick. It might even have a snake that could bite him. But the idea of getting back in that car *again* was so much worse. He took a few hesitant steps into the grass.

It was kind of spooky being out in the middle of night, but it was also exciting. The sky looked purple and blue and he could see the moon. He felt like he was an explorer, like he was the only person in the world who'd ever dared to walk into this place. When he made it all the way to the other side, he wanted to tell Hannah, but she was hunched over, staring at her phone.

After a while, he was getting a little bored. He'd walked back and forth, back and forth, and he'd even stepped carefully on one of those tree limbs. He was afraid the limb would snap back and hit him in the face, but it didn't. He wondered how much it weighed, and then he decided to see if he could lift it. He put his hands on the narrow part and tugged and tugged, but he only moved it a few inches, closer to the big tree on the far side of the yard—the one that sort of scared him because the branches looked like a giant's arms, but sort of excited him, too, because it was what the kids at his last school called a *climbing tree*. There was a place where the branches divided that was so low, he'd barely have to lift his foot and he'd be up off the ground.

His hands were dirty from lifting the limb, but he wiped them on his shorts and forgot about it. Hannah wasn't watching what he was doing, which kept surprising him. She seemed too upset about the phone to notice anything. In the car, when she was talking nonstop, she'd told him she was not actually a grown-up. "I'm seventeen, but I'm almost eighteen. Then I'll be able to do whatever I want. Maybe I'll move in with Grandma. If she wants me. I don't know. But what I'm trying to say is I remember being your age." She told him about kindergarten, and her school bus and her lunch pail and a bunch of other things. She also told him about a hill by her house. "It was really steep, but I thought if I got to the top, I would be the king—queen, whatever—of the mountain. And when I made it, it was even cooler than I imagined." She laughed. "Five was one of my best years."

He was still standing by the big tree. Every day at school, he'd wondered what it would be like to be one of the climbing kids. He knew he could fall and break his neck, but none of them ever fell. They were always laughing as they climbed higher and higher, so high that all he could see was the bright colors of their clothes flashing in the sunlight as they moved from branch to branch.

When he put his foot in the tree, he glanced at Hannah to make sure she wasn't going to tell him to stop. Part of him wanted her to, the scared part, but the explorer part was already grabbing the branch above him and pulling himself up. The bark was scratchy against his hands. The leaves tickled his face. He stood there until he decided he wasn't actually *up* in the tree, since he was at the bottom. So he climbed up higher, to the next branch. His hands were burning but he didn't blow on them until he climbed to an even higher branch, where the tree trunk and two other branches formed a little seat for him to sit on.

He sat there until his hands didn't hurt and then he found another place to climb. Every time he moved, he listened carefully to make sure none of the branches were the old kind that could snap off. He only moved to branches that were so solid they didn't budge when they felt his weight. He was trying to be safe, but he couldn't try too hard or he'd get scared and not have any fun.

He was about halfway up the tree when he saw a car pull into the dirt driveway. He could see Hannah talking to a lady with red hair, though he couldn't make out their expressions or hear what they were saying. Then the red-haired lady was in the yard, calling his name. She sounded out of breath, like Mommy did when she was worried about him, so he yelled, "I'm up here."

He watched her shiny hair move closer. When she was standing at the foot of the tree, she said, "Hi," and smiled really big. She didn't look like a grandma. He waited for her to say who she was, but the only sound was the fluttering of the leaves.

"I'm getting down," he said, because he figured that was what she was waiting for. But then he didn't move. The branch below him suddenly seemed very far away. If his foot slipped a little bit, he would fall to the ground like an acorn, except an acorn couldn't break its neck and have to go to the hospital.

When she asked if he needed help, he said no. Only cats got stuck in trees, and he was a boy. He took a big breath and held the branch he was sitting on as he eased himself down until his foot was snug on the branch below. It wasn't that hard. He just had to make sure he didn't look straight down.

"You're a good climber," she said. "You must do this a lot."

He was so pleased that it was easy to make it down to the next branch, and the next. His arms were shaking a little, but he held on tight and kept going until *crack*, a branch he'd just put his foot on broke off. His foot was dangling in the air, and then his shoe fell off!

"Hold on!" the lady said. "Oh God. Wait! I'll come up and—"

"I'm okay," he said, because he was. His hands were sweating and all of him was shaking now, even his teeth, but he'd already swung the sock foot to another branch, a bigger one. "I can do it myself."

He rested for a minute once he was safely on that branch. Then he went down again, and again. Finally he was on the last branch, the one that was just a small step to the ground, and then he was standing in the yard right next to her.

The shadows on her face made her seem not quite real, like a girl in a fairy-tale book. He felt like he wasn't just an explorer, but king of the tree, and she was a princess who'd appeared to tell him what a good job he'd done—and hand him his shoe.

"You did it!" she said. "Great climbing!" She was smiling and kind of dancing around while he smashed his sweaty sock into his sneaker. "My name is Courtney, by the way. I'm a friend of your grandmother's."

He wasn't sure which grandmother she was talking about, but it didn't matter. He was glad when she took his hand. He wanted to make sure she didn't trip on the tree limbs as they walked back across the yard. They made it over to the driveway, where Hannah was sitting on the hood of her car, leaning back against the windshield, looking at the sky, like nothing had happened.

When Courtney asked if he wanted to sit on the hood of the car, too, he said okay. He was so tired all of a sudden that he let her lift him up and sit him next to Hannah. He wondered if he'd been asleep the whole time, and the yard and tree were just a great dream.

Courtney sat down on the hood, on his other side. For a few moments, nobody said anything and Michael was examining the stars, trying to decide which one to make a wish on. He never picked the biggest star or the most twinkly one, because he felt like the other stars needed his wish more. Then Courtney and Hannah started talking so fast the words seemed like ping-pong balls flying by in the air above him. Hannah said their grandmother was on a date, and she'd texted that she'd be home as soon as she could. All they had to do was wait here. It couldn't be too much longer. But Courtney said that Hannah deserved better, and she shouldn't wait. "You can come home with me," Courtney said. "Or your aunt." Then Hannah said a bunch of stuff about her mother and her grandmother and her aunt that Michael didn't really follow. She sounded so sad, but there was nothing he could do. His head had fallen onto Courtney's shoulder and his eyes were closing again. Even the big light couldn't keep him awake.

He woke up when Courtney sat up straighter, and his head jerked forward. Another car had driven into the dirt driveway. He could tell by the engine sound that it was his father's Subaru. His parents had come to get him, just like he knew they would.

Courtney was scrambling to stand, easing him down so he was standing, too. His legs felt rubbery and tired, but he was running anyway. He ran to the driver's side door and then his father was picking him up, lifting him in the air. His mother was there, too, touching his face and his knees and his arms. He thought they were both about to cry, but then they were giggling. He was giggling, too, because he knew this wasn't a dream. None of it was, not even the best parts, which he blurted out because he wanted them to know so badly. They were his best friends. He wanted to tell them because that's what you do with best friends, you tell them all the stuff you're really happy about.

"I went on a boat and saw a real whale! I climbed a big tree!"

What happened next was very important to Michael; in fact, it would turn out to be the only thing he remembered about the time after his parents arrived. He would forget about all the grown-up talking that night, a lot of which, admittedly, he slept through, and all the confusing tears: Courtney's, after his father thanked her and gave her an awkward hug; Hannah's, after she noticed his mother's watch and knew she was finally face-to-face with the person she'd been dreaming of; and even his mother's, who hardly ever cried, but couldn't help crying when she saw how thin her niece was, how broken, but also because she felt so sure she would have Hannah back that she was already thinking of what she would do for her, how she would ask Sandra and maybe even Courtney to help her love this sad, motherless girl back to health. Though she'd lost her sister, her sister's daughter had found her again. This wasn't fate or karma; this was grace.

But what Michael would always remember was his parents' reaction after he told them about the boat and the tree. They continued to giggle and smile as they said how proud they were of him. When he took them over to see the tree and they didn't say anything about it being dangerous or even give each other that *doubt* look he knew so well, he might have gone back to his original theory that this was only a great dream, except for the fact that his parents were wearing the same clothes they'd been wearing that morning, when he left. They were still his mommy and daddy, and they would still worry the next time he climbed a tree. They would worry when he learned to swim and ride a bike and drive a car, when he went to school and went to camp, and even when he was a grown-up himself and they were very old, like Grandma. Nothing had changed at all, except that something had.

ACKNOWLEDGMENTS

This is my sixth book with Simon & Schuster, and I know I am lucky to have this wonderful company continue to support my work. My deepest thanks to everyone at Atria, especially Judith Curr, Greer Hendricks, Lisa Keim, Chris Lloreda, Peter Borland, Sarah Cantin, Rachel Zugschwert, Hillary Tisman, Paul Olsewski, Cristina Suarez, and Nancy Tonik. I'm also grateful to everyone on the S&S sales force, especially Michael Selleck, Terry Warnick, Barb Roach, Liz Monaghan, and my buddy Tim Hepp.

Again, my heartfelt thanks to Megan Beatie and Lynn Goldberg of Goldberg McDuffie Communications. To all the booksellers who have championed my novels and all the readers who have written me. To my dear friend Joe Drabyak, who read the beginning of this novel and loved it. I think of you every day, Joe. I wish you could know how deeply you are missed.

ACKNOWLEDGMENTS

To my family and friends: Marly and Michael Rusoff; Kevin Howell; Melisse Shapiro; Scott Tucker; Ann Cahall; Pat Redmond; Jim, Jeff, and Jamie Crotinger; Emily Ward, and, finally, Laura Ward and Miles Tucker, who were there. I will never forget waking up, coming back to you.